Alan Burt Akers

Swordships of
Scorpio

Illustrated by Tim Kirk

Futura Publications Limited
An Orbit Book

An Orbit Book

First published in Great Britain in 1975
by Futura Publications Limited
49 Poland St, London W1A 2LG

ISBN 0 8600 78361
Printed in Great Britain by
C. Nicholls & Company Ltd.
The Philips Park Press
Manchester

Futura Publications Ltd
49 Poland Street
LONDON W1A 2LG

CONTENTS

List of Illustrations

A Note On The Tapes
From Rio De Janeiro

I had assumed, along with thousands of readers who I am sure shared the same genuine sorrow, that the saga of Prescot of Antares must come to an end with the final transcriptions of the tapes from Africa. The editing of the tapes that chronicle the incredible story of Dray Prescot on Kregen beneath the Suns of Scorpio, a task which by a fortunate chance had fallen to me, had been so arranged that each volume might be read as an individual story in its own right.

But this meant that there were but few pages left to see publication after the first three volumes.

After that—nothing. I had hoped that Dray Prescot might in some way have been able to see a volume of his saga and perhaps be moved to contact me. So far this hope has proved vain.

But the ways of the Star Lords, no less than the Savanti, are passing strange and beyond the comprehension of mere mortal men.

I had just written the words, ". . . and then I yelled," and pushed back in my chair in my old book-lined study, feeling as though I had screwed down the coffin-lid on the face of an old friend, all glory fled from two worlds, when the telephone rang and it was Geoffrey Dean, long-distance from Washington. The coincidence affected me profoundly for it had been Geoffrey, an old friend and now connected with the State Department, who had given me the tapes from Africa. He had received them from Dan Fraser, a young field worker, who had provided Dray Prescot with the cassette tape recorder in that epidemic-stricken village of West Africa where Prescot had saved the situation. Geoffrey was wildly excited.

His first words were: "I have more tapes from Dray Prescot, Alan!"

By the time we both had calmed down, I had arranged to

fly out to see him at once. A mysterious box had that moment arrived, and he had opened it, all unknowing; but he began to suspect as he saw the packed cassettes, played the first one for a few seconds only—and then had phoned me. There was a letter he was having translated. The box had been all over the world, it appeared, but had been mailed from Rio de Janeiro. Geoffrey met me at the airport and I drove with him to his Washington hotel in an impatience I could barely control. As soon as we entered his room I saw them. The box had been left as he had opened it. The manila-wrapped cardboard box, carelessly slit open, rested on a chair, and paper and string hung down. From the box a whole heaping pile of tape cassettes lay tumbled—and I knew that they contained a great wonderful El Dorado of exotic adventures on Kregen beneath Antares, that fierce and beautiful, mystic and awe-inspiring planet four hundred light-years from our Earth.

Geoffrey was waving a letter in my face.

"Read this first, Alan!"

The letter in translation was curt to mystification.

Dear Mr. Fraser:

I have been asked by Mr. Dray Prescot to forward to you these cassettes. Mr. Prescot was instrumental in foiling a skyjack attempt upon a jet liner in which I was a passenger. The bandits were after ransom without political aims in their act. We crashed in the jungle. None of the passengers would be alive today if Mr. Prescot had not guided us all to safety and taken care of us along the way. We would have done anything for him. All he required was the use of my tape recorder and a large number of cassettes. And a promise to send them to you. With great pleasure this I now do. I regret I have been unable to listen to any of them as my English is imperfect. Mr. Prescot has now left Rio de Janeiro. If you see him please convey my deepest regard and warmest admiration.

(signed) Francisco Rodriguez.

"And a hotel address in Rio," I said.

Geoffrey sighed. "No trace of Rodriguez, I'm afraid."

I looked at the heaping pile of cassettes and my hands shook as I placed that marked *One* in the machine. The opening was garbled; but then a voice sounded out clearly. I knew that deep, powerful voice; I would know it anywhere. I cannot vouch for the truth of his story, but that calm sure voice inspires confidence—more, it demands belief.

The precious box had been sent by sea mail to Dan Fraser's address in Africa, had been shipped back to Washington by the agency and, because Dan had been tragically killed in an auto accident and had no relatives, had found its way to Geoffrey Dean, Dan's boss. Geoffrey had made inquiries about this skyjacking, but had discovered nothing at the various embassies he approached. "Whatever happened down there in South America we may never know. No one is talking."

But, beside this wonderful cache of undreamed-of treasure, I did not care. Now the world could once more share the adventures of Dray Prescot on Kregen under the Suns of Scorpio and revel in the barbaric color and headlong action of his life.

As described by Dan Fraser, Dray Prescot is above middle height, with straight brown hair and intelligent brown eyes that are level and oddly dominating, compelling. His shoulders made Dan's eyes pop. Dan sensed an abrasive honesty and a fearless courage about him. He moves, Dan said, like a great hunting cat, quiet and deadly.

Born in 1775, Dray Prescot had clawed his way up through the hawsehole to become a ship's officer; but thereafter had little success in this world. I believe it is clear that, even then, he perceived with an inner conviction that he was destined for some vast and unimaginable fate. When he was whirled away to Kregen he positively reveled in the perils set to test him, and through his immersion in the sacred pool of baptism in the River Zelph of Aphrasöe he is assured of a thousand years of life, as is his beloved, Delia of the Blue Mountains. Banished to Earth he was recalled by the Star Lords—of whom he tells us nothing—as a kind of interstellar troubleshooter, and he quickly rose to become Zorcander of his clansmen, and then Lord of Strombor, an enclave house of the city of Zenicce on the west coast of the continent of Segesthes. Hurled through the void once more he suffered the horrors of the overlords of Magdag and was instrumental in raising his army of slaves and workers in an attempt to overthrow them. In the midst of his final onslaught he was whisked to another part of Kregen's inner sea, and plunged once again into the Star Lords' schemes. He had become a member of the famous Krozairs of Zy, entitled to be called Pur Dray, dedicated to the red-sun deity Zair.

Determined to reach Vallia, and Delia, he set off toward the east. But Delia had set her emperor father's air service in motion to find him, and had come herself to the inner sea in search of her lost love. Delia and Dray Prescot flew through The Stratemsk, as Prescot describes them a truly horrific range of mountains walling off the inner sea from the land to the east, the Hostile Territories. With two companions, Seg and Thelda, they crash and go through adventure after adventure until, at last, with the death of the beast-man Umgar Stro at Prescot's hands and the rescue of Delia, they make a dash for it astride Umgar Stro's own impiter—a gigantic coal-black flying beast. Seg and Thelda, so Prescot relates with great sadness, had been ridden down by a host of half-men. A Vallian Air Service airboat picks them up; but there is treachery aboard this flier, *Lorenztone*, for Prescot awakes beneath a thorn-ivy bush. He has been drugged. He finds weapons and food tossed down to color the impression that he has fled because he is frightened to face Delia's father, the emperor. This is the work, he believes, of the Vallian Racter party, who do not wish the Princess Majestrix of Vallia to wed him, a man not of their choice.

At this point Dray Prescot picks himself up and says: "On my own two feet, then!"

At this point the present volume, *Swordships of Scorpio*, takes up the narrative. At the junction where the tapes from Africa end and the tapes from Rio begin, I have made a note. They do not run consecutively on; there is a gap. From study of the cassettes I am sure there are other gaps to come in the story we have. I repeat, we are superlatively lucky even to have what we do of the fascinating and pulse-stirring saga of Prescot of Antares.

Kregen under the Suns of Scorpio is a real world, savage and beautiful, marvelous and terrible. Dray Prescot is there now, I feel sure, carving out fresh adventures by the side of his Delia of Delphond, his Delia of the Blue Mountains.

Alan Burt Akers.

CHAPTER ONE

I march toward Vallia

On my own two feet, then, I would march all the way across the Hostile Territories and take ship at whatever port I came across and sail to Vallia, and there I would march into the palace of the dread emperor of that proud empire and in sight of all claim from him my beloved, my Delia, my Delia of Delphond, my Delia of the Blue Mountains.

I would!

The deadly Krozair long sword felt good in my fist.

My head still ached from the effects of the poison and my insides felt as though an insane vintner of Zond were trying to stamp a premier vintage from my guts. But I went on. There was no stopping me now—or so I thought then, wrapped about in rage and frustration and the unhealthy desire to smash a few skulls. . . .

The plain continued on in gentle undulations to the low hills ringing the horizon. Long pale green grasses blew in the wind sweeping past. Over all the scene that streaming mingled light of the twin suns of Antares scorched down. The water bottle was half-full. Evidently, whoever had poisoned me and thrown me into the hole beneath the thorn-ivy bush had tossed down the scarlet silk wrapped about weapons and food to fool those aboard the airboat. The food and water had not been meant to keep me alive; I had a shrewd idea that the poisoner thought me dead.

If I, Dray Prescot, with weapons at my disposal could not live off this land, then I did not deserve to survive.

As you will know I was no soft innocent from a big city who always walked on stone sidewalks, who took automobiles everywhere riding on concrete pavements, who pressed buttons for light and warmth, who ate pre-packaged food. Although I am a civilized man from Earth, I was then and

11

have remained when circumstances require as much a savage
barbarian as any of the primordial reavers ravaging out from
the bleak northlands.

The first river I came to I swam across and the devil take
what monsters might be lurking beneath the water.

Along the banks were mounds of bare earth. These I
skirted respectfully.

Ahead the tall grasses gave way to a lower variety, and
the ground lay bare and dusty in patches here and there. The
long black and red-glinting column I did not wish to see
advanced obliquely from my right. I had no hesitation whatsoever in turning in my eastward tramp and heading off to
the northeast.

From a low hillock—a natural hillock—I could see the
seemingly endless stream of ants. I give them their Earthly
name, for the Kregen names for the varieties of ants would
fill a book. These were shining black, active, prowling restlessly toward some destiny of their own. The twin suns sank
slowly behind me and the land ahead filled with the flooding
opaline radiance from Zim and Genodras.

The first screams ripped from the gathering shadows.

Now I knew where the stream of ants was headed.

Soldier ants, large fierce fellows, their mandibles perfectly
capable of shearing through ordinary leather, kept watch on
the flanks of the columns of workers. The soldier ants, I
judged, were all of six nails in length. Six nails make a
knuckle. A knuckle in Kregen mensuration is about four-
point-two inches, say one hundred and eighty millimeters.

These were big fellows.

The screams continued.

I hurried on, parallel to the column, seeing the sinking
suns-light glancing off armored bodies, glinting red from joint
and mandible.

Ahead the column spread out. It seemed to me like some
blasphemous inkblot, spreading and pooling, ever-fed by new
streams.

The man had been staked out.

His wrists and ankles were bound with rawhide to four
thick stakes, their tops bruised and battered from the blows
of hammers. He twisted and writhed; but the tide of black
horrors swarmed over him, a living carpet eating him to the
bone.

There was only one way to get him out of it.

My Krozair long sword had been in action against mighty

foes before; now it would have to go up against tiny killers four inches long.

Four quick slashes released the thongs. I bent and hoisted the man, holding him in my left hand, swatting with the sword. Already the horrors were scuttling up my legs, over my back, along my arms. Agonizing pains stabbed my flesh. I danced and jumped and ran and shed crushed black bodies like a mincer.

The man was clearly dying. I had merely saved him from the kind of death the people—or things—had planned for him.

By the time I had got rid of the last ant, and had rubbed my skin and felt the slick blood greasy there, and had placed the man down gently against a grassy bank, I knew he had mere moments to live. Most of his lower abdomen and legs had been eaten away, his chest cavity was partially exposed, only his head—with the exception of the eyes—remained to appear as a reasonable facsimile of a man.

He was trying to speak, now, croaking sounds from his throat, gargling, his useless arms attempting to lift toward me.

"Rest easy, my friend," I said in the universal Kregish. "You will sleep soon, and have no more pain."

"So—," he said. "Sos—" He choked the words out. "Sosie!"

"Rest easy, dom." I uncorked my water bottle, filled it at the river, and poured water over his face and between his lips. His tongue licked greedily. Some of the blood washed away.

"Save my Sosie!"

"Yes."

He knew he was dying, I think, and his voice strengthened.

"I am Mangar na Arkasson. Sosie! She—the devils of Cherwangtung took her—they took her—they—the ants! The ants!"

I moistened his lips again. "Easy, dom, easy."

His black skin shone now with a sweat-sheen in the pink radiance from She of the Veils, the fourth moon of Kregen. He had been a proud and imposing man. His face, despite the contortions his agony wrought in his countenance, still showed hauteur and pride. His features were not the hawk-like ones of Xoltemb, the caravan-master I had met on the plains of Segesthes, who came from the island of Xuntal. This man, this Mangar na Arkasson, had features more

Negroid in their fashioning, hard and firm with a generous and mobile mouth.

"Swear!" Mangar na Arkasson whispered. "Swear you will save my Sosie from those devils of Cherwangtung. Swear!"

He was dying. He was a fellow human being.

I said, "I will do all I can to save your Sosie, Mangar na Arkasson. You have the word of Dray Prescot, Krozair, the Lord of Strombor."

"Good—good—"

His mind was wandering now and although I knew he did not have the slightest notion what a Krozair was, and had never heard of Strombor, yet I believe that he took with him into the grave the conviction—and I hope the comforting one—that I was a man who would do as I had sworn.

When he died, after a few mumbled and almost incoherent blasphemies and pleas, cries of strange gods, and, at my questioning, the statement that Cherwangtung stood at the confluence of two rivers, by a mountain, away to the northeast, I buried him. There was no way of judging what marker or memorial he would want, so I contented myself with manhandling a great stone over his grave. That would hold the plains lurfings at bay, for a time at least.

Few lurfings would attack a single man, even, unless there were a round dozen of them. Low-bellied, lean-flanked, gray-furred scavengers are lurfings, equipped with probing snout-like faces well-suited to the tasks nature has set them.

I stood up.

Four moons wheeled across the sky now, and their combined radiance lit up the night-land of Kregen, here on the eastern plains of Central Turismond. Far away to the east lay the coast. On the coast stood port cities, of Vallia, of Pandahem, of Murn-Chem, of a number of trading countries from overseas. I had to reach one, take ship, sail to Vallia. . . .

But, first, I had given my word to a dying man.

I do not believe you, who listen to these tapes cut in this stricken famine-area of your own Earth, can condemn me for what I had sworn to do. I knew my Delia was safe. She was even now aboard the Vallian Air Service airboat *Lorenztone* securely on her way back to Vallia and her father the emperor. I need no longer suffer the cruel tortures for her safety I had recently gone through, when I believed her dead, then the captive of Umgar Stro whom I had slain, and so released her. No. With a clear conscience I could do what I had sworn.

My Delia, Delia of the Blue Mountains, would understand.

At that time I had, of course, had no experience of motive power for shipping other than the wind and the oar. The swifters of the inland sea with their massed banks of oars could sail independently of the wind—but I had gained the strong impression that I should judge the Vallian Air Service more from my own experience as a naval officer of a King's Ship of my own planet rather than from the wild times I had spent as a swifter oar slave and captain on the Eye of the World. I had in the nature of my profession heard of Claude François, Marquis de Jouffroy d'Abbans, who in 1783 had invented a paddle-boat and sailed her on the Seine at Paris, thus being, as far as I knew, the man to sail the world's first successful steam vessel. The first practical steamer had been built by the Scotsman, William Symington, whose *Charlotte Dundas* in 1801 proved herself by towing exercises. Robert Fulton, an American who would work for whoever paid him, had designed a paddle-steamer, *Demologos*, with the paddles between two hulls and armed with twenty-four thirty-two pounders. I wondered, then, as I strode across the pink-lit night-lands of eastern Turismond, just what this independence of the wind would mean in a vessel, in these sky ships built in far Havilfar.

All of which meant that I had no idea how long it would be before Delia reached her home in Vallia.

If the plans of the man who had poisoned me and dumped me under the thorn-ivy bush went as he envisaged, would Delia believe I had run off? Could she think I had quailed from meeting her formidable father, the emperor?

If she did so think—then I refused to contemplate that.

If she did not think so she would very well do as she had done before and send a fleet of airboats scouring the world for me. That, I confess, was a comforting thought.

The men of Cherwangtung, having staked out Mangar na Arkasson for the soldier ants, had merely removed themselves from that immediate vicinity before they got up to their devil's tricks with Sosie na Arkasson.

She was not screaming and so the first sounds I heard were the stamp of naked feet on hard earth, the throbbing of drums, the chanting and leem-keening of the men of Cherwangtung as they danced around the central stake.

This was a scene I did not relish.

Bound to that stake the lissome form of Sosie gleamed in the torchlight, her black skin in startling contrast to the fish-belly white of the men who danced about her shaking axes and spears, their ankles festooned with bells and bones and feathers. They danced two forward, one back, stamp, stamp, slide, stamp, stamp, slide, and they shook their weapons and in the torchlight their faces showed corpse-white and lascivious and incredibly evil.

Sosie held her head up proudly. They had stripped her garments from her. Her hair, done in the fashion we know on this Earth as Afro, bristled. Dust and grass stems covered it, and there were long scratches on her thighs. I could not see her back, lashed to the stake; but I guessed that, too, was lacerated in like fashion as these men had dragged her here for sacrifice.

What the sacrifice was about, what they were going to do, what blasphemous gods they worshiped—of all that I knew nothing. It could be I was interfering in a ritual demanded by law and custom. Both Mangar and Sosie na Arkasson could have been criminals, meeting a just end.

But no civilized man binds a young naked girl to a post and dances around her in the torch glare, his every intention obvious. I felt sure that I was not committing a gross error as I took the bow contemptuously tossed down from *Lorenztone* into my hand. This was not a great longbow of Loh. I shut my mind to thoughts of Seg Segutorio, who was of Erthyrdrin, and who was a master bowman, and who was now—I had seen him fall beneath the nactrix hooves—dead and gone and best forgotten.

How could anyone forget Seg Segutorio?

I lifted the bow. I must put thoughts of Seg from my mind. There were twenty of them out there, and after perhaps the fourth or fifth shaft the rest would flee into the pink-lit shadows. They would not escape by running; but I would have to be quick.

If only Seg were at my side now!

Angrily—furious that thoughts of my comrade Seg, who was gone, smashed into my mind—I loosed the shafts as fast as I could snatch up the arrows, drew back the string, and let loose.

One, two, three, four—the four went down, coughing, with shafts feathered into them.

The chanting and drum-throbbing ceased.

One of the men yelled and I put a shaft through his mouth.

Others were shouting, and running, their naked white rumps gleaming in the pink moons-light.

I pinned three more and then they were gone, in every direction. From now on I would be the hunted, not they.

Speed. . . .

Sosie regarded me as though I had appeared through the screen of a shadow play, in the round, flesh and blood, miraculously taking the place of a phantom.

"Sosie," I said. I spoke harshly. "I have come to take you away from these evil men. Mangar has sent me—" All the time I spoke I slashed her bonds free. As the ropes released, she buckled and fell. The agony of her returning circulation meant I must carry her. She was no Delia, who had been running fleetly at my side, wielding a sword, moments after I had cut her loose.

"Mangar, my father," she moaned. "I saw—I saw what they did! The ants! *The ants!*"

"Zair has him in his keeping now," I said.

Then, for a shocked instant, I wondered if these people of Arkasson worshiped Grodno, the false green-sun deity of the green sun Genodras. But Sosie gave no sign that she understood. I ran. Out from the torchlights and into the pink-shrouded darkness where that darkness was illusory, where the moons in Kregen's night sky cast down enough light so that one might read the small print of a directory, I ran—and then I stopped running. Sosie was bundled down by a small bush—not a thorn-ivy but, blessedly, a paline bush. Immediately she began to stuff the appetizing yellow palines into her mouth, drawing sustenance, refreshment, and surcease from them.

I scanned the horizon, lying down and looking up. One of the torturers showed against the skyline and he went down with an arrow in his guts.

His scream attracted two more, who ran, like fools, over to him, to be slain in their turn.

How many more were there? Another ten, I estimated, at least.

This crouching down was no way of fighting for me.

"Sosie." I spoke with an urgency that was not altogether feigned. I had to drive through to her mind. "Sosie! I am Dray Prescot. Your father made me swear to save you. Now, you lie hidden in this paline bush. Do not move. I will return for you."

She understood enough of that in her dazed condition for me to think it safe to leave her.

Then I went a-hunting men who tied girls to stakes, all black and naked, and tortured them.

They went down, one by one, until in the end five of them clumped together, brandishing their axes and spears, and charged me as I shafted one of their number who attempted to cast his spear into my belly.

Now was the moment I had hungered for, to my shame.

The bow went into the grass. The Krozair long sword ripped from my belt—that belt given me aboard the airboat by Delia—sliding against the fold of scarlet cloth on my thigh. I gripped the hilt in both fists, spreading them, the left against the pommel, the right hard up against the guard. That way the two-handed sword wielded by one cunning in its use could strike past and through the spears and axes of these white-skinned barbarians. They rushed against me, whooping, charged with anger, probably unable to comprehend just where I had come from or who I was—a man like themselves and no half-beast half-man of Kregen.

Like any man of Kregen who carries weapons they were skilled. But they could not match the swordsmanship of a Krozair. There is no boast in this; I merely state a fact.

By the time they had realized this, it was too late, and as I chopped the last of them—a wild and reckless stroke that took his head clean away from his shoulders—I was aware of the ostentatiousness of my behavior. They were men and not half-men; but they had been behaving like subhumans. That, I submit, is the only excuse I can offer for my savage conduct.

When I reached Sosie she was crying. Her slender body shook with her sobs. As tenderly as I could I lifted her.

"Where lies Arkasson, Sosie?"

"Over there."

She pointed due north.

I grunted. North in the compass bearing had bedeviled my progress through the Hostile Territories.

So, bearing a naked black girl in my arms, I set off to take her home.

CHAPTER TWO

Of the black feathers and gemmed quiver of Sosie na Arkasson

"You cannot just go walking off across the Owlarh Waste, Dray Prescot!"

Sosie na Arkasson glared at me in a positive fury, her hands on her hips, her eyes bright; but her full lower lip quivered betrayingly.

"I have to, Sosie, and I must."

"But, Dray! There are leems, and stilangs, and graint, and even risslaca, besides those devils of Cherwangtung. You just can't go!"

I have never been a man who laughs easily—except in moments of stress or passion—and I could not force a laugh now. Had I done so, it is doubtful if it would have soothed Sosie's real fears. Arkasson had proved to be an interesting town, built against a sheer cliff of stone in which giant gems twinkled in the mingled light of Scorpio. The architecture ran to much convoluted tracery and scrollwork carved in stone, and massive drum towers capped with round pointed roofs built from the heavy slates from local quarries. There were open spaces in which greenery grew; but, still, echoing the inflexible rules of all towns and cities to the west within the Hostile Territories, no handy perching places had been overlooked. The defense against aerial attackers was not carried out with quite the same fanatical attention to every detail in Arkasson, and the walls cincturing the town were battlemented against ground troops as their first priority; but a force of aerial chivalry would stumble attempting to alight in Arkasson.

Mangar, who had died so cruelly, had been a leading man of the town; and although I met a number of the notables and was treated with universal kindness by them, I itched to press on to the east, to Vallia, and to Delia.

My pale skin, tanned by the Suns of Scorpio though it was, aroused intense interest in the black-skinned people of Arkasson. Sosie, indeed, had had to speak with rapidity and with lucidity to prevent a spear degutting me on that first arrival.

The people of Cherwangtung roamed the land all about during the nights, the land that hereabouts was called the Owlarh Waste, and retired to caves and hidey-holes during the day. From Arkasson they were regarded with loathing as beasts who made life difficult and dangerous. The farms ringing the town were all heavily defended by wall and moat; but the fiends from Cherwangtung would creep through by night and raid and burn and kill. Sosie's farm lay in ruins, blackened by the flames, her mother dead and now her father dead, also. The white-skinned savages had done that.

I still retain a vivid mental picture of that torture stake with the slim black form of Sosie bound naked to it, and the torchlight flickering wildly on the gyrating bodies of the white savages in their bells and feathers as they circled her screeching their menace, shaking their weapons, lusting for her blood.

"If you go, Dray Prescot—I shall never see you alive again."

"Oh, come now, Sosie! I can protect myself."

This was, in truth, a strange conversation.

When, at last, Sosie and her friends and the relatives with whom she was staying in Arkasson—until she had found a man and married and so ventured forth to rebuild her farm—understood that I fully intended to walk on toward the east, they insisted on loading me with presents. Any town must have food brought into it, and manufactures to sustain it, and Arkasson was no exception. The farms were the lifeblood of the town, and the white savages of Cherwangtung were attempting to bleed that lifeline dry.

Similar situations must exist all over the Hostile Territories; this one was none of my business. I had fulfilled my oath to Mangar na Arkasson; now I must be on my way.

From Sosie I accepted only food and drink, and a finely built Lohvian longbow. Memories of Seg ghosted up, to be firmly repressed. The longbow was all of six feet six inches in height, and the pull I judged to better a hundred pounds. It was a bow with which I would acquit myself well; had I not been trained by Seg Segutorio, the master bowman of Erthyrdrin?

Sosie smiled as she handed me the quiver fully stocked with shafts. There was in her eyes the look of a woman who bedecks a corpse for its final journey to the Ice Floes of Sicce. Out of politeness I examined the quiver, and noticed the exquisite bead-embroidery covering it, animals and flowers and border motifs, all stitched in brilliant colors. The beads glinted in the suns-light—and at that I frowned.

"These gems were gathered by myself from the cliffs, Dray. I have spent many years stitching this quiver. It—" She stopped, and her black face shone upon me and her everted lips trembled and she lowered her eyelids with their long curling black lashes. I thought, then, that I understood.

Her aunt confirmed my suspicions.

"A maiden of Arkasson, on marriage, is expected to hand to her bridegroom an embroidered quiver, and tunic, and shoes of buckskin, stitched with gems she has gathered from the cliffs with her own hand, and polished to perfection, and drilled without a flaw or chip. You are a strange man, Dray Prescot. But for the color of your skin you would be a worthy member of the noblest of Arkasson."

"And will no young man take her to wife if she cannot provide him with these trinkets?"

The aunt—one Slopa, with a lined face and graying hair, which meant she must be well over a hundred and fifty— looked affronted. "No."

"Sink me!" I burst out. "I can't take the quiver from Sosie! It's taken her years to make. If no gallant will have her without it, then she'll wait years and years more, gathering gems, polishing them, drilling them, stitching them to a new quiver. And what of her farm? Aunt Slopa—I can't take it!"

"You will hurt her cruelly if you do not."

"I know, by Zim-Zair, I know!"

Aunt Slopa pursed her full lips. "Sosie would not have done this just because you saved her life. There is more to this business than that."

"Can you bring me an undecorated quiver?"

"I can. But that—"

"Just bring it, please, Aunt Slopa."

When I had transferred all the shafts from the brilliant embroidered quiver into the plain one and had time to mark the perfection of the feather-setting—every feather was jet black—I took up the quiver that was the gift of Sosie na Arkasson and sought her out where she sat on a bench in a courtyard, the anti-flier wire stretching above her Afro hair style. She was reading a book—it was *The Quest of Kyr Nath,** a rollicking tale of mythical adventure at least two thousand years old and known all over Kregen—and as I approached she put one slim black finger between the leaves to mark her place and looked up at me with a smile.

"Nath," I said. "I know a man called Nath, a dear comrade, and I intend to go drinking and carousing with him and Zolta again one of these fine days."

She looked at the quiver.

"I would like to live, Sosie, and yet you put me in mortal peril."

"I! Put you in peril, Dray Prescot! Why, how can you think it?"

"See how these marvelous gems and this incredibly lovely stitching gleam and wink and glitter in the light of Zim and Genodras!"

She reached out her free hand and stroked down the embroidery and the gemstones. Her face showed satisfaction and pride, as was right and proper for a young girl who knows she has stitched well.

"Indeed, they do look fine. Over your back they will proclaim to the world that the quiver was made for you by a girl who—" She stopped. Again her soft everted lips trembled. She did not go on.

I said, in something of that foul and harshly-dominating tone I so much deplore in myself, "The quiver is beautiful, Sosie. I am a rough adventurer, who must travel in wild and perilous lands. It could be the death of me. It would show the world where I was; it would show the world that I carried a fortune on my back. I would have no peace." She started to say something, quickly, hotly, but I shushed her and went on. "This should hang in the house of the man you marry, Sosie, the man you will love. For him, it will be a

---

*The Word "Kyr" has been used by Prescot many times in his narrative but I have generally changed it to "Lord." It begins to look as though this usage may be incorrect, and the honorific "sir" is a better translation. As part of the title of a book its use here is perfectly justified. Also we have here, I suspect, the root reason why there are so many Naths on Kregen.

source of unceasing joy and pleasure. For me, it could bring death."

"But—Dray—" She was confused.

"You do see, Sosie. I appreciate—"

As I spoke, as I held out the scintillating quiver to her, she leaped to her feet with a choked cry. *Kyr Nath* went flying. Her arms went about me and she kissed me with a full fierce passion that held in it only an innocence and a sweetness.

That hot wet pressure on my lips shot through me with a spike of agony. Then Sosie released me and fled into the house.

I sighed. Bending, I retrieved the book.

Kyr Nath. Well. I read at random: "And in this wise did Kyr Nath astride his coal-black impiter smite the legions of Sicce, so that they recoiled from him in thunder and lightning, and Kyr Nath smote them from beyond the sunrise to the day of judgment, so that they fell to the ground and crawled into the caves beneath the Mountains of Pearl and Gold from whence issueth their fiery breath even to this day."

I put the book down. Sunrise. It said sunrise. I was still, as an Earthman, bothered over saying "suns-rise" instead of sunrise. Those ancient people of the Eye of the World who had lived and laughed along the coasts, who had built the Grand Canal and the Dam of Days, they were called the people of the sunrise or the people of the sunset. There were mysteries here that I had no way at all of unraveling.

Perhaps Maspero, in distant, unknown Aphrasöe, could have explained.

Also, and significantly, this copy of the book had Kyr Nath flying an impiter. Those coal-black flying animals with their huge wingspread were well known here, in the Hostile Territories, and I had alternately cursed and blessed them, as I had fought Ullars screeching wildly on their backs, and flown with my Delia astride Umgar Stro's great impiter away to find safety with the airboat *Lorenztone* from Vallia. In Sanurkazz the story would have had Kyr Nath riding a sectrix. Certainly, the story as I had first heard it, declaimed among the wagon circle of my Clansmen of Felschraung, had Kyr Nath riding a vove.

The culture of a whole planet is an intricately-woven tapestry—and, I can remember now, that I turned with that duly solemn thought to find Aunt Slopa regarding me mournfully.

"Sosie asks me to say to you that she quite understands."

Although I had faced many wild beasts, as you have heard, I felt the strongest disinclination to probe into the details of the scene that had preceded that announcement. What had been said between Slopa and Sosie was nothing to do with me. It was to do with me, really; but it could not be allowed to become of me.

The subject of conversation being turned, Aunt Slopa said in answer to my question: "When a man dies, his embroidered quiver and tunic and buckskins are laid up with him in the Glittering Caves."

"The Glittering Caves?"

She nodded to the overbearing cliff face dominating Arkasson. "The cliff is riddled with the caves. The gems within the rock glow and glitter."

Further comment from me did not seem required; but I did think that a fortune beyond calculation lay within that cliff, embedded in the rock and lying beside the dead bodies of generations of men in the Glittering Caves.

Before I left Sosie appeared. She had dried her tears and made herself look presentable, which, in reality, meant that she looked dazzlingly beautiful with her black skin gleaming and her Afro hairdo a puffed-up nimbus. She wore a simple dress of a dark orange color, heavily spattered with sewn gems, and her feet were clad in yellow slippers. I remember those yellow slippers.

I started to say, "You will forgive me, Sosie—"

She hushed me at once, for which I was grateful. I make it a rule never to apologize; sometimes—not often—that rule of life becomes tricky.

"So you are determined to travel the Owlarh Waste, Dray Prescot! I know, now, I cannot prevent that. I thank you for your kindness to me—"

"Now, Sosie, it is you who are kind!"

"But not kind enough."

That was spoken tartly enough. She was no weeping willow, was this Sosie na Arkasson.

"I wish you all the luck in the world, Sosie—all the luck in Kregen. May you find the man of your heart, and marry, and the farm prosper. May you be happy. Zair go with you."

As before, she did not question my use of the name Zair. They were tolerant, in Arkasson, of any man's religion, unlike the primitives of Cherwangtung.

"And with you, Dray Prescot."

Before me lay what Sosie called the Owlarh Waste. I took a few steps away from the frowning stone walls, out of their shadow and into the streaming light of the Suns of Scorpio, and I turned.

"Rembaree, Sosie!"

She lifted her arm in farewell. "Rembaree Dray Prescot. Rembaree!"

With deliberate purpose I did not look back until the town of Arkasson had sunk into a blending gray against the lowering cliff upthrust beyond its walls.

During the midday break when I ate and drank sparingly was the time to take stock of myself.

Around my waist I wore the scarlet silk formed into a breechclout. Sosie had, without my knowledge, stitched up for me a scabbard and baldric from plain supple leather of lesten hide and the deadly Krozair long sword now snugged safely against my thigh. She had made some remarkably raucous comments on that sword which, to her eyes accustomed to the slender blades of the Hostile Territories, was so monstrous a brand. The broad belt Delia had given me aboard the airboat buckled up firmly about my waist, the silver buckle deliberately left tarnished, and kept the silken loincloth in place, for silk has this exasperating tendency to slip. The rapier hung at my left side. It did not hang parallel to the long sword but thrust out at a divergent angle. The main-gauche was scabbarded to my right side. You may smile at this plethora of weapons, and consider me a walking arsenal—remember Hap Loder!—but I was accustomed to be so accoutered and could manage athletic evolutions without the slightest inconvenience.

The quiver that had caused so much heart-searching I slung over my back, the black-feathered shafts protruding up past my right shoulder. This was for convenience in carrying. For rapid shooting the quiver would be carried slung low and angled forward on the left hip. The bow itself, all six feet six inches of it, I carried unstrung. In a waxed-leather pouch I had a dozen spare strings.

Also there were the food bag and the water bottle.

So, thus I found myself, Dray Prescot, walking on my bare feet toward the eastern coast of Turismond.

If I fail to mention the broad-bladed hunting knife sheathed onto the belt behind my right hip it is merely because a knife in that position has been my constant companion from the time I first stepped aboard a seventy-four.

In my long life I have handled many weapons and grown skilled in the use of weapons wholly strange to an Earthman. Armor in its right and proper place has also been of importance to me. Yet, however much I grow used to any one sword or rapier in particular, one special bow, I have never chained myself and my fortunes to just one single weapon. Many weapons have been presented to me, I have bought large numbers, and taken quantities from dead foemen; if I were to lose all this gaudy arsenal I would feel annoyance— an annoyance not, for instance, that I had lost this one particular Krozair long sword presented to me by Pur Zenkiren, but annoyance over the loss of any weapon in the midst of dangers.

The man who wishes to be an adventuring fighting-man had best not lock his fortune to one brand alone. Fate is all too often ready to snatch it from him, and seldom ready to offer it back—as I had snatched back my sword from Umgar Stro after I had snapped his backbone.

And with this goes the corollary that the true fighting-man can fight with whatever weapons come into his hands.

The twin suns of Antares passed across the sky, the smaller green Genodras now leading the giant red Zim, so that at the second sunset the land took on the tincture of rusted iron, a broad wash of orange and brown and crimson with the last few streaks and streamers of green pulsing through that ruby sky. Ahead the Owlarh Waste stretched in dust and thorn-ivy and prickly scrub. Finding safe anchorage for the night was not overly difficult and by the time Genodras reappeared ahead of me with its filaments of lacy green patterning the sky ahead and painting out the last stars I was well on my first leg of the day's journey.

There had been a noticeable lack of interference from the people of Cherwangtung and this could be explained in a number of ways, perhaps the best of these being Sosie's comment when I had left that the wild white men tended to lay up during the day and roam only at night. I was not naïve enough to believe they had spotted me and, remembering what I had done to their war party, were afraid to approach me. They might well have been; but that way lies arrogance, psychosis, self-delusion, and eventual destruction.

The land here in the Owlarh Waste was poor and getting worse as I tramped eastward. Arkasson was a town muchly cut off from the world, tending its own circle of farms and minding its own business. The problem facing me soon would be water. Dust kicked up at the unwary tread, behooving me to walk carefully. Leem prowled here, so Sosie had said, raiding into the farms if the fences were left unrepaired, at other times subsisting on the rabbit-like animals burrowing into the plain—animals on which I, too, must depend for food.

I had less concern that I might meet risslaca—of which there are innumerable varieties. The overlords of Magdag placed a bronze risslaca beneath the beaks of their swifters where the wales met. They more often than not took the fancy of using a mythical risslaca, a great lizard-dragon with fangs and forked tongue. Those that I had previously encountered during my runs ashore when I was fighting my way up as a swifter commander on the inner sea, the Eye of the World, had been impressive enough, saurian monsters, cold-blooded, fanged and clawed, armored with plate and scale, chilly of eye. Nath, Zolta, and I had fought our quota in defending Sanurkazz's southern boundaries. That all seemed a long time ago to me, now.*

As you may well imagine, having encountered dinosaurs in the flesh on Kregen, I have, whenever the opportunity offered, studied the dinosaurs of our Earth. They form a subject for study that fascinates everyone, from the school child to the paleontologist. Just why this is so can be explained glibly—or with much psychological insight. I had the idea of trying to trace any comparisons, any parallels, between the long-gone saurian kings of the Earth and the very present flesh and blood risslaca of Kregen.

There were, of course, many points of similarity. Equally, risslaca existed—had chased me and been slain—that were unlike anything that we know stalked the Earth at the end of the mid Mesozoic Era, the Jurassic Period, all of one hundred and forty million years ago.

Many were quite dumb. Many emitted shrieks like bursting boilers. Many hunted by eye. Many hunted by scent.

It was a trio of the latter who picked me up toward the middle of the afternoon, when I had entered an area where the ground, although still poor, offered perfect conditions for fern growth. A river had wandered athwart my path and I

---

*Here is another example of a reference to incidents in Dray Prescot's life on Kregen during the period he spent on the inner sea and in Sanurkazz lost to us with those missing cassettes, as related in "A note on the tapes from Africa" in *The Suns of Scorpio*.
                                                                    A.B.A.

"I saw a narrow head greedily gulping ferns."

had crossed it and carried on. The ferns grew in lush profusion. I felt the hunter's itch between my shoulder blades. The light from the twin suns burned down, orange and jade, shafts of sunlight striking down between the great ferns. The foliage curved over me. The unending stalks towered above. I walked very lightly, turning and twisting my head, and I had strung my bow with that practiced ease that Seg Segutorio exemplified best. I carried the longbow in my hand, an arrow nocked.

Walking thus lightly and alertly through the green and golden glory of the ferns with the jade and orange light falling all about me I came to a swampy area that I must bypass. Here and there the water gleamed like bronze. A wall moved before me. That wall rippled with scaled muscle. Blotches of color—amber, jade, jet—camouflaged the risslaca against the crowding ferns. I saw a narrow head greedily gulping ferns and the drooping leaves of the bristle-topped sickly trees that grew palm-like around the fringes of the water. A serpentine neck curled around. The head lifted from the ferns and cocked so that one eye could regard— *not* me! The eye looked coldly back down the twisted trail up which I had walked.

The three killers were there. They padded up on their three-toed feet—and I saw the first toe of each hind foot carried the long scythe-bladed claw, razor-sharp, that distinguished our Earthly deinonychus. The light from the twin suns of Antares fell luridly across their arrogantly gold and ebony-banded scales. Ten feet long, were the killers; seventy feet at least the camarasaurus-like herbivore.

And I stood between them.

The rudder-like tails of the deinonychus risslacas extended stiffly backward. Those long-curved scythe-claws caught the gleam of suns-light and glittered with deadly power.

With explosive, incredible ferocity, the three killers sprang.

CHAPTER THREE

Into the Klackadrin

With reflexive action so fast the movement was completed before I saw the first risslaca's hind legs leave the ground the black feathers drew back to my ear, the last extra urge of muscle snapped out as the bow bent, my fingers released the arrow, and the shaft loosed.

So fast had I reacted, my aim exact, that thereby I was nearly killed.

For I had not expected the incredible jumping power of the reptile. It sailed up into the air, its tail rigidly extended backward, its body straightening into the upright position that would enable those slashing blades on its feet to slice me to the backbone. I have seen kangaroos in Australia, larger than these risslacas, leap fantastic distances. The dinosaurs were no sluggish, lethargic movers; they were agile, rapid, deadly—and these were killers.

The risslaca leaped above my point of aim. The arrow skewered past its belly and struck deeply into the junction of tail and body.

Sosie had given me a selection of arrows, so that I had the alternatives of the thin armor-piercing bodkin, the body punching pile, the broad meat-cleaving barb, or the utility arrowheaded point. Against what I had fancied would be after me for supper I had chosen the great barbed meat-slicing head. This slashed its way through the scale and flesh of the risslaca, gouging deeply. Chance had driven that arrow with deadly precision.

For deinonychus of the type on Kregen has the thick bunched tendons and muscles around the root of the tail so that the tail may be extended rigidly and thus give the animal the balance necessary for it to spring and use its lethal scythe-claw.

The arrow slashed all those staying tendons and muscles apart. The tail flopped. The risslaca, hissing, somersaulted, all balance and control gone.

In the same instant I darted into the shadows of the giant ferns.

The two following risslacas hurdled their screeching companion. They sprang again. High and viciously they curved into the air. I heard the shrieking snorting roar of the giant camarasaurus as they landed on its back, one high against the junction of neck and shoulders, the other lower down, so that its curved claws sank bloodily into the belly of the herbivore.

At that instant, simply by stepping forward and loosing twice, I could have slain both killers.

But I do not kill unnecessarily. I regret that sometimes in my long life I have been forced to kill. Certainly, I own to the weakness of being willing to slay first the man or beast attempting to slay me. It is a defect of character, no doubt. Here, though, nature was merely being followed. Since long before I had arrived so unexpectedly on Kregen and, without a doubt, long after I am gone, the risslacas hunt and kill as do all carnivores. It is in the nature of these fascinating creatures—just as it was in the nature of the scorpion to sting my father to death.

Judging by the noise and the thrashing among the giant curving ferns the killers were not having it all their own way.

Circumspectly, then, I left that scene that might have been wrenched from the scarlet pages of Earth's Jurassic and walked delicately on around the swamp.

Perhaps, by taking out one of the hunting party of carnivores, I had given the herbivore the better chance, at that.

You may be sure I walked long into the night, constantly alert, until I was well away from the swamps and ferns of the meandering river and once again treading the poor, dry and dusty ground. I camped that night without a fire and merely dozed. Three days and nights later and with the land still as unfriendly and with only a mouthful of water left in my canteen, I had to revert still further to our barbaric ancestors. My shaft drove skillfully, and slew me a darting rat-like creature—not a Kregen rast, although no doubt a species allied to those unpleasant creatures—and I drank its blood to slake my thirst.

I strode on, having recovered my arrow and cleaned it on the animal's gray and dusty fur, ever vigilant for predatory enemies. More to the point, I was also constantly on the lookout for food. So, I suppose, as is the way with men or the half-men of Kregen, I was the greater predator crossing that dismal and hostile wilderness.

Toward evening of the fifth day I ran across one of the broad high-banked roads left by the conquerors of the Empire of Walfarg who had driven through here from the eastern seaboard in the old days and taken their suzerainty of all the Hostile Territories.

The debate I carried out did not last long. Of a certainty I could travel far faster along the road with its squared slabs than across the arid plain. Those stones were still in remarkable condition, squared, their edges only slightly crumbled and the greenery that attempted to struggle through the interstices could subsist only on drifted soil, for the old engineers of Loh had built well. But on the road I would be marked.

So, keeping the road generally in sight, I traveled more safely if more slowly parallel to it, heading east.

On the eighth day I began to discern a jagged appearance to the eastern horizon. The skyline there did not bear the kind of outline I associated with a mountain range, and I hoped there was going to be nothing like The Stratemsk ahead of me. I did not relish that thought. We had flown through The Stratemsk, Delia and Seg and Thelda and I. That mountain chain lofted so high, extended so sprawlingly vast, that it defied all rational comprehension. It walled off with chilling finality the western end of the Hostile Territories from the eastern end of the lands on the eastern border of the inner sea. What happened there, in the Eye of the World, might have been happening back on my Earth for all that the people of the Hostile Territories knew. And, now, I began to entertain the deepest suspicions that another and equally hostile barrier existed between the Hostile Territories and the eastern seaboard of this continent of Turismond.

If it did, I would have to pass through, somehow, so as to reach the coast, take ship to Vallia, and reach my Delia of the Blue Mountains.

The terrain continued unpleasant, much cut up with dry gulches and razor-backed outcroppings of naked rock. Here —although I knew I must have trended well north of the parallel of latitude on which stood Pattelonia, the city of the eastern seaboard of the Eye of the World from which we had set out—the weather continued hot with the brazen Suns of

Scorpio burning down. I had now to hunt my food and drink in earnest.

The jagged impression of the skyline before me continued when I was able to observe it from a higher-than-usual eminence, although the difficulty of the ground with its bare-bones, dessicated look meant I was more often than not confined between rocky walls. My back kept up an infernal itch and my head swiveled from side to side, constantly observing my back trail, like—if you will pardon the anachronistic image—the rear turret of a Lancaster. The only life that scraped a subsistence here larger than the insects and lizards and other burrowing animals seemed, from all that I observed, to be a kind of six-legged opossum and the wheeling birds, both of which fed on the life lower down the food-chain. You may easily understand how relieved I was that from day to day the birds that followed me were no larger in size than an Earthly vulture or kite. Why they were following me was obvious; but I had to reach my Delia of Delphond, and was in no mood to provide a meal for these scavengers of the air.

Harsh vegetation grew scrawnily along shadowed cracks in the uptilted rock faces. There were ants here, too, and I avoided their dwellings with great circumspection.

So it was that a quick and furtive movement beyond a boulder at the far end of a draw sent me at once to cover.

I waited.

Patience is not merely the virtue of the hunter—it is his life.

Presently a Chulik stepped out into the center of the draw.

I drew my breath in a gasp of amazement.

The Chuliks I had seen on Kregen before were full-fleshed men, with two arms and two legs, with a healthy, oily yellow skin. They habitually shaved their skulls with the exception of a long rope of hair that might grow to reach their waists. From the corners of their lips protruded two upward thrusting tusks a full three inches in length and, although they were human-seeming, they knew little of humanity. Normally they were highly prized as mercenaries and guards commanding higher prices than the Ochs or the Rapas, beast-men who performed similar functions. Some I had seen as slaves, not many.

This Chulik's hair grew matted and coarse and filthy. One of his tusks was broken jaggedly. He wore a scrap of black cloth about his middle, much covered with dust and dung

and his yellow skin was likewise befouled. In one hand he
carried a long pole fabricated from a number of spliced
lengths cut from the twisted and scrawny bushes that were
all that grew hereabouts, and the end of the pole carried a
yoke-like fork. A basket woven of dry stems enclosed four
of the little opossum creatures. The Chulik was busy about
the task of catching a fifth, poking and prying down into a
shallow hole beneath a boulder, moving with an alacrity
pathetic in comparison with the lithe and vigorous movements of the Chuliks I had known.

I waited.

Moments later another figure joined the first.

Again I felt astonishment.

This was a Fristle, a half-man with a face as much like a
cat's as anything else, furred, whiskered, slit-eyed, and fang-
mouthed. Although I still had no love for Fristles—for
Fristles had carried my Delia off to captivity in Zenicce so
soon after I had been taken to Kregen for the second time—
much of my dislike had been mitigated by the gallant actions
of Sheemiff, the female Fristle, she who had called me her
Jikai and had so proudly worn the yellow-painted vosk-skull
helmet when my rabble army of slaves and workers re-
volted in Magdag.

This Fristle wore a black breechclout, was as filthy and
downcast as the Chulik. He carried the curved scimitar
that is the racial weapon of the Fristles, but its hangings and
lockets were tarnished and broken.

What had brought these two representatives of proud and
haughty races so low?

The impression grew in me strongly that I had nothing to
fear from them.

The strangeness of that feeling must be apparent to you
who have listened to my story so far.

I stepped out and lifted my hand.

"Llahal!" I called, using the double-L prefix, after the
Welsh fashion, to the word of greeting, as was right when en-
countering strangers.

They looked up sluggishly.

After a time the Fristle said: "Llahal."

The Chulik said: "Why do you not work?"

"I am going to the coast."

For a moment they did not understand. Then the Fristle
cackled. I know, now, that laughter for him and the others

here occurred so infrequently that it might never have been invented; it came almost as seldom to them as it does to me.

"I have marched from the Hostile Territories, through the Owlarh Waste, and I have not come here to be laughed at— by a Fristle least of all."

In response the Fristle merely blinked. His hand did not even fall to his scimitar hilt.

The Chulik cowered back, but he did not lift the forked pole against me.

I rolled out a vile Makki-Grodno oath.

What had happened to these men? What power had so ferociously tamed them into pitiful wrecks of their former selves?

Also, the thought occurred to me, it is said there is hereditary enmity between Chulik and Fristle, except when they are engaged by the same employer.

Knowing that, I was profoundly impressed when the Fristle helped the Chulik hoist the cage containing the four opossum creatures onto his back. I caught a glimmering, then, that whatever horrific experiences these men had gone through had brought them closer together and by stripping away the artificialities of race and species had displayed them to each other in adversity as creatures together beneath Zair and Grodno.

"The grint has gone, now," said the Chulik. He spoke in the whine habitual to the slave. "Four will not be enough, but that is all the Phokaym will get."*

At this name, this name of Phokaym, both Chulik and Fristle gave an involuntary shudder.

Before I could say another word they hunched around and slouched off, quickly vanishing into the tangle of boulders at the end of the draw.

I ran fleetingly enough after them; but when I entered the rock-strewn area I saw quickly that they had taken themselves off and lost me, traveling by secret paths and passages they would know well.

Pushing on through this country grew more difficult in the following few burs and so, at last, I chanced striding out along the old road of empire.

---

*Prescot spells out this name, Phokaym, giving it the "Ph" and the "Y," although he nowhere tells us where he learned that these were the correct spellings, in place of the "F" and the "I."

A.B.A.

One vital fact was very clear. In this area lived some power of such strength that it could reduce arrogant beast-men to a cowering state lower than that of a whip-beaten slave. From the evidence of the Fristle's scimitar I judged that they were not slaves. All resistance had been knocked out of them, and warriors who had strode victoriously over a score of battlefields had been reduced to a state of abject degradation. All this was proved to be true—as I found to my cost, as you shall hear.

Occasionally I glimpsed over the twisted and fantastically jumbled landscape on either side of the road more of these subdued people, men and women, Ochs, Rapas, Fristles, and Chuliks, as well as Ullars and other half-beast, half-men I had not so far encountered closely enough to identify. They all scuttled at my approach, disappearing into crevices in the rock. None ventured onto the squared blocks of the road surface.

That night I camped uncomfortably in a rock crevice of my own close to the road and, apart from a few strips of dried meat hung on my belt, I went supperless to bed. I had the strongest conviction I should save as much food as possible for what the future held.

In the morning with that jade and ruby fire mingling and pulsing down I stood up and stretched and was at once alert and ready to face the terrors of the day. As I walked along that ancient road I saw that scummy water filled pools and hollows among the rocks, and that a weird and gnarled vegetation grew, all twisted and stunted, its roots curling like petrified serpents from the rocks into the fetid water. Indeed, the smells of indescribable foulness grew every yard I progressed. I began to feel a dizziness. I blinked and shook my head and pressed on. The road appeared to me to waver as does tar macadam at the brow of a hill in hot sunshine; a shimmering stream of interconnecting and vibrating images at once obscuring vision and lending it a fraudulent magnifying quality.

Now I walked all alone. No other living soul I could see stirred in that dismal expanse.

Ahead of me lay the east coast, and a ship, and Vallia— and Delia. No fainting fit would hold me back. I staggered as I marched. I hauled up, the sweat starting out all over my body as I stared directly ahead along that ancient road, there on the continent of Turismond on the planet of Kregen beneath the Suns of Scorpio—and saw a three-decker of a hundred and twelve guns lift her scarlet-lidded gun ports and saw the thirty-two pounders and the twenty-four pounders and the eighteen pounders run out, grinning at me, and belch in silent flame and smoke!

That smashing broadside would pulverize me in an instant. The familiar yellow smoke engulfed me and I could not prevent the old prayer rising to my lips—but even as I said, "For what we are about to receive," the three-decker vanished. In her place I saw a swifter of the inner sea, a lean deadly hundredswifter turning toward me so that her bronze rostrum aimed directly at the rib beneath my heart!

I yelled—and in that wavering mist and confusing smoke, the glint of the twin suns and the smothering feeling of madness rising in my mind I saw my friend Zorg—Zorg of Felteraz—smiling at me, his moustache curling. Zorg, dead and gone and food for chanks in the inner sea.

His face was ripped away and next I saw Nath and Zolta, my oar comrades who with Zorg and I had labored at the oars as slaves, Nath and Zolta, chuckling, the one with a leather blackjack slopping wine, the other with a giggling wench on his knee.

I shouted.

I lurched forward—and now I saw Gloag, my good comrade from Zenicce who was not a full human being and yet who knew more of human kindness than—than Glycas, that cruel and cunning man of Magdag, and his sister, the beautiful and evil Princess Susheeng—and I saw Queen Lilah, the Queen of Pain of Hiclantung—and I saw Hap Loder and all of my clansmen in headlong cry astride their massive voves —I saw Prince Varden Wanek of the House of Eward. I saw many people, then, all replaying the roles they had played in my life.

I saw Seg Segutorio and Thelda—and I wept.

And then—then I saw my Delia, my Delia of Delphond, as she had walked with so lithe a swing down toward Great-Aunt Shusha and me. Delia I saw, wearing that flaunting scarlet breechclout and with the dazzlingly white ling furs I had given her aswing about her form, her long lissome legs very splendid in the suns-light.

Then I knew beyond a doubt that I dreamed.

I shook my head.

Knowledge of hallucinatory drugs is more widespread on this Earth than heretofore, and armed with modern knowledge I might have appreciated far more rapidly just what was happening to me. Opium and hashish were known to me, as was the more luscious and gentle if treacherous kaf used by the weak-willed on Kregen beneath Antares. Drug-taking for escape from life is generally the mark of a decadent or bored society—and on Kregen life was too vivid and head-long and demanding for those who sought life out for the taking of drugs to be more than a marginal nuisance. It has seemed to me that I have never had the time to investigate properly all this modern to-do over the drug habit and on Kregen I have always had far too much to do, even as slave, when my every thought has normally been set on escape.

So now I staggered and lurched along the old imperial road and the phantoms from my mind took on form and substance and came to leer and gibber at me, to mock, or to smile and hold out their hands in friendly Lahal.

That first time I attempted to cross this barrier to the eastern coast—the barrier was called the Klackadrin, as you shall hear—I entered on the task as a young and innocent. Those scummy pools fed minerals to the scrawny plants, which breathed out their miasmic bedevilment, betraying the wits of men and beasts. The Klackadrin sealed the eastern flanks of the Hostile Territories as effectively as The Stratemsk sealed the western.

Delia's counterfeit image swung away and in her place pranced all the might of the cavalry aswirl about me at Waterloo. I brushed a hand across my eyes, and when I looked again I saw Umgar Stro, huge and ferocious, charging upon me with the ghostly replica of the sword I now carried!

Tendrils from the marshy pools set amid deep crevices of the rocks at the side of the road wriggled across the road at me. At first I thought them figments of my imagination, perhaps a reminder of those morfangs we had battled in that cave of the Hostile Territories. Then a thick and clutching tendril wrapped itself about my ankle. It hauled.

A single slash from my Krozair long sword severed the thing.

More of them crowded the road ahead, writhing, seeming obscenely beckoning arms, beseeching me to walk into their embrace. I would have to hack my way through.

A fresh sound obtruded. A hard, ringing clash of steel-like claws on the flagstones of the road.

I swung about.

I really believe, even now, that I thought I was bewitched still, seeing phantoms, seeing things that never were.

That belief, sluggish and obstinate, held me in a stasis that came from the foolish belief that of all these hallucinations none could harm me and that only from the beckoning and writhing tendrils had I any physical danger to fear.

What I saw impacted with the sense of physical nausea and yet, with all my experience of Kregen and its beast-men to give me a guide, I realized that these beast-men were not half-men half-beasts; these were half-beast half-monster.

They were the Phokaym.

They rode cousins to those risslacas I had previously met, huge lumbering dinosaurs that yet moved with a quickness that would tax a sectrix to match. The Phokaym themselves, quite clearly, were racial descendants of risslacas. They were cold-blooded, as I discovered, with the wide-fanged mouth of the carnivorous risslaca, the small front legs that had adapted into manipulative arms and clawed hands, and the powerful hind legs and tail of the carnivorous dinosaur. They were perhaps twelve feet tall. They carried their tails curled up and around behind the ornate saddles. Each one was armed with spear and sword. They wore barbaric ornaments, and their scales were painted and lacquered into geometric patterns of cold reptilian beauty.

Were they real?

Intelligent, armed, cold-blooded carnivorous dinosaurs riding spurred and bridled herbivorous dinosaurs?

They were real.

Had they been more alien, more weird, more unearthly than their very forms suggested, I might have believed. There are so many unearthly life-forms on Kregen that one can understand the profusion of life and its multiplicity; had they been like those morfangs, or the wlachoffs—incredibly alien in appearance—or any other of the many unterrestrial creatures I have encountered on Kregen, I might have reacted sooner. As it was their very suggestion of Earthly dinosaurs riding Earthly dinosaurs, a conception staggering to me then, if not so much later, with its immediate impact of rejection and dissociation in that bath of hallucinogenic compounds, made me laggard and late.

Thick blood-red strands fell about me, tacky and binding, dragging my arm and long sword into my side, entangling my bow and quiver, wrapping me from shoulder to ankle. I fell.

The smash of the hard stone against my cheek awoke me.

But it was too late.

Enmeshed I was dragged along the hard stones of the road, back toward the west, back away from the coast, back into a slavery of the kind I had seen in those unfortunates skulking among the rocks and fetid pools.

Triumphantly shrilling, the Phokaym dragged me away.

Had they had eight limbs each, I would have believed in them, and my long sword would have drunk cold reptilian blood. Had they had eight legs, I would have believed.

Six legs, even. . . .

CHAPTER FOUR

The Phokaym

An old crone of an Och came to me in the corner of a cave where the Phokaym had flung me, still tightly bound in the thick blood-red strands. She was old and her stringy bleached hair hung lankly down. She stood before me on her legs, holding the pannikin of foul water with her middle limbs, and brushed the scum from the surface of the water with one of her upper hands, while the other dipped the stone spoon and so dribbled water between my lips.

"They want you alive and healthy for the voryasen."

The spoon was merely a dumbbell-shaped piece of stone with one end hollowed out. Most of the water trickled down my chin and into my beard—which was longer and more ragged than I customarily allowed—but the drops I sucked in, despite my knowledge of their stinking condition, tasted like the best Zond wine.

The Och made no attempt to free me. She cringed at the slightest sound, shutting her eyes and hunching her head down into her neck. She spilled more water than I got, but at least I felt a little more myself. I asked her impatient questions, and when I mastered myself enough to soothe her, she was able to speak, albeit falteringly and with many frightened glances over her shoulder. Outside came the noise of people moving about, the rhythmical gong-like notes as stone struck against stone. The suns had set, but it was still hot.

"The Klackadrin." The old Och woman sighed. Her name, she said, was Ooloo. She had no clear memory of any life before this; yet she must have been brought here in some way, if she had not been born here. She did not remember. "The Klackadrin. It is evil, weird, ghosts and bad spirits dwell there. No one can cross it at all—only the roads, only the roads—"

41

How many of these poor devils had sought to escape via the roads, only to have the fearsome Phokaym astride their risslacas hunt them down and bind them with the blood-red cords and cast them to the voryasen?

"Devils," she said, muttering, and cast a terrified glance toward the cave mouth.

The Klackadrin, she told me, was not a great distance in an east-west direction, although its north-south axis, meandering and curving, stretched she did not know how far into North Turismond and ended, she thought, far down into the south, perhaps as far as the Cyphren Sea where the Zim Stream sweeps up from unknown oceans.

"Evil dreams, nightmares, madness, that is all the Klackadrin can offer. There are monsters there—monsters—" She shut her eyes. I had had no food and when I asked she brought me a piece of raw opossum which, as a warrior, I knew I must eat to keep up my strength, yet tasted hard and stringy and needed much chewing.

"One day, perhaps, the Phokaym will go away and leave us in peace," said Ooloo. It was pathetically transparent that she did not believe this would ever happen.

By continuous perseverance I discovered I could move my fingers a little within the constriction of the blood-red strands. I kept working away, pushing and pulling one muscle against the next in well-remembered drill, seeking to keep them flexible and the blood coursing through my body. If I was to escape I could not have the agony of blood returning to circulation slowing me down.

I was working on my upper arms when the Phokaym amid a loud noise of clashing weapons and scaled armor came for me.

"The voryasen!" whispered old Ooloo. As I was dragged out with a great shouting and much buffeting I heard her say, "Jikai, Jikai," and I thought she sobbed.

We warriors always felt a trifle contemptuous of Ochs with their little round shields when it came to combat; but I think I can trace my emergence of a better feeling for them from that encounter with old Ooloo there in the fetid caves of the Phokaym.

Clouds drifted across the sky and She of the Veils, the fourth moon, shone more fitfully even than usual, while the first moon, almost twice the size of our own moon, the Maiden with the Many Smiles, was already setting far across the Owlarh Waste.

The collection of food and the production of tools and utensils were the primary concerns of the crushed-down people, both men and half-men, under the despotic rule of the Phokaym.

Tonight was to be a spectacle night, an occasion when the risslaca Phokaym emphasized their absolute power. A man was to be tossed to the voryasen. Consequently, so I gathered, more torches than usual were lit, painfully gathered by the slaves from the waste, twisted and gnarled branches they had so painfully gathered set alight gleefully by the Phokaym to illuminate their celebrations.

I saw stone jugs passing from claw to claw as the Phokaym gathered. Their scales glittered in the torchlight. It was difficult to distinguish just what was armor and what was their own scaly hide. I was dragged toward the stone lip of a great pit. Above the pit an arrangement of wooden supports lashed together projected, like the boom of a crane. The Phokaym crowded toward this pit. I was hoisted upside down and my lashed ankles were fastened by a rope painstakingly woven from dry stems. Torchlight glared upon the scene, ruddy and orange, streaming light and driving weird shadows cavorting among the rocks and the stunted bushes.

Up I swung, twisting and turning, upside down, hanging from the rope. The boom moved and turned and I was carried out over the pit. I looked down.

A voryas is a form of risslaca one might imagine in nightmare, part crocodile, part tylosaurus, a giant fang-filled mouth, all jaw and muscle, and an agile scaly body and bludgeoning tail, that one would do well never to imagine, even in nightmare, let alone care to encounter.

Bound and helpless, with all my weapons about me and unable to use them, I swung upside down above a water-filled pit crawling with the saurian horrors.

They lifted from the surface of the water, hissing and spitting, their jaws wedges of fangs, their eyes red and wicked and glaring upon me with voracious intent.

The Phokaym had fun.

They kept paying out the rope and lowering me down toward the surface of the water so that the voryasen would leap up at me, giant scaled forms gleaming dully emerald and amber, surging upward to fall back, baffled, hissing their rage, as the rope was hastily hauled in.

Up and down I went, and the voryasen leaped and hissed, and the world turned scarlet from the thrum of blood in my

"I was dragged toward the stone lip of a great pit."

head and my eyes threatened to start from their sockets, and my body grew numb.

By a stupendous effort I managed to jackknife my body and look upward. A Phokaym, his teeth glinting as carnivorously as any voryas in the pit below, held out a blazing torch. He was touching the fizzing and sputtering torch to the rope holding my bound body above the pit.

Furiously I struggled with the blood-red cords, but they would not yield.

If I could swing, I could reach the timber support of the boom from which I hung suspended. The smells, the shrieks, the whole cacaphony of noises spurted up to rumble and roil in my head. I was helpless. Below me the carnivorous water-predators saw the flame of the torch and their hissing redoubled.

They knew what would happen when the torch burned through the rope.

They knew!

I was sweating now; everything whirled about me. One crunch of those gigantic fanged jaws below and I would be cut into two bloody halves.

There could be no last-minute rescue. There was no one within a hundred dwaburs who could aid me now—no one anywhere on this wild and savage world of Kregen.

The pit yawned beneath my dangling head. Torchlight splintered back from the scales and the eyes of the voryasen below. Now their hissing bounced back in magnified echoes from the pit walls. I craned up again—the rope was burning!

I could see the frayed and blackened strands parting, one by one, curling out like spent matches.

The torchlight burned into my eyes.

The shrieking and yelling of the Phokaym deafened me.

I swung. . . .

My mouth was wide open, but I was not yelling.

This might be the end of it all, of all the high dreams I had had, here on Kregen, of winning my princess and of taking her to my palace and estates in Zenicce, of once more riding with my loyal clansmen across the great plains of Segesthes. . . .

I swung. . . .

The world dizzied before my swimming eyes. Smoke and flame mingled and blinded me.

But I could see the fire of burning rope, see the strands

parting, see the evil flickering flame gnawing through the only thing that supported me above the fangs and jaws of those merciless risslacas below. . . .

I saw—I saw the last strand burn, the rope part and break and then I yelled—

At this point the tapes from Africa end.

The following narrative picks up the story later on in Prescot's life on Kregen. It begins in the middle of a sentence.

The end of the last cassette came with a noise—a sound— of such unimaginable ferocity as to chill me to the heart when I first heard it, and which I hesitate to play over again. After that the tape spins emptily through the heads. Whatever it was that made that frightful sound, I have grave doubts that even the African jungle harbors its creator.

The beginning of the fresh cassette is garbled and there is some confused noise as of laughter and—I guess—the popping of champagne corks. This, as I think you who have followed the saga of Prescot this far will agree, is well in keeping.

The writer who has been giving me invaluable assistance in editing these tapes, a distinguished author with an international reputation, when he heard this portion observed, with what I took to be wry admiration: "Dray Prescot has successfully pulled off one of the oldest classical clichés in the book."

"Of course," I told him. "That's Dray Prescot's style."

I do wonder, though, if we will ever be privileged to hear what failed to record at the beginning of this tape. Just how *did* Dray Prescot do it? Those of you who have followed his saga so far will have no doubts whatsoever that he *could* do it. . . .

And, there is the yellow fang of the Phokaym Prescot gave to Pando to act as a clue. . . .

Alan Burt Akers

. . . bringing me up out of the light doze into which I had fallen and this time louder and more urgent. I opened my eyes and cursed and stretched out a hand across the wide rumpled bed where the fused jade and ruby light from the twin suns threw a miniature landscape of mountain and valley. The light glinted back from the hilt of my rapier as I took it up into my fists. Again the scream knifed up the narrow black-wood stairs of *The Red Leem*. I cursed, and groaned, for my legs were still rubbery and my head throbbed as though an impiter smote me with his coal-black wings.

"What in the name of Makki-Grodno's diseased armpit is going on?" I yelled.

By the time the third scream ripped out I recognized Tilda's voice. I staggered a little, and gripped onto the bedpost. The wooden floor with its scattered rugs of bright Walfarg weave swayed under me like the deck of a frigate blockading Brest. I shook my head. I had my old scarlet breechclout wrapped around my middle and my rapier in my fist. Hastily I snatched up the main-gauche and started for the door.

The door burst open and young Pando appeared, his hair wild, his eyes reflecting more of the red light than the green, his whole body animated with anger and furious defiance. He shouted at me, his words tumbling over one another, a little dagger in his fist that shook with his passion.

"The Pandrite-forsaken devils!" He danced up and down. "They're insulting Mother—Dray! Come on! You've got to help!"

"I'm coming, Pando." I set straight for the door and bounced from the jamb. Pando grabbed my arm and steered me through the doorway. "You'd best not stick 'em with that toothpick, Pando," I said. "You'll only upset them."

"I'll degut 'em all!" he shrilled. He was only nine years old, as I had to remind myself, and he thought everything in life was black and white.

Then, as though commenting on my thoughts about him, he gave me a kick to help me on my way. I wobbled toward the black-wood stairs, twisted, my feet shot from under me on one of the Walfarg rugs, and down the stairs I went, bump, bump, bump, to the bottom. The bottom hit me hard.

Through the arched opening into the main room of the inn I could see the counter with its ranked amphorae, its trim rows of sparkling glass cups, the covers over the food, everything neat and tidy and waiting for evening when the men and women of Pa Mejab would crowd in for their evening's entertainment.

The chief source of their entertainment was now struggling in the grip of three men. They were ruffians, all right, intent on their prey. As I stood up, smarting, and stared blearily at

them I fancied they were leem-hunters, men from the back
hills away to the west and probably men who would venture
almost to the Klackadrin itself. They wore clothes made
from leem pelts, and broad leather harness, with swaggering
rapiers and daggers and large riding boots and all seeming to
me to be very powerful and blurry.

I blinked.

Tilda's blouse had ripped down over one shoulder and then
the other, and the men laughed.

"Let go, you stinking cramphs!" Tilda was yelling. Her
long mane of black hair floated freely from her head, swirling out, in truth, very much like the wings of an impiter.
She got one arm free and slapped a leem-hunter across his
leathery, whiskered cheeks, whereat he roared with laughter,
and, catching that arm, bent it back and drew his face close
to Tilda's.

"You won't dance for us, ma faril, when we ask all polite-
ly, so you'll dance to another tune now."

"Wait until we open our doors, rast!"

"Hold on!" shouted another of the men, too late, for
Tilda's naked toes slammed into him. He doubled up,
clutching himself, and rolled away, both laughing and retching.

Yes, they were ruffians, all right. In from the country and
wanting their fun. Pando ran past me, straight up to them,
and struck wildly with the dagger at the man gripping his
mother.

"Pando!" I yelled, alarmed.

The man back-handed Pando off. He staggered back, can-
noned into a table, went over spilling the vase of moon-
flowers onto the floor. The man roared his good humor.
About to bend again to Tilda he caught sight of me, in the
doorway, the rapier and main-gauche in my fists.

He straightened up and threw Tilda into the arms of the
third man, who grabbed her—most familiarly, I thought—
whereat she squealed and tried both to kick and bite him.

"So what have we here, by the gross Armipand himself!"

He ripped his rapier from its sheath, and the dagger followed as quickly. The man Tilda had kicked hauled himself
up, turning to face me, his features still twisted and the tears
still in his eyes. For a moment the tableau held in the main
room of *The Red Leem*. I was conscious of the stupidity of
all this. My head rang as though a swifter's oars were beat-

ing my skull all the way along the hull of a two-hundred-and-tenswifter.

"You had best release the lady," I said with some difficulty.

They guffawed.

"A tavern wench a lady! Haw, haw!"

I shook my head in negation—and that was a mistake. All the bells of Beng-Kishi clanged resonantly inside my skull.

"She is not a tavern wench. She is Tilda, the famous entertainer, a dancer and actress. She is," I added with words more like myself, "not for scum of the likes of you."

"Ho! A ruffler!" The leader of the leem-hunters abruptly threw himself into the posture of the fighting-man. "A swagger with a rapier and dagger! Come on, little man, let us see you back your words with your sword point."

When I say my legs felt like rubber, it would be more correct to say I could hardly feel them at all, and my knees seemed like mashed banana. I took a step forward, and my rapier point described trembling circles.

The three men laughed hugely.

"Serve him as you served the landlord, Gorlan!"

Portly Nath, the landlord, lay huddled beyond an overturned table. All I could see of him were his legs and feet in their satin slippers, and his balding head, the face turned away from me, and a small trickle of blood. He was not dead, for he moaned; but he had been struck a shrewd blow.

"I am not a fat old innkeeper," I said.

"Then I will open your tripes and find out!" said this Gorlan, flickering his blade very swiftly before me.

He lunged.

My dagger seemed—of its own volition and without any conscious effort of my muscles—to do as it pleased. It sliced up, deflected the rapier blade in a screech of metal, and so drove Gorlan back, with a spring, his face abruptly blackening with thwarted anger.

"You miserable cramph!" he bellowed.

He drove in again, powerfully, overbearing me by sheer weight and ferocity. My twin blades beat him off. The metal slithered and clanged, sliding and twisting with many cunning tricks and turns. He scored a long slicing cut across my left arm and then my rapier point pressed into his throat and his dagger flew spinning across the inn. I did not hear it land.

"Oh, Gorlan," I said, rather thickly and with the world

jumping and dancing with purple spots and streaks of white fire. "Oh pitiful little Gorlan!"

His face blanched. It was a very wonderful sight to see that swarthy visage drain of blood, the eyes glare in terror upon me, the lips go suddenly dry.

"Dray!" screeched Tilda.

I swiveled to my right, taking the rapier around ninety degrees and showing its point to the man Tilda had kicked and who was now rushing upon me with drawn sword. My left hand gripping the main-gauche swung around with my movement and my fist smashed sloggingly into Gorlan's jaw. He dropped like a sack.

The second man hauled up, his rapier engaging mine, and for a short space we circled. With an oath the man grasping Tilda flung her from him, drew his own weapons, and charged in upon me at the side of his companion. The difficulty of focusing nearly betrayed me; I did not want to kill these two, as I knew they would not wish to kill me. This was a tavern brawl over a woman—as far as they were concerned a tavern wench—and they knew the arm of the law of Pandahem stretched here to Pa Mejab. As for me, the same strictures obtained. That Tilda was in very truth a famous actress, here in this colonial port city of Pandahem only because she had married for love, and her soldier husband had been killed here, leaving her stranded with her nine-year-old son Pando, meant nothing to them, although it meant a great deal to me.

So I engaged, and parried, and feinted, and took their blades upon my dagger, and thrust in the attempt to disable them. And all the time the world pressed roaring and swirling in upon me, my sight dimmed. I felt my banana knees bucking, and their onslaughts grew stronger and stronger as I grew weaker.

By a desperate piece of sheer outrageous Spanish-style two-handed fencing that would have had my old master, the cunning Spaniard, Don Hurtado de Oquendo, foaming with outraged professionalism, I managed to disarm the second man and send him reeling back with blood spurting from a pierced bicep.

But the other fellow bored in and my sluggish legs wouldn't drag me around in time to meet his attack.

Then—like an avenging angel—Tilda rose up at his back and, two-handed, brought down a jug of purple wine upon his head.

He grunted and lurched forward and his rapier skewered the floorboards as he smashed on past, the blade vibrating backward and forward and hilt seesawing like an upside down metronome.

As though hypnotized by that rhythmic motion I went to my knees, toppled slowly forward, and so came to rest beside the leem-hunter—and all of Kregen fell on me in blackness.

CHAPTER FIVE

A zhantil-skin tunic for Pando

Tilda would not tell anyone—not even me—any other name by which she might be known in Pandahem. Tilda was her professional name, her stage name, and by it she had become famous. What personal tragedy lay as the cause of her moldering, as I termed it, here in a distant colonial port city she also would not reveal. I gathered this had something to do with her husband, and of him all she would say was that he had married her against the wishes of his family. As a soldier he had been posted to Pa Mejab and, leading his squadron one day, had been slain.

She was fanatically proud and possessive of Pando, who was, as you have seen, an engaging imp of a rascal. She fretted continually over his safety and welfare, constantly chiding him for not wearing enough clothes, for not eating enough, for fighting the other children thronging the busy streets. But, in all this, she never lost sight with a clear-headed practicality that Pando was the son of a soldier, that she must look to him one day, and that he must develop as a man.

I confess that I grew to a better liking for both of them with each day that passed. My room at *The Red Leem* had always a vase of colorful flowers, and the sheets and sleeping furs were changed with hygienic regularity. Old Nath, the landlord, recovered of the knock on the head, consented to allowing me a reduced rent when I went on the guard duties by which, perforce, I earned my daily crust. He was only too well aware of the business Tilda brought into his inn. In the evening when she sang and danced, when she gave recitals of the great parts in Kregen drama, tragediennes and comediennes, performances so moving in both cases that they brought tears to the eyes of her audiences, rapt in silent admiration, Pando and I would sit companionably together and listen.

Pando, at nine years old, had the most fanatical admiration for his beautiful mother.

For, as I have said, Tilda was a beauty with her ivory skin and ebony hair, all swirling and glowing, with her firm figure that had no need of the theater's contrivances to drive men's blood singing through their veins. Her violet eyes and her voluptuous mouth could melt with passion, could become stern and regal, could blast all a man's hopes, could urge him to fire and ardor and unthinking gallantry—and all this on the tiny scrap of stage mounted at the far end of the main room of *The Red Leem!*

Pando is a familiar name for children of Pandahem, the great rival trading island to Vallia. It was only on the second day of my stint as a caravan guard that he was discovered hiding among the calsany drovers.

The overseer, a tough and chunky man with a cummerbund swathing the results of many a night at *The Red Leem,* and, probably, all the other inns and taverns of Pa Mefab, hauled Pando out by an ear and ran him up to me where I strode along on the left flank of the leading flight of calsanys.

"Dray!" roared the overseer, one Naghan the Paunch. "Dray Prescot! Look what has dropped with the nits from the hides of the calsanys!"

I sighed and stared at Pando with a greatly feigned air of complete despair.

"We have no room for passengers, Naghan. Therefore he must either be slain at once, or sent back alone—or—?" I cocked an eye at Naghan the Paunch.

He pondered deeply. "To slay him now would probably be best, for he would never reach Pa Mefab against the leems and the wlachoffs who would rend the flesh from his bones and devour him until not a morsel was left."

Pando, squirming against the brown hand that held his ear in so tight a grip, looked up, and the whites of his eyes showed.

"You wouldn't do that to me, Dray! What would Mother say?"

"Ah!" said Naghan the Paunch, enjoying himself. "Poor dear Tilda the Beautiful! Tilda of the Many Veils! How she will grieve for this limb of Sicce himself!"

"Dray!" yelped Pando.

I rubbed my beard. "On the other hand, Naghan, Pando

did run with his dagger to protect Tilda the Beautiful when
she was attacked by leem-hunters. If he could do that, might
he not thus also attack the leems themselves?"

Naghan twisted the trapped ear. "Have you a dagger,
boy?"

Pando was thoroughly aroused now. He tried to kick
Naghan. "Had I a dagger, oh man of the Paunch, I would
have stuck you with it long before this!"

"Oho!" quoth Naghan the Paunch, and laughed.

And I laughed, and so—I, Dray Prescot, laughing!—because we could not send Pando back across that dangerous
land we had perforce to take him with us. He was a bright
lad, full of wiles and mischievousness, and yet with an en-
dearing streak of pleasant loyalty and quickness of wits, and
a readiness to learn that I knew would stand him in good
stead on Kregen, where a man must be a man if he wishes
to survive.

His greatest vice was his inveterate untidiness. Nothing he
touched could be found in the same condition, and even
to enter his tiny cubicle-like room in *The Red Leem* was
usually impossible for the chaos strewing every surface and
the floor, unless one did as he did and took a flying leap onto
the trundle bed.

The caravan, with its long lines of calsanys head-to-tail in
their stubborn purposeful swaying movements and with the
smaller numbers of plains asses separated from the calsanys,
pressed on toward Pa Weinob in the northwest. Pa Weinob
was an outpost town, part of the spreading web of influence
the men of Pandahem were spinning along the seaboard and
hinterland of eastern Turismond. There was set a definite
limit to their western expansion as the same limit was set for
all the peoples seeking to extend westward. The Klackadrin with its cold hallucinations and its Phokaym waited out
there.

I have spoken a little at my chagrin at finding myself in
a port city of Pandahem when I had wished to reach Port
Tavetus, of, failing that, Ventrusa Thole, both colonial port
cities of Vallia. The difficulty of finding a ship at all to take
me to Vallia had been further compounded by this enforced
arrival at a port locked in mortal combat with Vallia. Mention of Vallia here was—almost—as mad as mention of Sanurkazz in Magdag, or of Magdag in Sanurkazz. There was
a faint gleam of light in that I detected less vicious acrimony
between the men of Pandahem toward Vallia, more a kind of

grudging respect and a direful determination to do them down, than the out-and-out obsessional hatred on the inner sea between the red and the green.

Tilda often wore a green gown; and I was used to that now.

Naghan the Paunch kept Pando very busy about the calsany lines, and the youngster learned very quickly not to be anywhere near them when they became frightened. Naghan himself rode a zorca—a fine powerful specimen of that graceful riding animal. It had been a long time since I had seen a zorca—a long, long time. In the lands fringing the Eye of the World men rode sectrixes, and in the Hostile Territories they rode the near cousin of the sectrix, the nactrix. I looked at that beautiful zorca and I felt my hands clench in envious longing, for I had to pad along on my bare feet.

This zorca, like all the breed very close-coupled and with four impossibly tall and spindly legs, possessed a particularly fine horn, twisted and proud, flaunting from the center of his forehead. I would march along and look at the zorca and think.

What little money I earned—heavy silver pieces of Pandahem coinage called dhems, and duller and often-chipped copper coins called obs, one eightieth of a dhem—I saved for my food and keep and lodging, and, most particularly, to buy myself a zorca. I had seen no voves. You must remember that this city and zonal region of Pa Mejab was civilized, or as civilized as any area of Kregen given its situation had any right to be, and I could not just knock over the first person I ran across and take his gear and weapons, mount and cash, as had been my lamentable habit in more savage times. I had to earn what I needed, as I must earn a passage to Vallia. Often I have laughed since to think that the great and puissant Dray Prescot, Krozair of Zy, Lord of Strombor, had been placed in this position; but there was no shame in it at all. Nothing had happened to me here to give me an opportunity, and a great deal of the blame for that must lie at the door of my terrible weakness that debilitated me as a result of my experiences. You will know that after my immersion in the pool of baptism in the River Zelph of far Aphrasöe I could look forward to a thousand years of life, and, equally, that I did not take to disease and mended quickly from wounds, so that my weak state gives some inkling of the ghastly passage of the Klackadrin.

Here I was once more in the sphere of influence of men and institutions that had surrounded me when I had first carved my way in Segesthes. Between this eastern coast of Turismond and the western coast of Segesthes lay the northern tip of Loh, that mountainous and mysterious land of Erthyrdrin, and Vallia, I was back among rapier and dagger men, among tall ships, among zorcas and voves—gone were swifters and sectrixes and the Krozairs of Zy.

Although—the Krozairs of Zy held now my undying loyalty.

Gone, too, were impiters and corths, although it was foolish to dream that those great flying beasts of the air might bear me across all the pitiless dwaburs to Vallia over the shining sea.

When I made inquiries to discover if the Pandaheem possessed airboats, those fliers manufactured in distant Havilfar and widely used by the Vallians, I was met by a curse and a shrug. Evidently, Havilfar did not sell their fliers to Pandahem. Equally evidently, the snub to trade was resented.

A light cheerful voice singing fragmentary snatches of the robust ditty "The Bowmen of Loh" brought me back to the present with a start. How that cunning and hilarious song brought back memories of Seg! Of how he and I, with my Delia and poor Thelda, had marched through the Hostile Territories singing!

Before I could yell, Obolya, an exceptionally tall and heavily-built man with a bristle of black hair all over his muscular body, cuffed Pando around the head.

"Sing somewhere else, you pestiferous brat! Little rast! Your screechings make my guts rumble!"

Obolya was a guard, a man whose profession as a mercenary had made him a man embittered, callous, unfeeling. Whatever he once had been, growing as a young man at his mother's knee, seemed all to have been wiped away during his years of hard fighting and long tramping. He owned a preysany, a kind of superior calsany, used for riding by those whose estate in life did not extend to the purchase of a zorca. He considered himself invaluable to the caravan, and Naghan the Paunch treated him with some respect.

It was with Naghan himself that I had taken service, as I have related. Now Obolya was being tiresome again.

The word "one" has many definitions and names on Kregen, of which "ob" is—if you will pardon the pun—one.

Obolya,* a common name in various forms, indicates that its recipient was the firstborn of the family's children. The Obolya who had just knocked Pando flying was tall, over a knuckle taller than I. Others of the guards on this left flank of the caravan with a few drovers crowded across to see the fun. Zair knew, walking caravan duty was monotonous enough so that any break in the routine was welcome. And Obolya was known of old; until every fresh guard knuckled down to him he would be ever seeking to force a confrontation which poor Naghan the Paunch, who valued Obolya's massive thews in defense, must condone.

Pando just managed to avoid the nearest calsany's instinctive response and scrambling up flew toward me.

"Just rest quietly, Pando," I said, "while I speak with this limb of Armipand."

Armipand was one of the devils in which many of the more credulous of the Pandaheem believed devoutly.

"Cramph!" roared Obolya. "You have a mouth wider than the Cyphren Sea! I must fill it—with my fist!"

"May Pandrite aid you now, Dray Prescot!" said Pando, overwhelmed by what had happened. He had known me long enough to know I would not shrug off an insult; but also he had seen me only as a weak and ill man, lucky to be employed by the overseer Naghan on the personal request of Tilda of the Many Veils. Pando sucked in his cheeks, and his eyes grew very round.

"Crawl back into the hairs of a calsany's belly where you belong," I said to Obolya.

He stuttered. The black bristles on his cheeks and chin quivered. He pointed at me, and threw back his head, and roared his contempt.

"You! Cramph-begotten rast! You who carry the leavings of a blacksmith's shop upon your back!"

This was a reference to the Krozair long sword. Now, in this culture of rapiers and daggers, I carried the long sword on my back, still in the sheath Sosie had made, beneath the quiver of which I have spoken. The weapon was in many respects anachronistic here. The guards carried short broadbladed stabbing spears for butcher work until the rapiers

---

*I think it worth pointing out that the suffix "A" clearly does not invariably denote the feminine gender in Kregish, as Prescot suggested in "Beng" and "Benga," the Kregish for male and female "Saint." We have also the example of Zolta—a man if ever there was one.
                                                                                      A.B.A.

came into action. This would be after the bows had taken the
first toll, and it was as a bowman that I had been engaged by
Naghan.

He would say to me, half surly, half jesting: "You carry
your bow in your hand, strung, and with an arrow nocked,
Dray Prescot, when you guard my caravan. That is what I
pay you for."

The hope that by carrying the long sword over my back
and thereby escaping its notice had not, in the case of Obolya,
succeeded. Just how long he would go on hurling insults before he got down to action I did not know. I was almost back
to my full strength, the fresh air and the suns-light and the
daily marching had all combined in my recuperation. But, as
always, hot though I am to resent authority, I attempted to
avoid an unnecessary clash and a dangerous enmity. Pride
and a hot temper are all very well for those who do not
think; my trouble is that I think first—and then still go berserk, to my sorrow.

Obolya wore a bronze breastplate of a reasonably high
standard of workmanship; but for more complete protection
he had under it only a leather tunic. On his arms and legs
were boiled-leather strappings, and he wore a boiled-leather
cap reinforced with straps of iron. He was as well-enough
armored as many men who work as mercenary guards for a
living; his armor, of course, would have made my clansmen
smile and evoked mirth from the mail-clad men of the inner
sea. I wore only my scarlet breechclout. My sleeping gear,
along with Pando's, was carried aboard one of the guard
detachment's plains asses.

"You affront me, Obolya. But, as I do not wish to deprive
you of your few remaining teeth, black and stinking though
they be, I will refrain from fighting you now."

The crowd roared at this and Naghan the Paunch came
running up, sweating, starting to yell and drive us back to
our duties. But Obolya waved him down and Naghan, seeing
how the wind blew, took himself off, sweating even more
over the safety of the caravan he had contracted to protect.
The crowd roared again as Obolya threw down his spear and
crouched. He used a large and variegated collection of foul
Makki-Grodno oaths. He advanced on me to, as he informed
me with great relish, tear my head off and stuff it between
my knees.

He wouldn't kill me, as he knew I would not kill him.

This was a bull moose confrontation, to decide who was who in the hierarchy of the caravan guards.

I handed the longbow to Pando. "Hold it off the ground, Pando. The bow is more valuable than this kleesh."

A kleesh is violently unpleasant, repulsive, stinking—and the name was guaranteed to drive Obolya like a goad.

His infuriated roar was quite up to the standard of a leem caught in a pit.

He charged.

He sought to grapple me to his breastplate and, holding me there, bend me back until I cried quarter. I stepped to one side and drove my fist into his jaw—and Obolya was not there. His speed was surprising. He hit me higher on the chest than he'd intended, because I moved; and in that I was lucky, for a blow from those massive arms would have taken my breath.

"Dray!" yelled Pando, mightily excited.

I did not deign to rub my chest, where the dint spread a pain I ignored. This time I rushed—halted, with a twist—took the blow on my upraised forearm—smashed Obolya in the breadbasket—drove him to a knee—chopped down on the back of his neck—and so laid him on the grass, insensible.

Someone let out a screech. Someone else was swearing by the gross Armipand. Another was laughing.

In truth I had welcomed the exercise and now I regretted hitting Obolya hard enough to knock him out. A little more of fisticuffs would have suited me, then, for I was strangely slow in getting back to my usual form. The Phokaym and the Klackadrin had drained more from me than even I realized.

Pando bent and retrieved a yellow object from the grass. He held it out to me, holding it gingerly.

"This fell from your loincloth, Dray, when you fought."

I took it. It was a six-inch fang I had taken from the jaw of a Phokaym as a memento. About to stuff it back, I stopped. Pando was looking at it with undisguised curiosity.

"What is it, Dray? It looks like—like a risslaca fang."

If I told him what it truly was, he wouldn't believe. No one who did not know me, Dray Prescot, Lord of Strombor, would or could believe.

"It's a risslaca tooth, Pando. Here." I tossed it to him. "Keep it as a memento of the fight. Boys collect anything—your friends won't have anything to match that for a space, I'll wager."

Pando took it eagerly. But, turning it over in his hands,

he said: "Young Enky has a risslaca fang almost as big. And Wil had a claw he said his father cut off a risslaca himself."

I was, as you may imagine, duly cut down to size.

Pando went babbling on about the fight. I took my bow and nocked an arrow—for Naghan the Paunch only half jested—and resumed my station. Guards who had felt Obolya's fist were helping him up. I saw him shake his head, looking dazed, and he dragged his feet as they helped him along. All this time the caravan had not halted, and we were well into the outer cultivated areas surrounding Pa Weinob.

I said, "Don't let your mother hear you singing 'The Bowmen of Loh,' Pando. You're only nine."

At his reproachful glance, I went on, "As for me, it is a fine song, and you may sing it as you will. I do not think anyone else will tell you to stop."

"By the glorious Pandrite, they will not, Dray!"

A shouting at the head of the caravan followed by a series of shrieking roars heralded fresh trouble. I doubled up past the plodding calsanys, but by the time I reached the van the problem had been solved. The zhantil had been slashed to death by many thrusts from the broad-bladed spears of the advance guard. This zhantil was of moderate size, about the length of a leem, although his massive mane and forelegs lent much greater weight to his foreparts than has the weasel-shaped leem. He was magnificently banded in tiger-stripes of glowing umber and ruby, and his richly golden mane fell about him. His blood pumped out to foul all that rich and gaudy marking. I felt sorry for the beast, and I know many of the caravan felt as I did. Although, of necessity, we must defend ourselves from zhantils when they attacked us, we did not feel for them the loathing and determination to destroy with which we regarded leems.

Naghan the Paunch, puffing, rolled up and at once began berating the guards.

"Fools! Imbeciles! Look at the pelt! Aie, aie—that would have brought many dhems had you not slashed it to pieces!"

An archer guard, one Encar the Swarthy, cursed and said, "We slashed it, good Naghan, because it was trying to slash us!"

"Well," persisted Naghan, wiping his forehead and neck, "you might have slashed with a little more care not to spoil the pelt."

Pando and I looked at each other, and Pando broke first, and held his belly and roared. Some of the other guards and drovers, knowing Naghan the Paunch, chuckled at the jest.

I said, "Naghan—will you spare a portion of the pelt—a trifle—to give Pando here a fine new tunic? Remember, he is the son of Tilda the Beuatiful."

Naghan put a foot into the stirrup of his zorca, who sniffed once at the zhantil, and finding it smelling dead, thereafter ignored it. He twisted around, his paunch straining that brilliant blue cummerbund.

"A tunic for Pando? Of zhantil skin? Ho—I think Tilda of the Many Veils would like that. Ay! She would part with a whole amphora of the best wine of Jholaix for such a zhantil tunic for her adored son!"

Jholaix, I knew, was the extreme northeastern country of Pandahem, which island is split up into a number of nations of the Pandaheem, and, further, I knew Jholaix wine to be scarce, dear, and extremely potent and pleasant to the tongue.

"You mercenary old rascal, Naghan the Paunch!" I said.

But he merely mounted his zorca, with an almighty belch, and winked down at me, whereat I nodded and said, "Done."

Between us, Pando and I took enough of the zhantil skin to make him a fine tunic, and, also, I cabbaged enough to make a belt for him, also. I would pay the cost of the amphora of Jholaix wine—and, thereby, put back the time when I could buy a passage out of Pa Mejab. But, looking at the rosy glory of Pando's young face, and the sparkle of sheer delight in his eyes, I knew my Delia of the Blue Mountains would forgive me.

Zair knows, she had much for which to forgive me. . . .

Naghan's servant, a one-eyed shaven-headed Gon, remained with us to take the rest of the skin and the mane, all of which, by virtue of his office, were the property of Naghan. The caravan had gone perhaps a little farther on than was altogether advisable by the time we had finished, and I made Pando step out smartly. The bloody pelt, rolled, I slung over my left shoulder.

The shout for help, when it reached me, made me whirl about and fling the pelt down and draw my bow fully.

There was no need immediately for violence.

The man who crawled toward us from a clump of missal trees was smothered in blood, and the long ax he bore glistened with gore. He tried to stand up to run toward us, but collapsed and fell. He twitched once and then lay still.

"Dray!" yelled Pando.

"Pick up the pelt, Pando. Go back to the caravan—and hurry!" I shouted at the one-eyed Gon. "Run, too! Warn Naghan—the caravan is attacked!"

For, beyond the man collapsed in his own blood and that of his enemies, I could see the wolfish shapes of halflings riding preysanys coursing toward the caravan, their fleet forms half-hidden by the missals. The opaz glitter from the twin suns speared back blindingly from their brandished weapons. In scant seconds they would be upon the caravan.

I loosed at the nearest rider and then slung the bow, ran roward the fallen man, and hoisted him upon my back. He was incredibly tall and thin. As I lifted him his eyes opened and he gasped. His right hand did not relax its death-grip on the haft of his ax.

"Bandits!" He choked the word out, and I knew from the way he spoke he had summoned up all his strength of purpose to run and warn the caravan and had been struck down. "Bandits!"

"Quiet, dom," I said. "Rest easy."

Then I raced back toward the caravan where already I could hear the shrieks of men engaged in mortal combat, and the slither and clang of iron weapons.

CHAPTER SIX

Concerning the taboos
of Inch of Ng'groga

The guards around the center flight of calsanys were already in dire trouble. The caravan had come to a halt and the beasts were milling. Hastily dumping down that impossibly tall man with his ax beside Pando, and yelling to him to keep out of sight and trouble, I drew the longbow.

The time had almost passed when archery could help; but I was able to feather four of the bandits before a gang of them swung their preysanys and coursed in at me, waving their spears.

Getting the long sword out of Sosie's scabbard over my shoulder demanded a convulsion of effort, and I had to jump up and bend over in a most undignified fashion to do it. But, once the deadly Krozair brand was in my fists, I was ready to meet these throat-slitting bandits, and to earn the wages Naghan the Paunch paid me.

Since that long-gone day when I had met Hap Loder on the beach and we had made pappattu and then I had taken obi of him, I had learned much of sword-fighting. Then I had been accounted a useful man with a cutlass, and had learned a great deal with those wonderful swords of the Savanti; but, all the same, when my clansmen armed with broadsword and short sword had gone up against the sophisticated rapier and dagger men of the city of Zenicce, I had worried about them. Now, I had all the skills and scientific knowledge, and the art and mystic practice, of the Krozairs of Zy to drive my nerves and impel my sword arm.

The rapier and the left-handed dagger are excellent weapons, as I have indicated, and they can between them take on much variegated weaponry. By this time the bandits and the guards were at it hammer-and-tongs, their broad-bladed spears flung down, and the rapiers and main-gauches, the Jiktars and the Hikdars, flaming and slicing, cutting and stabbing, in a welter of slivers of finely-honed steel.

I charged the bandits running at me with a great shout of: "Hai! Jikai!" and at once that terrible Krozair long sword was whirling a path of destruction through the bandits.

My own rapier and dagger bounced scabbarded at my side.

The long sword took the head off the first bandit—he was a man of uncertain origin (but of certain destination)—and sliced back to lop the rapier-wielding arm of the next one. They spurred their preysanys in to get at me, and this, I believe, led to their own destruction, for I could reach them with the long sword and they could not reach me. This fight roared and bloodied away. At least to me it appeared topsy-turvy, for the mounted men used weapons shorter than they should, given the fine length of their rapiers, and I had no long pole arm. In this fight I did not learn, truly, of the full problems of long sword against rapier and dagger. The fight taught me only that I had to get it over fast, for I caught a distorted glimpse of young Pando, with a snatched up dagger, trying to hamstring a bandit preysany. If anything happened to him . . . !

Already Tilda must be frantic with worry over where the little devil had got to—and if I returned and told her he had been with me, and had been killed . . . I couldn't face that.

So my long sword became a bloodied blur. The bandits fell before me. They were of many races of men and half-men: Fristles, Ochs, Rapas, Gons; alike they fell before my brand.

Obolya I saw, fighting like a demon, spitting his man, taking another's attack on his dagger, twirling with a laugh full of braggadocio, lunging into the belly. Naghan the Paunch I saw, also, striking about him with a broad-bladed spear that from his height on the zorca kept the bandits at bay.

I shortened the long sword and drove it carefully into the neck of an Och, sliding above his out-thrust shield. I body-swerved to avoid the thrust that his last involuntary movement impelled. I jumped over his falling body. Right-handedly I slashed away a Rapa who, wasting time screeching, tried to spit me. He went over with his beak sheared off.

I jumped over a preysany, my Earthly muscles back to

full power and tone, chopping short and hard down onto the man who ducked far too late. I landed neatly enough, removed another Rapa beak, swung and slashed and so forged my gory way toward Pando.

He came up screeching, scooped under my left arm. I laid the flat of the sword across his rump, whereat he yelled like a trapped leem, and left a long blood smear there.

"Quiet, you imp of Sicce!"

Obolya was down.

A Rapa, his fiercely predatory bird face gobbling with blood-lust, was in the act, seeming so deliberate, of thrusting his rapier down into Obolya's belly. Without pausing in my run I swung the long sword in a flat arc that intersected first with the Rapa's right arm, thus removing it and the rapier from Obolya's intestines, and then sheared on into the Rapa's side. He was wearing a bronze corselet. The Krozair blade smashed through in a screeching splintering of metal.

I wrenched the brand free, spun, caught a rapier and, with the supple wrist-twist that is easy enough with a rapier, damned difficult with a long sword, managed to thrust the blade into the bandit's throat. He vomited blood and went over.

Obolya was up. He glared at me.

"How many more are there, Obolya, in Zair's name?"

"Enough for me to repay you my life, Dray Prescot."

There was no time to wonder about that. The bandits pressed and we guards earned our money. When I had contrived to deposit Pando back among the plains asses—who were more restful and far less impossible than the calsanys, to whom everyone fighting gave a wide berth—and sorted out another group of bandits, I began to think we would best them.

They had waited for us here, on the outskirts of the cultivated areas, thinking that having traversed the dangerous lands we would relax our guard. As it was, with Naghan yelling us on, with Obolya fighting like a demon, and with my long sword that simply destroyed them, they had had enough.

The last we saw of them was the dust their preysanys kicked up as they ran.

Without pausing I ran across to a preysany from whose saddle a man hung with his foot entangled in the stirrup. I put my foot on his face and kicked him free. Then I swung up into the saddle.

Naghan yelled: 'Don't pursue them, Dray! They won't be back."

I rode across to another preysany which stood nuzzling the bloody rags around the head and shoulders of the Gon, its late master. The head and the shoulders were separated by a space of bloody grass. I remembered that one. Grasping the reins, I pulled the animal away and, a little reluctantly, it followed.

I said to Naghan the Paunch: "I claim these two prey-sanys, for Pando and me. Agreed?"

He huffed his paunch more comfortably in the saddle and nodded. "You may claim them, Dray Prescot, with pleasure. Under the terms of our contract they are mine, as you well know. You can work them out of your pay."

"Naghan the Paunch!" I yelled.

He was chuckling and wiping the blade of his spear and reveling in it. I did not chuckle; but I suddenly shouted: "Hai!" and the zorca started and leaped and Naghan went careering across the grass, wildly grasping anything to keep from falling off.

I heard a deep belly-rumble of laughter and turned and there was Obolya with his black-bristle face all crumpled with malicious mirth.

"You treat men hard, Dray Prescot."

No surprise showed on my face. This was only a petty border skirmish, a thing to be done and forgotten and not to be placed alongside the great battles and campaigns of my life; but a man can be killed as easily in a skirmish as a world-shaking battle.

"True, Obolya. To their deserts."

He eyed me a moment, and then went off about the business of a mercenary guard—stripping the dead of their valuables. In this I heartily agreed. Pickings are hard-come-by. But when I saw Pando engaged in the same occupation I started off at once to check him, outraged, wondering what Tilda would say if she could see her son—and then I stopped. This was life. This was what fighting and killing were all about. Let Pando learn the true facts, and then, perhaps, in later life he would not be so quick to provoke a quarrel or to seek to kill.

I went back to see about the tall and thin man I had rescued, with a parting shout to Pando: "Don't waste time on trifles, Pando. Pick the best."

On the way back I took three rings from bandit fingers. As

it happened the rings came off easily enough, greased by blood. Had I had to hack the fingers off to get at the rings this I would have done. I needed cash to buy a passage to Vallia and my Delia.

The drivers were sorting out the calsanys now and soon the caravan got under way again.

The tall man, still smeared with blood, was loaded face-down onto one of the preysanys I had acquired and the loot obtained by Pando and myself bundled in our sleeping gear on the other. Pando was hopping wild with excitement still, running up and down and emitting shrill Red-Indian-like war whoops. I let him blow off steam. Any fancy modern notions that his mind had been affected by the horrific sights he had seen, of course, did not apply on Kregen, where the absence of such sights usually indicates abject slavery on one side. He was growing up into a world of great beauty and wonder, for Kregen is a planet at once gorgeous and barbaric and highly-colored; but at the same time he was also preparing himself to face the other side of Kregen, the terror and the horror and the continuous struggle for existence.

Young Zorg, the son of Zorg of Felteraz, Krozair of Zy, my friend and oar comrade now dead and eaten by chanks, and his sister Fwymay, were both preparing themselves to enter the adult world of Kregen, far away there in Felteraz on the shore of the inner sea. Their mother, Zorg's widow, Mayfwy and Tilda had little in common except a love for their children and the sense of loss for their husbands—but I thought of them both, then, as I strode along, thinking, as I always do, mostly of my Delia of the Blue Mountains, my Delia of Delphond.

When we camped that night the man I had rescued had so far recovered as to consent to being washed. I discovered that most of the blood splattering him was not his. He kept that great ax close by him. He had had a thwacking great thump on the head, that I judged had smashed beyond repair the helmet he had lost, and was still a little muzzy. After some wine—mediocre red stuff from a local Pa Mejab vintnery—and a morsel of bread from a long Kregan loaf, liberally smeared with yellow butter, he sat with his back wedged against a tree bole munching a handful of palines. They would soon clear his headache.

"I am Inch," he said. "From Ng'groga."

So far had I come from Magdag that all those "G's" did not worry me. Inch told us that Ng'groga was a nation situated on the southeastern part of the continent of Loh, facing the unknown southern sea. He was, himself, a somewhat amazing individual. He was, as I have said, incredibly tall, some seven feet of him from toe to the top of his head. That head was covered in long and silky yellow hair that hung to his waist and which he would bind up and coil when in action. He was thin, also, but I did not miss the bulge of muscle about that sinewy body. At the moment his only clothing was an old and tattered brown tunic, gathered in by a leather belt of lesten hide. Beside his great ax, which reminded me of the Danish pattern carried by the clansmen of Viktrik, with the addition of a daggered head after the fashion of my own clansmen of Felschraung and Longuelm, he bore at his waist a long knife. He had no sword.

"I shipped out as a mercenary, as so many youngsters do," he said. "The life suited me but ill. Then I was betrayed—that does not concern me now—and was sold as slave. So I escaped and joined the brigands. But, that life, also, was not for me."

"Then what happened?" demanded Pando. He was hunched up, eagerly listening to the story, which Inch embroidered far more than I have indicated.

"At last the bandits said they were going to attack the next caravan, slay all the men and—ah—" He cocked an eye at Pando, and went on after a cough. "Abduct all the girls. I had an argument with the chief of the bandits and left him, I fancy, with his ears wider apart than they had been."

As he spoke he moved his hand across the ax, and I could well imagine that mighty weapon splitting down through the skull of the bandit chief.

"And?"

"That was a foolish thing to do. My taboos had not warned me adequately, which was passing strange."

This was the first I had heard of Inch's taboos; but not the last, oh, certainly, not the last! As you shall hear.

"So I ran from them, and they pursued, and I killed many; but then Largan the Wily hurled a stone, and I fell, and they would have beaten my brains out but for my old helmet." He reached a long hand up to his head, and felt his yellow mane of hair. "I am sorry I lost that, by Ngrangi, yes!"

"Yes, yes!" said Pando. "And then?"

"Then, when I thought I was done for, and the caravan gone, I called out and this monstrous man here, Dray Prescot, came and took me up and shot Largan the Wily with that bow that, if I mistake not, is a true bow of Erthyrdrin."

"Yes," I said. I could not speak of Seg, not yet, to Inch.

For, from what Sosie had told me, I knew this Lohvian bow she had given me was a true bow of Erthyrdrin, made from true wood of the Yerthyr tree, long matured and sweetly seasoned. I thought even Seg Segutorio would be happy with this bow, although comparing it always unfavorably with his own stave he had cut himself from the private tree of Kak Kakutorio.

Gone—those days, gone and dead and best forgotten!

In Pa Weinob, a city of wooden, high-built houses and a wooden stockade with watchtowers, we waited for the goods to be collected for the caravan to take back to the coast in exchange for the manufactures we had brought here. During this period I had a local woman recommended to me cure and prepare Pando's zhantil skin. Another woman, a clever seamstress, sewed him a fine tunic and belt. When he donned the gear and turned to let us see, both Inch and I made all the necessary noises of surprise and gratification. In truth, Pando did cut a dashing figure, and he was as pleased as a woflo eating his way through a whole Loguetter cheese.

By the time the country produce had been baled and loaded and we set forth to return to Pa Mejab, Inch had been taken on as guard by Naghan the Paunch, and he and I and Pando had palled up in a way that surprised me, although Pando took it all in his stride.

One night when the Maiden with the Many Smiles shone down from a cloudless sky, Inch approached the fire where we were cooking a tasty vosk haunch purchased in the town. He crinkled up his nose at the delightful smell. Over his long fair hair he wore a huge mass of cloth, like a sloppily-wound turban. Not a scrap of his hair was visible.

Pando let out a yell.

"Hey! Inch! That's my sleeping cloth!"

Pando started to pull the bundle of cloth from Inch's head. Inch went mad.

He jumped up, waving his arms, screaming words no one understood, words clearly of his local language of Ng'groga. A strand of hair fell loose. Inch shrieked as though his flesh was being wrung out by red-hot pincers. He jumped toward the fire—he jumped *into* the fire!

"Inch!"

"You have made me break a taboo!" he shrieked. He

gyrated in the fire and his sandals smoldered and then burst into flames. He didn't seem to feel a thing. He gyrated around, scattering hot coals, and the guards yelled and scrambled away, beating at their clothes.

"When the Maiden with the Many Smiles is alone in the sky, she may not shine down upon a Ng'grogan's hair! It is taboo!"

I grabbed Pando and shouted to the other guards and we cleared off. We knew when to leave a fellow alone with his taboos.

After that when Inch went berserk, or solemnly took a cup of wine and threw it over his left shoulder, or dropped onto all fours and stuck his rump into the air and beat his head against the ground, we left him to it. It was a chancy business, living with Inch and his taboos.

Pa Mejab looked most welcome with its streets of wooden houses, some brick ones already shouldering out the earlier timber structures, and its cool groves of fruit trees, its harbor and vista of the sea. We were paid off by Naghan the Paunch, and precious little I had left after I had settled all my debts, what with the preysanys and the zhantil tunic, paid for by the amphora of wine from Jholaix.

"At least, Naghan, Inch and I can have a cupful of Jholaix with you tonight, eh?"

"Surely," he said, patting his paunch. "Naghan is the most generous of men."

"Ayee!" said Pando, most impudently.

We walked from the caravansary through the crowded streets to *The Red Leem*. If we walked with a trifle of a swagger—well, had we not crossed dangerous lands and fought wild beasts and wilder bandits, and brought the caravan safely home?

A shriek as of a Corybant broke upon our ears as we walked up to the tavern.

Tilda, trailing a green gown, her glorious black hair swirling about her like impiter's wings, flew down upon Pando. She caught him up, kicking and squirming, against her breast, and smothered him with kisses.

"Pando! My son, Pando!"

Then—

"Pando! You limb of Sicce! Where have you been?"

And with that, Tilda the Beautiful started laying into him with the flat of her hand, applied to the bottom of that brave new zhantil tunic, until Inch and I winced.

"He's been all right, Tilda," I said—like a fool. "He's been out with the caravan, with me—"

"With you! Dray Prescot! Out there—out there, wild beasts, bandits, drought, hunger disease—out there—Dray Prescot, I'll—I'll—" She left off beating Pando long enough to scream: "Get out! Get out of *The Red Leem!* If you show your face in here again, you vile abductor, I'll scratch your eyes out!" She spared a hand to rip off a slipper and hurl it at me.

"Out! Out!"

Inch and I walked off, hurriedly and without dignity.

"Nice class of friend you have, Dray," was all Inch said.

CHAPTER SEVEN

How Tilda the Beautiful fared at *The Red Leem*

Tilda's anger against me did not last long when Pando managed to tell her what had happened. For his pains he was sent supperless to bed that night, as Inch and I quaffed best Jholaix in company with Naghan the Paunch and Obolya. Inch disappeared for a time and when he came back he winked at me and leaned over, whispering.

"Climbing the back wall was easy, Dray. That young devil is munching a vosk-pie now, and probably getting disgustingly drunk of a thimbleful of Jholaix."

"If Tilda catches him and he tells on you, Inch—"

Inch looked pleased with himself. "Sending boys to bed supperless is against my taboos," he said, and winked.

I perked up. Inch was turning into a comrade, rather than a companion. Now, if Seg were here—or Nath, or Zolta. Or, Gloag, or Varden, or Hap Loder . . .

I must not think of Seg, I thought then.

Inch was laughing and telling how a friend's taboos had given him a pair of horns, and Naghan and Obolya were laughing, too, and I could understand Naghan the Paunch, not Obolya.

If I was asked to describe the Pandaheem succinctly, I would show my interlocutor Naghan the Paunch. He was Pandaheem to the very last nail of him. Built for comfort, the Pandaheem, as were their ships.

Obolya, now, while he had changed since I had knocked that Rapa off him, was still as surly and vicious as ever to everyone. To me, he maintained a watchful respect, the result, I imagined, of our fight. He did not, to me, fit in with the men of Pandahem at all. I had discovered that the island of

72

Pandahem, which lies to the east off the coast of Loh, due south of Vallia, was divided up into a number of separate nations, most of them governed by kings jealous of their own power and prestige, continually at loggerheads with their neighbors. They seldom united even against Vallia, whose single mighty empire operated from the secure base of an island under one government. This division weakened Pandahem. Pa Mejab, which lay well to the north of Ventrusa Thole and just tucked into the bay south of the great promontory projecting from Turismond into the Sunset Sea, was a colony city of the human nation of Pandahem called Tomboram.

Tomboram, as I learned, is a pleasant place in almost every respect, situated in the northern and eastern part of Pandahem, with Jholaix as a smaller country to the northeast. The Tomboramin are a happy folk, they had made me welcome, and although they would fight their neighbors, and Vallia, and the mysterious pirate ships that sailed up out of the southern oceans, they much preferred to sit in a tavern and drink, or watch and applaud a great dramatic performance. Industrious when working and idle when playing, the Tomboramin were people with whom I got on well.

And yet—I could not forget the bitterness with which Thelda, of Vallia, had spoken of the Pandaheem, of how she had sworn by Vox that they must all be destroyed one day.

My Delia was a Vallian—she was the Princess Delia, Princess Majestrix. These people among whom I sat and drank and sang were her bitter commercial rivals, and deadly foes upon the seas.

Even now a great deal of talk was in the air of the next expedition to probe southward to attack the Vallian colonial port city of Ventrusa Thole.

My distress you may imagine; my determination to reach Vallia, I assure you, was in no way impaired by all this newly-found good fellowship as we drank and roistered in *The Red Leem* and watched the incomparable actress, Tilda the Beautiful, perform so gracefully and movingly for us.

When Vallia was mentioned by the Tomboramin, it was with a curse and a bitter feeling of betrayal, a sense of dejection and doom. No, these good people of Pa Mejab did not care for Vallians. Listening to them, hearing tales of treachery and deceit, I absorbed some of that feeling. Vallia was overbearingly powerful, omnipotent, almost. Vallia scorned all other nations. Vallia made treaties and broke them, contemptuously, careless of good faith. Vallia was as perfidious as, I suppose, the England of my day was considered by France.

Albion Perfide was now Vallia Perfide—indeed!

These days I habitually left my long sword in my room and in deference to local custom wore only the rapier and dagger about the town.

Tilda, in conversation one day, mentioned that political difficulties were growing worse every day with the Pandahemic nation immediately to the west of Tomboram, a nation she called The Bloody Menaham. I took little notice, although I knew that Menaham had sited a colonial port at what appeared to be perilously few dwaburs to the north, being more concerned over my own problems and being a trifle irritated that the wrangles on one island of Kregen were preventing me from reaching another.

In this I should have been more careful; for The Bloody Menaham, no less than Tomboram, was to play a large part in my life before I found Delia again.

We discovered that it was taboo for Inch to eat the tiny and delicious fruit called squishes and Pando took a fiendish delight in bringing in great baskets of them from the orchards, for they were in season, and leaving heaping bowls of them everywhere in *The Red Leem*. Inch doted on squishes. This convinced me that his taboos differed radically from what is considered a taboo on Earth; there, had the squishes been taboo, he would never have eaten one in the first place. As it was, whenever we came upon Inch standing on his head, his face expressing the greatest anguish, we knew he had broken his taboo and gone munching squishes.

And Pando, the imp of Sicce, would laugh.

"I wonder, Dray," he said to me, very solemnly, with Inch on his head in a corner close by. "If I had to stand on my head every time I ate vosk-pie, would I go off vosk-pie?"

"Such gratitude!" said Inch, and succulent squish juice dribbled down into his eye.

"Stick to palines, Inch," I said. "There is nothing more sovereign."

He groaned, and shut his eye, thus winking at us when he had nothing in his head to warrant a merry wink—at all.

The time was fast approaching when the armada might be expected in from Pandahem and the caravans would be loading again and Naghan the Paunch would be hiring guards.

Due to the depredations of pirates—call them corsairs, rovers, buccaneers, privateers, as you will, to honest sailormen of Kregen they were renders all—abroad on the outer oceans ships tended to sail whenever they could in great convoys called armadas. I heard Naghan shaking his chins and his paunch and saying, "The swordships make life hard for a merchant, may Armipand drag 'em down by the short and curlies. I sometimes make myself remember, when my caravan is attacked, that I am lucky not to be a ship's captain."

"Come now, Naghan!" I protested, out of my ignorance. "Surely the Sunset Sea and the Cyphren Sea do not harbor so very many swordships?"

"Enough and to spare, Pandrite rot 'em!"

Well, I had been to Segesthes and I was now in Turismond; but I had never traversed the seas that lay between.

When the bells began to ring and the people streamed out of their houses and ran in wild excitement down to the harbor you may be sure that Pando was well up with the leaders and I not far behind.

Everyone looked out over the sea, toward the southeast and a great cry went up when we saw that armada of sails.

The commotion and seething rushes, the fluttering scarves, the hats tossed into the air, the cheering, the ringing of bells, the frenzied scamperings of children and the mad gyrations of dogs through the crowds, the gusts of happy frothy laughter—all were prodigious.

With a somewhat more cynical eye, I, an old sailorman, looked at that distant white-glinting armada of sails, and the sea between, and felt the wind, and I remembered days hanging around in the Downs, and said to Pando, "I am thirsty, Pando, and am going back to *The Red Leem* for a drink."

"But the fleet, Dray! You'll miss the ships!"

"They will still be in the offing when I return, never fear." He wouldn't budge. "If you fall in," I told him, "apart from realizing that I told you so, swim to the steps and take your time. The seawall breaks the force of the waves."

After I had sunk a couple of glasses of the local red biddy —not for me the best of Jholaix when I needed every ob— Inch joined me and we strolled back to the harbor. I was surprised. The first ship was already entering the stone-built entrance past the pharos, gulls swinging whitely about her three masts, her sails coming down, her crew gathering on her forecastle with ropes. A band was playing and the music

"The ships of the armada were sailing into Pa Mejab harbor."

lolloped into the air as this broad-beamed ship lolloped through the sea. I studied her lines critically.

The Pandaheem called these high-charged ships of the outer oceans argenters. They were rigged with square sails; had they been rigged with lateens they would have looked remarkably like caravels, with their high forecastles and their half decks, quarterdecks and sterncastles. As was to be expected they were decorated lavishly with much gilding and carving, fine gingerbread work that glittered in the opal glare.

They were broad in relation to their length, solid, heavily-built, comfortable ships—and, therefore, slow. They carried courses and topsails on their fore and mainmasts, and courses —a crossjack—on their mizzens, with a spritsail on the bowsprit. I gained the impression, watching the argenters glide solidly and squarely into port, of rolling argosies of sail, dependable, unimaginative, lofty as to hull, cautious as to sail area and plan.

As you know it has been my custom not to jump about in this narrative but, rather, to attempt to tell you of what happened to me on Kregen beneath Antares in as good a chronological order as I can contrive. Maybe that skyjacking has loosened up my time-sense. I will, therefore, quickly say that when I—at last, at long last!—saw the ships of Vallia I saw immediately how like galleons they were. And I mean a real galleon, the type of ship invented by the English: low, streamlined, fast, daringly sparred, superb sailers. Despite the plethora of names the Vallians use for their ships I have always thought of Vallian ships as galleons, and will so refer to them when the time in this narrative is ripe.

By contrast—and I thought of it then, as I stood with Pando and Inch and saw the Pandahemic argenters without knowledge of the Vallian galleons—these ships of this armada sailing into Pa Mejab were reminiscent of Portuguese and Spanish caravels and carracks. Maybe history does repeat itself, even though it takes place on different worlds separated by four hundred light-years of interstellar space.

To finish this anachronistic comment; the reason—or one of them—why I could never seem to catch a Vallian ship on the inner sea lay simply in the galleon's superb ability to drive on in wind that would have overset a swifter in a trice.

As well as varters—the ballistae as used by swifters of the inner sea—these ships carried as well catapults powered

by many twisted strands of sinew and hair. Watching critically the evolutions of the ships as they lost way, brought
their canvas in, dropped their hooks, and swung to, I was
reasonably satisfied that they were seamanlike enough. They
were not in a hurry. The reason they had gained the mouth of
the harbor before I had expected was explained by their use
of sweeps thrust through a few ports cut in their sides. People around me commented on this, giving as their judicious
opinion that great news was carried aboard the ships, for
using the sweeps meant hard work, and the Tomboramin only
worked hard when a definite end lay in view.

The wind was free, was it not, dom? So why sweat at the
oars?

If these men *were* in a hurry—I shuddered to think what
their customary seamanship would be like.

With the taking in of the fore and main courses disappeared the huge and gorgeously painted devices of Tomboram. Tomboram proudly flaunted the pictured representa-
tion of a quombora, a mythical monster of devilish aspect,
with much fangery and toothery and clawery, spitting flames
and smoke, as her symbol. The fore and main topsails carried
the painted devices of the individual ships and owners. Many
bright blue flags fluttered.

A swarm of boats put off to the ships, and the first pair
were being warped alongside the jetty to begin unloading.
The show was over. My next and most immediate plan was
somehow to arrange a passage on one of those ships when
she returned to Pandahem. I would have to sign on before
the mast. That procedure must—given the physical facts of
sailing-ship travel in relatively primitive ships across many
dwaburs of open ocean—entail prodigious suffering and discomfort which meant nothing, of course, beside my determination to seek out Delia.

In a directly straight line from Pa Mejab to the chief
port of Tomboram the distance is approximately eight hundred dwaburs. Distances of this order might be covered by a
ship without calling in for water and supplies; normally the
armada would make port somewhere in northern Loh, along
the coast of that great thrusting promontory of Erthyrdrin
As I understood it ships of many nations shared port facilities here, docile under the constraint of the sufferance of the
Erthyr. From thence a journey due east or northeast would
bring a ship to Vallia. For Pandahem the course would be

southeast, either outside or inside the long chain of islands that parallel the northeastern coast of Loh.

Inch and Pando went back to *The Red Leem*, for there would be new customers to care for and probably, if old Nath was lucky, passengers to be accommodated, while I went to find Naghan the Paunch and explain that I would be unable to go with him on the next caravan. I knew he would shout and swear and call me an ingrate; but my purpose was set.

Naghan the Paunch did all these things. In addition he threw a wine bottle at me, for I found him soaking in the small room of *The Marsilus and Rokrell*. I ducked.

"Peace, good Naghan. Oh man of the Paunch, I have served you well and taken your silver dhems, let us then part in friendship."

He glared at me. Then he pulled up another glass and bottle, and poured, and lifted his glass to me, as I did to him. "You are the finest bowman I have ever engaged, Dray, you and that great Lohvian bow of yours. I have seen many bowmen, and some almost your equal." He drank and wiped the back of his hand across his lips. "But never, no never, have I seen anything like that damned great cleaver of yours!"

I drank to him, and said, "I shall not forget you, Naghan the Paunch. Care for young Pando, if you can, and Tilda the Beautiful, his mother."

"That I will always do. By the glory of Pandrite, I swear it!"

"Remberee, Naghan the Paunch."

"Remberee, Dray Prescot."

I went back to *The Red Leem*.

People were moving about the streets, all of them still excited over the arrival of the armada, and passengers were already coming ashore. I saw a cart trundle along, the two calsanys drawing it impatiently goaded by the imp in charge, the cart's master dragging them by their stubborn jaws. Bundles and bales and casks and kegs would be coming ashore, and Pa Mejab was coming alive again, fed through all those dwaburs of sea by the mother country. It was a gala day. Pa Mejab was not forgotten by the king and the nobles and the merchants and soldiers and all the people in their far-off homeland.

As you may well imagine, I had made all my usual inquiries, but no one had heard of Aphrasöe, the Swinging City.

About to put my foot on the fantamyrrh, the habitual un-

thinking act performed by every Kregan entering a house, I
paused. Pando shot out of the doorway, wild-eyed, his hair
tousled. He did not see me at once and just as his eyes fell
on me a hand at the end of a long arm reached after him,
clapped around his mouth and neck, jerked him back. He
disappeared.

That long hand and arm did not, I thought, belong to Inch.

Young Pando was a handful, I knew that well enough, and
an imp of mischief, and it could well be that he had so upset
a new guest in the inn that chastisement had been considered
necessary. Yet I hurried inside, anxious that no real harm
should come to the lad, and, if the truth be told, growing
indignant that someone else other than his mother should
lay hands on the child.

The noise of people in the main room drowned out any
sounds of beating that might be coming from the upper floor.
Quite a crowd had gathered already as the news and gossip of
far-off places were detailed, and the merry sound of clinking
glasses and the throaty exclamations of amazement accompanied me, along with the heady smells of wine and cooking
food, up that narrow black-wood stair.

As I reached the top I saw Tilda's door slam shut.

I stopped at once, making a face to myself. No man with
a pennyweight of brains interferes between a widow and
her son in moments like these. But then—a stir of unease
ghosted over me. That had not been Tilda's slender and
shapely ivory-skinned arm that had so roughly pulled Pando
back, and I had not passed the owner of the offending arm on
the stairs. Strange.

With a certain hesitation—an unfamiliar sensation for me
—I moved quietly toward Tilda's door. I listened. I heard
nothing except a hoarse breathing, close up against the
polished wood. I kept my own breathing steady and quiet.

Then a man yelped in sudden pain—as though, for instance, a woman had driven her bare toes agonizingly into
his middle—and a woman's voice rang out. Tilda's voice.

"Help! Help! Murder!"

CHAPTER EIGHT

Wedding plans for Delia,
Princess Majestrix of Vallia

I smashed the door open with a single kick and leaped into the room.

These were no rapscallion leem-hunters out for a good time, unwilling to kill, ready for a bit of rough-and-tumble.

I knew this breed. These were killers. There were four of them. They were tall, lithe, poised men, all bronzed from the suns-light, muscular and predatory. Their rapiers and daggers were plain, workmanlike, efficient.

They wore dark clothing, plain tunics and well-oiled leathers, high black boots, and their broad-brimmed gray hats with the curling blue feathers cast shadows across their faces from which the gleem of their eyes in the suns-light through the windows struck leem-like.

One held Tilda around the waist and his dagger lifted above her ivory throat, poised to strike. Another stood holding his middle and retching—I did not smile—and the other two swung around to face me. Reasonable odds for the Lord of Strombor.

There was no time to consider. The dagger was about to plunge down into Tilda's throat, and all Pando's despairing yell as he struggled between the legs of the assassin would avail nothing. My rapier and dagger were in my hands. I threw the dagger. It flashed across the room like a streak of sunlight, buried itself in the neck above the squared tunic. The man gulped and dropped his own dagger. His knees buckled; but I could watch him no more for with a clang and a screech of steel the two assassins hurled themselves upon me.

Our blades met and parried and I had to dodge and skip

for a few wild heartbeats as I avoided their attack, my left hand empty.

I spitted the first one in the guts, recovered, slashed savagely at the next and did not complete the stroke, leaping back so that he parried with his dagger against the empty air. I ran him through the heart, aiming delicately between the requisite rib members. As I withdrew, the meanness of these men showed itself in the last one's actions—for, knowing he faced a master swordsman and knowing he faced thereby his own death—he turned and dived headlong through the window taking the glass and the framing with him in a great splintering crashing.

One spring took me to the wreck of the window. I looked down.

The assassin was picking himself up, his face still with a greenish hue from Tilda's kick and blood on his face from the smashed glass.

Inch was walking up toward *The Red Leem*, whistling.

I shouted, "Inch! If it is not against your taboos, kindly take that fellow into custody. Don't treat him gently."

"Oho!" said Inch, and ran in and planted a tremendous kick upon the assassin's posterior as he attempted to stand up. I jumped out of the window, landed like a leem, grabbed the fellow by the tunic, and hit him savagely on the nose. Blood spurted. I did not knock him out.

"Talk, you rast! Or I'll spit your liver and roast it!"

He gabbled something, something about Marsilus, and gold, and then blood poured from his mouth and he collapsed.

Inch looked offended.

"I did not kick him hard enough for that, Dray. Nor would your blow upon the nose have hurt a fly— So why is he dead?"

I was annoyed.

"He must have smashed his guts up jumping through the window and falling awkwardly. By the disgusting nostrils of Makki-Grodno! The fellow is dead and that's an end to it."

We left him there to be collected by the mobiles of Pa Mejab, who were later fully satisfied with our explanation of four dead men, and went back to Tilda and Pando.

The assassin I had first run through was in the act of dying as we entered the room. There was nothing to be discovered. Pando collected four rapiers and four daggers, which I was pleased to sell later for good silver dhems, and

Inch took the best of the leather boots which fitted him, for his feet were inordinately long and thin. I had a pair, also; as an addition to my wardrobe, just in case. Two of the broad-brimmed hats, also, with their curled blue feathers, might come in useful. The tunics would not fit either Inch or me—I was too wide in the shoulder and Inch too narrow —so we sold the rest of the gear.

"If they have any friends come asking for them," I said to Nath, the innkeeper, "then let us know, by Zim-Zair, and we will wring the truth from them."

But no one else bothered us thereafter on the score of the four assassins while we were in Pa Mejab.

"They swaggered in and demanded to know if the actress Tilda and her son Pando lodged here," said old Nath, mightily shaken up by the event. He kept a respectable house, as, indeed, he must, otherwise Tilda would not have lodged and performed there. These goings-on were not to his liking. They might be common in *The Silver Anchor* and *The Rampant Ponsho* along the waterfront, not here in this respectable street and *The Red Leem*.

Not one of the four dead men yielded any personal identification to prying fingers. Apart from money and the usual items to be found in the pockets and gear of any man they were devoid of information. Inch wondered if we might make a few discreet inquiries among the ships; but Tilda, rather alarmed, vetoed this idea at once.

Looking at her, I caught the impression that perhaps she knew more about this business than she was prepared to discuss with us. After all, Inch and I were strangers.

A considerable number of people had taken lodgings with old Nath and he had let all his rooms. The main room was crowded that evening. Tilda had insisted that she was perfectly all right and could go on. Old Nath, gallantly protesting that she should rest up after her ordeal, visibly showed his relief that she would give her performance, whose fame accounted for his vastly increased trade and profits. But I do not condemn him for that; he was good to me as well as others.

When Tilda made her final exit to rapturous applause that thundered to the rafters and set all the glass wine cups on the shelves ajingling, she came over to my table as was her custom. Old Nath did not mind me occupying a table just so long as I paid for what I consumed in the same way as an ordinary customer. Most often I did not bother, saving my scraped

wealth, but this night was different. Just as we were preparing
to listen to the beginning of Tilda's impassioned rendition of
the execution scene from the music drama—not quite the
same thing as an opera—known over most of Kregen as *The
Fatal Love of Vela na Valka*—I had heard the light musical
voice of a young woman say: "Oh, Pando—there is not a
table left!"

A young couple stood in the doorway, looking disappointed.
She was young, lissome in the normal way and with fine eyes;
at the moment she was pregnant. Her husband was a soldier,
a Hikdar, handsome in his Tomboramic uniform. Naturally,
I offered them seats at my table, and Wil, who had been
brought in to help, quickly brought glasses and wine—a
yellow wine of Western Erthyrdrin—so that when Tilda
joined us we had already been thrown into the quick and
casual friendships of the frontier. Inch had discovered a taboo and now came across, brushing sawdust from his long
fair hair, and sat down.

The young couple told us all the news. The Hikdar was a
calvaryman and burning for adventure out here on the
borders of the spreading empire of Pandahem. His name
was Pando—the cause of my immediate reaction when they
had entered—Pando na Memis. His wife's name was Leona.

"Memis," said Tilda, gracefully drinking the yellow wine.
"I know it well, those tall red cliffs falling to the sea, the
islands and their gulls—oh, millions of gulls!—and the wine
there." She laughed. "It is far smoother on the tongue than
this Erthyrdrin—"

Pando na Memis looked somewhat confused and beck-
oned quickly. I watched the byplay. Young Pando trotted
up, he also having, for a change, been conscripted.

"Bring a better vintage than this, young one," said Pando
na Memis. "It is not to the lady's liking."

Pando—the urchin of that distinguished name—made a
face at me, whereat I lifted my fist, so that he scuttled off,
laughing. Tilda looked gracious, oblivious of the exchange.
Pando na Memis pushed the bottle of yellow wine away
across the table—and a long lanky arm reached out from
somewhere and Inch grasped the bottle by the neck. Leona
na Memis had not missed a single nuance.

Much of the traffic and trade of Kregen is devoted to this
kind of mutual exchange of commodities. It is an infuriating
fact of human nature that the grass is always greener over
the neighbor's fence; and that is why wine from Western

Erthyrdrin reached Turismond, why in Zenicce we drank Pandahem wine when the good vintages of Zenicce were shipped to Vallia. As to Vallia, her wines were carried to the far corners of Kregen. Despite all that, I still preferred the fragrant tea brewed by my clansmen in far Segesthes.

Inch, I considered, would be happiest with a bottle of dopa, that fiendish stomach-rotting drink that I had seen at work in the warrens of Magdag.

Drunkenness is relative on Kregen. Few Kregans consider getting drunk the occupation of a fully rational man, and my two oar comrades, Nath and Zolta, although they might become as merry as nits in an eiderdown, seldom ever achieved that disgusting paralytic sick drunk common in certain so-called civilized countries of this Earth. Kregans love to roister; and that means enjoying themselves. Getting sick drunk and puking over everything is not, really, much idea of fun.

The conversation wended on, and we heard of Pando na Memis' plans for the future, of how he craved for action— at which Leona looked alarmed—and of how, soon, the Tomboramin would advance along the old Lohvian roads through the Klackadrin.

"After the old Empire of Walfarg fell," said Pando, "The land must have gone back. The Hostile Territories are still there, waiting for strong men to ride in and take over. One day, and soon, we of Tomboram will do just that, before the rasts of Vallia or Menaham or anyone else!"

I made the right noises, saying nothing.

Then the name Marsilus came up. A great noble of that name, old, crotchety, more than half-mad, had just died back in Tomboram and his estates, reputed valuable beyond price, had fallen into the hands of a nephew, who was also a nephew to the king. Pando na Memis whistled when Tilda, rather sharply, I thought, said: "Are the estates then so valuable?"

"Are they not! They rival the king's. Now that Murlock Marsilus, the nephew, has inherited, the king must be greatly pleased, for the kingdom may inherit also when the king dies. There was a son to old Marsilus. Unfortunately, he died."

Speaking very precisely, Tilda said, "Was the son disinherited, then?"

"By no means. But he is dead and—there was a story—he was banished in disgrace. Married out of turn, so the story goes. Everyone has heard it—you must have, surely?"

"Yes."

"I haven't," I said.

After I had given some explanation of myself, brief and almost totally untrue, Zair forgive me, Pando na Memis went on: "Murlock Marsilus is now Kov of Bormark, but the story goes that the old Kov, old Marsilus, screamed and shouted for his son on his deathbed. He relented of his punishment of the boy when he married. There was a grandson—but, of course, he stands no chance of the title and estates now that Murlock holds them under the king's agreement."

"The old man was stricken with the shrieking horrors," said Inch, wisely. "It is known. He wanted to go to the Ice Floes of Sicce with a clean mind and with clean hands. One can visualize the scene. Poor benighted of Ngrangi!"

I leaned forward. "The king," I said, "and this Marsilus, Kov of Bormark, who had died. They were brothers?"

"Yes," said Leona, smiling at me. "You must be from some wild and untamed part of the world!"

"I am," I told her. "Oh, yes, indeed, I am!"

The conversation changed course then; but I noticed Tilda was very quiet after that. The hated name of Vallia came up and with it tidbits of gossip and scandal. Of these I felt my heart lurch when Leona, speaking with a gentle malice quite natural in the circumstances, said: "The Princess Majestrix of Vallia! Such a proud hoity-toity madam! Her father, the emperor has ordered her to marry—"

"To marry!" I shouted—and they all leaned back from me, their faces shocked, expressive of bewilderment and disgust. They must have seen that devil's look on my face. I made myself calm down. My Delia! My Delia, Princess Majestrix of Vallia, ordered by the tyrant emperor, her father, to marry—to marry some blundering oaf of his choice. I had to hold onto my sanity and my temper then. I do not apologize, so I just said: "You were telling us of Delia, Princess Majestrix of Vallia, Leona. Please go on."

In a voice she struggled to keep from quavering, Leona went on speaking. And, as I listened, I felt a warm sweet relief flooding me, and I breathed easier.

For my Delia had defied her father!

She had flatly refused to marry the oaf picked out for her! She had stood up against his puissant majesty the emperor of Vallia, and told him flatly she would not marry. Not marry at all.

This made my heart lurch afresh.

My Delia vowing never to marry?

Did she—could she—believe that I had abandoned her, as that scheming villain had planned when I had been drugged and dumped under the thorn-ivy bush? Had that foul scheme worked?

I had to get to Vallia—and yet, was there any greater urgency now than there had been? At least I knew my Delia was safe and well. She refused to marry. The emperor was still hale and hearty and, so the scandal went, quite prepared to wait and let his only daughter rot in maidenhood until she decided to marry the man of her choice. He would not force her; he would let time and nature take their courses.

Once I had held Delia of the Blue Mountains in my arms and pressed her dear form close to my heart I had known that no other woman in two worlds could compare with her, no other woman could take her place. And I had known many women, blazingly beautiful women of arrogance and power, lovely women of lissome grace and refined artifice, women of passion and glory; and one had been to my Delia as as a candle to the radiance of the red sun Zim. I had felt absolute confidence that Delia felt in exactly the same way about me, however little I deserved so marvelous a wonder. Delia was everything. No—she would not despair of me— she would not, she must not!

"You all right, dom?" said Inch.

"Assuredly, my long friend. Do I thus break a taboo?"

He chuckled and pushed the wine over to me and I drank and pushed the problem of Delia's father, the emperor of Vallia, away for a space. At that time I had not settled the question. It rankled. I had to walk away from it for a space.

Leona, having exhausted herself on the scandal of a princess majestrix disobeying her father the emperor, had harked back to the Kov of Bormark, and was saying how lovely it would be if all that money were her Pando's. Pando laughed. With what I considered to be deep wisdom, he said: "The money might be fun, Leona, my dearest; but what comes with it—ah, that is a different matter."

Tilda was still sitting silently and sipping her wine and I saw her face suddenly tauten. I swiveled. Young Pando, his naked legs flashing, his brave zhantil tunic laid aside for the humble job of waiter, his hair tousled, was fleeting between the tables. A big fellow in the blue of a sailorman reached out and cuffed Pando alongside the head.

"Bring me a flagon, you rast of an imp of Sicce! Hurry, you little devil!"

Pando picked up his tray and what glasses were not broken. Someone else—a newcomer off the ships—kicked him irritably as Pando bumped into his legs; but that was a reflex action.

Tilda put a hand to her breast. Her violet eyes were large with anguish. Her supple voluptuous mouth shone, half open, pained, vulnerable.

I stood up.

Old Nath waddled across. "Now, Dray, please . . . !"

The sailorman laughed coarsely among his mates. He was big and bluff, with the tattoos across his forehead and cheeks that some sailors believe indicate heightened sexual potency or, perhaps, will give them immunity to the demons and risslacas of the seas.

"You, Nath, have a stinking clientele in here, lately."

"Please, Dray—"

I went across to the sailor who was already roaring for the little rast of a waiter and picked him up by the scruff of his blue tunic. He started to thrash his legs about so I clouted him—once was enough—and carried him outside horizontally. It was done quickly and decently, and old Nath put his hands together and cast his eyes up to Zair and Grodno.

Outside I stood the big fellow up and said, "You hit a young boy, you kleesh. This may be wrong, it may be savage and barbaric, it may be against the divine dictates of Zair; but I do not like men like you who hit young boys."

So, somewhat sorrowfully, for I know I sinned, I struck him in the belly. I stood aside as he was noisily and smelly sick. Then I kicked him where Inch had kicked the assassin and told him to clear off. I went back into *The Red Leem* and I managed to force out some sort of smile for Tilda.

Old Nath had quickly whipped a round of drinks onto the sailor's table and his mates were drinking and ogling the local dancing girls Nath had hired especially for the night. Tilda never performed more than once an evening. These girls were fine strapping wenches who danced like chunkrahs. They made great play with gossamer veils, they were heavily made-up, and each one would roll a sailor this night, or she was no true daughter of Pa Mejab!

Pando na Memis said to me as I sat down: "That was the captain of an argenter, you know, Dray."

"I should hope so," I said. "Nath runs a respectable house."

Tilda said she was tired and we all stood up as she left the table. The night roared on and presently, mindful that I must see about a ship the next day, I, too, went to bed. Tilda stood by her door, beckoning to me. She had waited for me to retire. A lamp burned in her room. I had made plenty of noise coming up the stairs. Even then, I believe I knew what she was going to ask me.

I sat on the bed, but Tilda prowled restlessly. She wore a long gown of jade, a green glinting and glorious. How strange, how incongruous, that I, Pur Dray, Krozair of Zy, dedicated to the utter destruction of the Green of Grodno, could sit and watch and not be moved!

Her ivory skin gleamed against the silk. Her black hair swirled as she walked. She prowled like a caged leem, like one of those leem stalking in the leem pit below the palace of the Esztercari in far Zenicce when my Delia clung in the cage above their ferocious fangs and claws.

"You need not whisper, Dray. Pando is fast asleep and it will take the wrath of the invisible twins to wake him. I sent him up to bed after—I saw that." Her voluptuous lips tightened. "I saw that, and I made up my mind."

I said, "What kind of life can he have, out here, on the frontier, Tilda?"

She clenched and unclenched her hands. She padded up and down those carpets of Walfarg weave, up and down.

"Old Nath runs a respectable house, for Pa Mejab. Yet already you have seen what can happen, Tilda." I tried to make my face smile for her; but I gave that up, and said flatly and, I fear, brutally: "You must take him home and claim what is his right."

Her white hand flew to her throat. She halted, stricken, and gazed at me, those violet eyes enormous in her white face.

"What? You know—how can you know?"

"It is not difficult, Tilda. By Zim-Zair. His father must have been a man!"

"He was! Oh, yes, he was! Marker Marsilus! Who would have been Kov of Bormark this day, had he not died out here in this pestiferous hell-hole. And Pando is his son."

"You mean, Tilda, that your son Pando is really Pando Marsilus, Kov of Bormark. He is, rightfully and legally. Is this not so?"

She looked at me, still and alert, like a risslaca watching a bird. "He is, Dray Prescot. Rightfully and legally." She took a breath so that the green gown moved and slithered. What she said next rocked me back with surprise.

"I am going home to Tomboram and I am going to claim what is his right for Pando. Dray Prescot—will you come with me and help Pando and me? Will you be our champion?"

CHAPTER NINE

We sail southeast past Erthyrdrin

Ochs, Rapas, and Fristles do not make good seamen. Chuliks may be trained, given the methods to which I had been born and grown accustomed, the system of the late eighteenth century, consisting of the lash, the starters of the bosun's mates, a wall of marines—and the lash.

Rum, in its counterfeit of shipboard wine, also helped.

As a consequence the vast majority of the crew of *Dram Constant*, Captain Alkers, were men of recognizable Homo sapiens stock. The few halflings were, and on their own wishes, employed in noncritical functions aboard ship—waisters.

No captain in his right mind would enroll a Fristle. I saw one being aboard—he was not Homo sapiens—who interested me mightily. His body was square in the sense that the distance across his shoulders, waist, and hips was the same, and equaled the distance from his neck to his upper thigh. He had but two arms, and they were as long and thin as Inch's, while his legs, also long, were nearly as thick as Inch's, which is another way of saying he was spindly-legged in the extreme. His face bore a cheerful rubicund smile at all times, his ears stuck out, he had a snub nose, and he could run up the ratlines and around by the futtock shrouds into the top with the agility of a monkey. This man, one Tolly, was a member of the race of Hobolings, inhabiting a chain of islands that I have mentioned, that ran parallel to the northeastern coast of Loh from the tip of Erthyrdrin southeastward to the northwest corner of Pandahem opposite the land of Walfarg.

Dram Constant, as Captain Alkers was happy to tell me, was as fine and tight an argenter as it was possible to find plowing the Sunset Sea. He knew that this report of his ship

had been the cause of our taking passage in her, our little
party consisting of Tilda and Pando, and Inch and I as
guards and champions to protect them and see they were not
molested and reached their destination safely. I believe it is
not necessary to dwell on the mental turmoil I went through
after Tilda's offer. As the days passed and the dwaburs
slipped past out keel, as we sailed in the armada toward Loh,
I had again and again to rationalize out my decision. Delia
of Delphond waited for me in Vallia; yet I was to travel to
Pandahem. Not only was I sailing away from her, I was
voyaging to a land in deadly rivalry with my own.

By taking an intense interest in every aspect of the argenter—an occupation easy to feign—I canceled out a great
deal of my own misery and indecision. I thought Delia would
understand, I prayed she would; and yet I doubted. . . .

This argenter was about a hundred and thirty feet long—
Captain Alkers told me she was a hundred feet on the keel
—and almost fifty feet on the beam. She was thus little more
than twice as long as she was broad. Captain Alkers also said
she was eight hundred and fifty tons burdened; but this I
tended to doubt. She was a fat, wallowy, comfortable ship,
with good stowage place below. We quartered ourselves aft,
within the three-decked aftercastle, and our cabins were of
a roominess that at first amazed me, used to far more
cramped quarters. One genuine improvement these sailors of
the outer oceans had made in their ships over the swifters of
the inner sea was in the use of a rudder and whipstaff in
place of the twin steering oars.

With her three masts and her square sails, *Dram Constant*
plunged gallantly onward, sheeting spray, and if she made a
great deal of fuss about her passage she did make a passage
over open and truly deep sea—if at a snail's rate of knots.

Pando loved to lie out along the bowsprit beneath the
spritsail mast and watch the water smashing against the
round cheeks of the bows, creaming and coiling away. *Dram
Constant,* as it were, squashed her way through the sea.

Tilda was continuously on at Pando, and me, for the lad
to come down where it was safe. After I showed him a few
of the necessary tricks of the trade any sailorman must
have, I felt a little more confident about him. But, all
during that passage, he was a sore trial.

Probably in an attempt to get his mind off ships and to
confine him to one spot, Tilda got me to teach him rapier
and dagger work. In truth, he was of an age when this

very necessary accomplishment would be vital for him to learn quickly.

A full-size Jiktar and Hikdar would have overweighted him, but we were fortunate in being able to borrow a practice pair belonging to one of the young gentlemen signed aboard *Dram Constant* to learn their trade. With these I had Pando puffing and lunging, riposting, parrying, drawing the main-gauche back in cunning feints, carrying out all the many evolutions of swordplay—the twin-thrust, the heart-thrust, the thigh stop, the flower, the neck riposte—until he was dripping with sweat and limp as a moonflower on a moonless night. Tilda would sometimes watch, and when the boy flagged, would say tartly: "Get on, Pando, get on! This is man's work now! Stick him!"

She did not, and for this I was mightily thankful, use that expression: "Jikai!"

Tilda and Pando proved excellent sailors.

Poor Inch lost a great deal of his dinner and his dignity over the side.

Memories ghosted up—to be instantly quelled.

For me to be back on the sea again was an invigorating experience, and I snuffed the sea breeze like an old hunter let out to the chase once more. The sky gleamed and glowed above us, a few clouds streamed in the wind, the breeze bore us on, all our flags and banners snapped and whistled in that breeze, our canvas strained, billowing with all the painted panoply gorgeous upon it. We plunged and reared in the sea and in our wake we left a broad swathing wash of creamy foam. Yes, for a time they were good days. I knew that I would reach my Delia; first I had to deliver Tilda and Pando—that imp of Sicce who was now Kov of Bormark—safely to Tomboram.

Tilda had not told Pando, yet, just who he was. That would come later. A wise decision, I felt.

We made landfall in due time at Northern Erthyrdrin, and took on fresh provisions and water and landed a man who had fallen and smashed up his pelvis. We shared berthing facilities with ships from other Pandahemic nations; but the peace was kept. I looked up at the gnarled mountains that thrust right up to the coast. Up there, in those mountains and valleys, lay Seg Segutorio's home. I could walk there. I knew the way, for he had told me often. But I was committed. I vowed that one day I would go there, for I could walk directly to where he had cut his bow-stave, where he

had held the pass, right to his home and greet the people as
though I had known them for years. But my honor and in-
tegrity—such as they are and have value—had been enlisted
in support of Tilda and the young Kov. Yes, one day, I
would walk the hills and valleys of Seg's home.

We were talking of the enforced amity of the different
countries of Pandahem here, and I heard more stories of the
horrors that did occur from time to time. There were mas-
sacres, and mutual extermination excursions, and tales of bitter fighting even when the Vallians laughed and stepped in to
steal the prize. I came to recognize the different devices and
characteristics that divided and marked one nation from another on Pandahem. In all this talk of division and what
amounted to internecine warfare I began to wonder if the
Star Lords had set another task to my hands.

As we sailed out in our armada and set our bows toward
the southeast I leaned on the larboard rail and looked back
over the larboard quarter. Out there, across the shining sea,
lay Vallia. . . .

As I stood there dreaming I heard a harsh and savage cry.
I looked up. Up there, slanting against the mingled rays of
the twin suns, a giant bird circled, a gorgeous scarlet-
feathered raptor, with golden feathers about its neck, and
wickedly clawed black talons. I knew that bird, circling in
wide hunting circles. The Gdoinye, sent by the Star Lords.
As I watched I saw the white dove fly smoothly above me,
circle once, and then rise and wing away. The white dove of
the Savanti!

I felt a tremendous sense of elation, of relief, of lightness.
I had not been forgotten. The Star Lords, who had brought
me to Kregen, and the Savanti, who also had brought me
here and then thrust me out of their paradise of Aphrasöe,
both were watching over me. They would not take a hand to
halt the cruel thrusting spear or sword. They wanted me for
their own inscrutable purposes. I wondered, again, if there
was work for them to my hand in Pandahem.

"What weird bird was that, Dray?" demanded Pando. His
mischievous face was all screwed up against the sun glare,
and quite serious.

"A bird, Pando. An omen." I could not tell him the Gdoinye
came from the Everoinye, the Star Lords. "It means that
everything is going to be wonderful in Tomboram."

"Of course, I am excited at going there, and the sea, and
the ships, and learning swordplay—but, Dray, tell me. Why

is Mother going home?" His eyes searched my face. "Home to me is Pa Mejab. She knows that."

"When you get to Tomboram, Pando, there will be many wonderful and exciting things to do. You will be a man. I know you will do your best to look out for your mother. She is a woman alone."

"She said to me once, would I mind if she married again."

"What did you say?"

"I said I would not mind if she married you, Dray."

I pushed myself off the rail and swayed gently with the roll of the ship.

"That cannot be, Pando." I spoke seriously, man to man. "Your mother is a most wonderful woman. You must cherish her. Yes, she will marry again, I feel sure, I hope—but I cannot marry her—"

But he was staring at me with such a black look that I felt sick. "You don't like her!"

"Of course I do." I looked around the wide deck, which was largely deserted on the larboard side, most folk being over on the starboard watching the last of the land. I bent toward him. "Can you keep a secret?"

"Of course I can." He was most ungracious, his lips in a pout.

"I am engaged to a girl—a wonderful girl—and I—"

"Is she a princess?" Scornfully.

I eyed him. He had been hurt. But I did not intend to lie. Clearly, not even a princess was better than his mother—and how right and proper that attitude was, to be sure!—but if my betrothed was a princess that, so Pando must be reasoning, might go some way to explaining my boorish behavior. But I would never, quite, be the same to him again.

He was growing up.

"Do you know what a Kov is, Pando?"

"Of course—anyone does. He has lots of money and rides a zorca and is covered in jewels—and he has a flag—and—"

"All right." A Kov, a similar rank to our Earthly duke, is what Delia had more or less confirmed me as, after my masquerade as Drak, Kov of Delphond, in order to avoid being killed by the overlords of Magdag. The title had been given me and she had confirmed it; I was not foolish enough to believe her father would do the same. As for the Lord of Strombor—as for all the other lords of the enclaves of the city of Zenicce—we were a cut above a Kov!

"As far as I am concerned, Pando, your mother is a Kovneva."

He screwed his face up to me. He was jigging up and down now, as all small boys do, being compounded of spring wire and rubber. "A Kovneva? So I'm a Kov, then?"

I tried to laugh. I did laugh, after a fashion.

"And I am the captain of a swordship!"

He laughed, then, and we were friends again; but it had been a near squeak. I sensed that Pando, young as he was, perhaps because of the insights of that youth, felt in me a secret that I could not utter, something vast and portentous that might move mountains. That it was in truth merely the love of an ordinary mortal man for his princess might have seemed far too commonplace for him.

Because of the action we had seen together, and my rescue of his mother, and the swordplay I was teaching him, Pando had come in his boyish way to hero-worship me. I had tried to choke this off, being not so much embarrassed as aware of the dangers; but had had little success. Now I felt I had succeeded, violently, and at a stroke.

The days passed and we bore on southeastward, the weather remained fine with a moderate breeze generally from a few points north of east, so we were continually on the larboard tack. Two alternatives now lay before the admiral of the armada.

He might choose to swing to the east and so outside the long chain of islands stretching down to Pandahem. This choice would offer attack opportunities to privateers from Vallia, scouring across the Sunset Sea. Or, he could run down between the islands and the mainland of Loh, which was here the homeland of Walfarg, progenitor of a once-mighty empire. This choice would lay him open to attacks from all the swordships which lay in wait in their festering pirate nests among the islands.

If he took the latter course, however, he would have to swing due east when he reached the last of the islands and run clear across the northern coast of Pandahem and the countries having their seaboards there before he could reach Tomboram in the east. Also, to figure into the calculations, there was over twice as much sea room outside as inside the island chain. To me, a fighting sailor, sea room is vital.

The admiral hoisted his flags and Captain Alkers, not without a fitting comment on the importance of the occasion, put his telescope to his eye. He nodded his head with satisfaction. He lowered the glass and turned to the helmsman. "Make it east!"

So we were to run clear of the islands, and then turn southeast for Tomboram directly—and to the Ice Floes of Sicce with the rasts of Vallia!

Every sixth day Captain Alkers conducted a short religious ceremony on the open quarterdeck. Most of the passengers attended and all the crew, both human and halfling. Tolly, I noticed, was particularly devout. In the inner sea the green of Grodno and the red of Zair hate and detest each other. In Zenicce they used to say: "The sky colors are ever in mortal combat." The people of Pandahem and Vallia had progressed some way along the path of a more live religion, for they held the view that the red and the green, Zim and Genodras, were a pair. They both shone down upon the one world, the twin suns mingling their light into an opal glory. They regarded their deity as an invisible pair, the invisible twins with which Tilda so often threatened Pando, and upon whom she called in time of trouble. The name often given to this twinned deity of invisible godhead was Opaz: a name conjoined from the light streaming and mingled from the Suns of Scorpio.

Despite my vows to the Krozairs of Zy, and my own half thoughtless swearing by Zair, I was happy to join the others in their worship, feeling no true blasphemy to my own God, feeling, rather, that these people were nearer to Him than many and many another I had known.

So we beat on east and then turned southeast and aimed for a quick run to Tomboram. The easting had cost us time, for we had had to make to windward by a long series of boards. But that weary tacking was paying off now. The spume flew, and the last of the gulls left us, and we were alone on the shining sea.

The lookouts were alert, and a most careful watch was kept at all times toward the east and northeast, from which we might expect the lean galleons of Vallia to pounce upon us.

As the days winged by and the weather remained fine we began to congratulate ourselves. Not a single speck of sail showed on the horizon rim. The galleons of Vallia had missed us, or were not at sea. The reason we discovered, to our disaster, when black clouds began to build up all along the eastern horizon. The twin suns shone down with a light I found uncomfortable. This was rashoon weather. When the blow came I discovered the difference between a rashoon of the inner sea and a hurricane of the outer oceans.

I have lived through many a hurricane and tempest, many a typhoon—on two worlds—but that was a bad one. We were driven helplessly toward the west. Our masts went by the board. We lost crewmen swept overboard. The blackness, the wind, the rain, and the violence of the waves battered at our physical bodies and smashed with a more awful punishment against our psyches. We suffered. We went careering past islands, seeing the fanged rocks spouting ghostly white, to see that spray ripped and splattered away in an instant. Onward we surged, a wreck, our seams opening, our timbers splintered, lost, it seemed, in the turmoil of the seas.

When the storm at last blew itself out and we poor souls, numbed and drenched, could crawl on deck and discover to our surprise that Zim and Genodras still smiled down upon us from a clear sky, the dreaded cry went up.

"Swordships! *Swordships!*"

The deck was in a frightful mess, cumbered with wreckage, raffles of cordage, splintered timbers, everything that had not been washed overboard. We rushed to the rail. There they came, long lean shapes spurring through the sea. With deadly intent they closed in on us. Helplessly, we wallowed in the sea as those sea-leem ringed us.

"*Swordships! Swordships!*"

CHAPTER TEN

Swordships

"Swordships!"

I eyed the lean low-lying leem-shapes surging through smothers of foam all about us. Slender, cranky, spray-drenched craft, they clearly had put out from some pirates' lair hidden on a nearby island. They were closing in for the kill. Soon our decks would run red with blood.

"Oh, Dray!" said Tilda, grasping my arm in a convulsive grip. Snuggled against her side and held by her other arm, Pando—who was a Kov although he did not know it—stared with all his boyish excitement and venom out to sea and those slender hungry shapes.

A hail from forward distracted my attention from the swordships for a moment. Then I saw the cause. Tangled together in a raffle of mutual destruction two other argenters from our shattered armada wallowed toward the shore. I saw the scheme of the swordships now. They would wait until *Dram Constant* had run athwart those other two dismal wrecks and then they would have us all, three fat ponshos, in the killing circle.

On the drifting wrecks the frantic forms of men ran and scuttled, and I caught the gleam of weapons across the water.

Very well.

We would fight.

Captain Alkers, pale but determined, gave his orders and his men were issued with axes and spears, boarding pikes and bows. Bows! Yes—to begin with, a little artillery might soften up the opposition. I disengaged my arm, very gently, from Tilda.

"You did Inch and me the great honor of asking us to be

your champions, Tilda the Beautiful. Now, we will see about honoring our side of the bargain."

"But, Dray!" she wailed. "There are so many of them."

About to make the habitual response, I checked, as Inch, with a gusty laugh, said it for me.

"All the more of them to kill, Tilda of the Many Veils!"

I cocked an eye at the suns as I went aft to the state-rooms to collect my Lohvian longbow that was built of true Yerthyr wood. How old that bow might be I did not know; but it was of great price, and I thanked Sosie once again as I brought it forth. I buckled my Krozair long sword at my waist, along with the rapier. There would be need of those later.

Ax in hand, Inch waited my return.

"It will be dark in three burs or so," I said. A Kregan bur, being some forty Earth minutes long, meant we had two hours before we stood a chance of escape in the darkness. Like any Kregan, I carried a kind of almanac of the motions of the seven moons in my head, and I knew we had a bur or so of true darkness, lit only fitfully by a small and hurtling lesser moon, before the twins, the two second moons of Kregen, eternally orbiting each other as they orbit the planet, would rise to cast down their pinkish light. Would they rise before we could escape? Would we all be dead before the last orange glow of Zim faded from the western sky?

Soon after the twins would rise She of the Veils. Then the darkness would be dispelled completely. We had to hold out against the swordships. We must!

The corsairs opened away before us and a single bank of oars flashed, dripping, rising and falling, from each lean flank as the swordships heaved and rolled in the running sea after the gale. Two-masters, the swordships, with a low profile extending into a familiar beak and rostrum forward, a compact forecastle, a sweeping length of deck packed with men and half-men half-beasts, and a single-decked castle aft from which blazed and fluttered many gaudy flags and banners. The swordships carried varters mounted forward and on the broadside. All our varter and catapult artillery had been smashed and swept away in the hurricane.

We were not entirely defenseless. I watched a swordship surging up alongside, as a ponsho-trag herding a straying ponsho, worrying, attempts to push the recalcitrant animal back among the others, and I saw the way the water broke

over her deck. I saw the spume shooting up, and the way
the oars flailed and lost their rhythm, and the quick falling-
off of the head to the wind to ease the swordship's motion.
Waterlogged, *Dram Constant* rolled sluggishly onward, steady
as a half submerged rock.

Lifting the bow and doing all the instinctive complicated
mathematics of wind and relative velocities instantly in my
head, without conscious thought, I loosed. The shaft struck
the helmsman. He threw both arms up and pitched forward.

A great yell went up from *Dram Constant*.

The next instant the swordship abaft the one I had so suddenly and summarily deprived of her steersman loosed her
starboard bow varter. The chunk of rock, as large as a fine
amphora, flew over our wreckage-cumbered decks and
splashed into the sea well forward of our starboard beam.

Again the crew of *Dram Constant* cheered.

But there were bowmen of Loh aboard the swifters, also,
and a dozen multicolored arrows sprouted from the timbers
of the argenter, and a crewman staggered back, cursing
wildly, a long shaft embedded in his shoulder, the dark blood
running down.

Wasting arrows has been a pastime in which I have never
been interested. I shot only when absolutely sure of hitting
a target; and I made of those targets the chief men of the
swordships, for one oarsman more or less will not halt a
galleass in full course.

The island richly clothed in a choked and brilliant vegetation toward which we drifted was appreciably closer now.
The swordships closed in. There were seven of them, and
they worked as one, obviously under the orders of a single
commander. I call them galleasses because, in truth, lean
and low in the water though they were, they were built
with a far greater freeboard than the swifters of the Eye of
the World. They would have need of that freeboard on the
outer oceans. To add to the correctness of my description
they carried varters in the broadside position, shooting over
the single bank of oars.

When an arrow feathered itself into the planking hard by
Pando, and Tilda screamed, I told Inch to take them both
into the aft staterooms. I wanted Inch out of this long-range
stuff, just as much as Tilda and her son, for his ax would be
invaluable at close-quarters; now he was merely a target.

The swordships kept on with their attack. I fancied they
were as unhandy in the sea as is any compromise between

the out-and-out galley form and the complete sailing vessel. They looked dangerous ships—dangerous to those who sailed them.

The very aftermath of the storm, the long deep-swell waves, were aiding us by preventing the typical galley tactic of ram and board.

Soon, however, we must tangle up with those other two hopeless wrecks and strike the shore. When that happened the swordships' crews would beach and board us. We had little chance, for the pirate ships carried large crews.

The long-range artillery duel went on as we drifted closer to the island and I grew more and more miserly in my husbanding of shafts. The swifters in which I had commanded varters had soon, under my brand of discipline, acquired accuracy and speed in rate of loosing. A King's Ship with the ever-present memory of Nelson to jog heart and mind and sinew is the best training ground for rapid shooting, even if accuracy is a subject scarcely mentioned, to my annoyance. But these swordship varter-men were plainly inept. Only twice they hit us. One chunk of rock smashed clear through the aftercabin and destroyed the crockery the storm had left unsmashed there. The other mashed three crewmen into a red puddle. That was all.

There is callousness and callousness. Do not think I did not grieve for those three men, still practically strangers; but I had seen all this before, and Tilda, Pando, and Inch were on my mind.

"Not long now, Dray Prescot," said Captain Alkers. He held his rapier in his hand, and he fiddled with the gay golden tassel dangling from the hilt. "We will give them a fight, though, before they take us."

I had seen on the nearest swordship a man strutting importantly on the low forecastle, shouting at the vartermen, and before I answered Captain Alkers I spitted the swordship varterist through the chest. He fell over the side and was much beaten by the oars, which pleased me. Then I answered the captain.

"We can hold them off long enough to get the women and children off and into the island, can we not?"

There is callousness and callousness, as I have said. That varterist did not merit overmuch regret, I warrant.

In this, as you will hear, I perhaps did the man an injustice.

On that particular swordship, a larger vessel with three masts, a bowman had been having a go at me with some consistency. His arrows had sung past my ears, three had buried themselves in the timbers of *Dram Constant*'s rail shaving close, and one had slain a Rapa waister who had been set to collecting incoming arrows. Captain Alkers cursed.

"I didn't mean the fool Rapa to collect an arrow in himself, Opaz take him!"

These arrows, of which I took only the automatic notice of a fighting-man engaged in an archery duel—which meant that I examined them with minute care—were feathered all with lush and lovely royal blue flights. Although I had never seen that gorgeous lambent shot-silk blue before, I knew exactly what they were and from which bird they had been taken. Seg had told me. They were the flights from the king korf, the largest bird of Erthyrdrin. The king korf was large; but it was nowhere near the size of the corth of the Hostile Territories; it was not a saddle bird. From this I knew I was up against a master bowman of Erthyrdrin on that swordship. It was extraordinarily difficult to pick him out on the deck clustered with men shooting. On the forepart of the aftercastle that extended into a quasi-quarterdeck stood a figure in brilliant and, the fleeting thought occurred to me, clashingly discordant clothing. A pendulous figure, with a mass of plumes waving above its helmet, the shine and wink of gems all about it, in a profusion; yet I caught the impression of uncaring scruffiness there. Twice I had shot at this figure, which appeared to me to be the captain of the swordship, and twice a mere chance had deflected the shafts.

Captain Alkers came back, cursing.

"We will strike the shore in a jumble of wreckage with the other two argenters. One is poor Captain Loki's *Tombor Adventurer*. The other is too far gone for me to be really sure just who she is—"

At that moment a blue-flighted arrow sprouted from the deck between us. I jerked it free, ran my fingers along the shaft to feel the sweet trueness of it, saw the head was a plain arrow-barb, nocked it, drew, loosed, and lost that flaunting blue in the mass of men crowding the deck of the swordship.

Now we were within close range of the shore the movements of the ships became more discernible. The swordships were swooping up and down in the sea. We surged on, sluggishly, and in a moment the shattered stump of our bowsprit tangled with the tattered bravado of the stern-castle of *Tombor Adventurer* and together, with the other argenter now a mere waterlogged mass disintegrating visibly, the three ships grounded. We swung broadside amid a great rending of wood. Outside of us now the swordships nosed in. Our keel grated on sand, we heeled, heaved as a wave caught us, and smashed down solidly onto the sand. *Dram Constant* had made her last landfall.

Some confusion ensued. I put it like that to let you understand that some of us wanted to stand and fight and some wanted to run into the shrouding vegetation of the island. Inch appeared with his great ax cocked over a shoulder, carrying our most precious possessions bundled into a canvas dunnage bag in the other hand. Tilda kept fast hold of young Pando, who was brandishing a dagger.

Captain Alkers formed his crew. The swordship carrying the blue-flight archer with whom I had been having that duel bumped our seaward side, going up and down like an elevator through the giant plants of Aphrasöe. I glanced back. People were pouring off the three ships and racing up the beach. A number of the swordships had landed farther along and pirates were running from them, waving weapons.

"Inch!" I put all the old deviltry and arrogance and unpleasant authority into my voice. "Take Tilda and Pando and get into those trees. Hurry! I will join you later."

"But—Dray—"

"Don't argue, man! *Move!*"

He looked at my face. He nodded, once, and his own lean face went tight and intense. He and Tilda and Pando hared off.

We met the first pirate rush in a smothering welter of blades that left many a sea-bandit screeching and toppling into the water in the gap between the two hulls. The swordship was going up and down confusingly. Men tried to leap aboard, and missed, and so were crushed. Others reached the decks and were cut down. I had been handed a fresh sheaf of arrows by a Fristle deputed to the task, and with these, standing back a little, I shot out those men who climbed the rigging in their passionate attempts to board. Arrows splintered the deck about me and one sliced my thigh; I did not think I could last much longer.

A quick glance showed me the beach deserted, and the pirates from the grounded swordships now preparing to attack us from the landward side. Men on the other two argenters were yelling and fighting and dying. Pirates forced their way onto the foredeck of *Dram Constant*. Captain Alkers was yelling his men on, clutching his left arm from which the blood splattered.

"Get into them, you calsanys! Fight! Fight!"

I slung the bow and ripped out my long sword. I leaped for the deck where the pirates were now shoving and pushing aft, shouting in triumph. I leaped—and I, too, shouted.

"Hai! Jikai!"

The Krozair brand gleamed brilliantly silver in the air; then it reeked a crimson gleam more dreadful as I lifted it for the next blow. With the argenter's crew I pressed forward. The pirates fought well, employing a miscellany of weapons; but we concentrated our strength and, just for the moment, were too many for the few who had boarded. We cleared the deck. But now, from the two shoreward ships came fresh sounds of conflict. In moments we would be attacked on two sides.

Captain Alkers' arm was bandaged; blood soaked through already. He glared about, panting, the rapier in his fist dripping blood.

"They want our valuables and our goods. They will overpower us for sure. We have done all we can, as honest sailors."

One of his mates, blood seeping from a slash across his forehead, shouted: "By Pandrite the Glorious! We have done that, Captain!"

"*Abandon ship!*"

Of that call so horrific to a sailor, Captain Alkers made a benediction and a curse, all in one. I knew he was right. I suppose, left to my own devices and being in the middle of a little fight, I might have stayed and tackled the swordship renders for the sheer hell of it. It is not in my nature to run from a fight. But I had the responsibility of Tilda and Pando—as well as Inch—and so I, Dray Prescot, also went with the crew as we jumped across the other argenters which were already deserted, leaped to the sand, and after a brisk rearguard action gained the shelter of the trees.

Tolly, the squat little Hoboling who knew these islands, took the lead and we hurried into the interior. We met up with the passengers and I was reunited with my three traveling companions. Tolly led us to a safe resting place and then went back to reconnoiter the coast. Inch, with a somewhat sour comment to me about staying with our charges, went with him. When Tolly and Inch returned they reported the argenters about stripped and the swordships preparing to leave.

After that, feeling empty and let-down, we trailed off to a fishing village Tolly knew, where we were welcomed by the headman, who looked remarkably like an older version of Tolly, and where we were able to obtain food and drink and a roof for the night. That bur or so of darkness had passed and now the moons of Kregen shone refulgently in the sky. Tilda and Pando fell asleep at once. I stayed up with Inch talking with Tolly and Captain Alkers and some of his mates with the headman, one Tandy. Tandy expressed a deep hatred and contempt for the swordships.

"They ruin trade," he said. "And our fishing. We are simple people and we live simply. But we are never likely to make contact with the outer world while the swordships by their depredations prevent commercial contact."

We argued and talked into the night and then I slept. But I made it a point to give Tandy a fine jeweled dagger I had picked up—I had severed it and the fist grasping it from its previous owner's arm—and tried to smile at him. I felt that he and his people would be valuable, situated as they were on an island in the midst of this strategic but isolated sea battleground. They'd be down to the stranded ships first light tearing them to pieces. The sea brought them harvests.

We made the necessary arrangements to secure a passage to the nearest port fortress of Tomboram, situated on an island a little to the southward. They existed in an attempt to suppress the swordships, an attempt, I fear, largely futile. They ran their own little fleet of swordships which flew hither and yon chasing the pirates—a thankless life.

From there we shipped aboard *Pride of Pomdermam,* Captain Galna, and made an easy passage direct to Tomboram's chief port and capital, Pomdermam, and so I sailed into the next period of my life in Pandahem. Vallia lay to the north. I would reach there, one day, soon. That, I vowed.

CHAPTER ELEVEN

"You ingrate, Dray Prescot!"

Pando had a toothache.

His face looked like one of those lusciously overripe gregarians grown in the lush gardens of Felteraz, a species of fruit of which both Nath and Zolta had been fond and so had converted me to their taste. A toothache in my own time on my own world was a serious, painful, and dreary business. On Kregen, of course, Pando saw a dentist who neatly twirled a couple of needles into his ankle and then yanked with professional skill. As first teeth, these should have given Pando no trouble in coming out and, normally, none did; this one had gone bad on him. The acupuncture gave him a completely painless time of the dentistry, and we came out and ate huge helpings of palines at the first restaurant we ran across.

But all this domestic business had blurred the edges of just why I was in Pandahem at all.

I told Tilda. I explained reasonably that she had asked Inch and me to escort her to her home; this we had done, and therefore it was time for me to be pushing on. Inch, when sounded out by me, had made the same reply he had made back in Pa Mejab.

"I'm a rover of the world, Dray, a wanderer. As a mercenary guard I can earn an honest crust. I'd as lief stay with you as not."

"I am heading for Vallia."

He whistled. "Vallia! May Ngrangi aid you! From Pandahem they'd as soon send you to the Ice Floes of Sicce as to Vallia."

"I know. Please don't mention our eventual destination. We have to push on. We'll find a ship, somewhere, never you fear."

Now, when I told Tilda as we squashed down ripe palines and Pando explored his cavity with a pink tongue, Tilda exploded.

"You ingrate, Dray Prescot!" Her fine ivory skin flushed with blood and her violet eyes clouded. She put a hand to her bosom, over the orange robe, and grasped the golden locket there. "You were to be our champion, Pando's and mine. And now, just when it is all to do, you are deserting us! Is this friendship?"

I sighed.

Tilda had made not the slightest sign of any advance toward me and I was comfortable in her company. Poor Thelda, now, had been all gushing, pushing and eagerness and help, and had thereby been a confounded nuisance.

Sosie, of course, had had her own secrets, and I felt a twinge of bafflement when I thought of her sweet black face and her great eyes and Afro hair. She had presented her own brand of problem. I got along with Tilda perfectly.

"What do you mean, Tilda? It is all to do? Surely, you are in your homeland—"

"Do you think this great untidy port of Pomdermam is my home?"

"Bormark?"

"Of course. Bormark lies on the extreme western border of Tomboram, and the lands run border with those of The Bloody Menaham. We have to reach Bormark, Dray, before Pando can claim his rightful inheritance."

I looked at Inch. He rubbed his ear and popped a paline into his mouth, and chewed, and refused to meet my eye—a mean and despicable act in a comrade.

"Is there no one here who can help?" I shot a shaft at a venture. "The king in his capital—"

"Him!" Scorn flashed from those lovely violet eyes. "King Nemo? He would as soon lock up Pando and me deep in a dark dungeon and throw the key away. I am sure he hates us, for being the relatives of his brother, Marsilus."

"All right, then. Anyone else?"

She picked up a paline and began to roll it on her palm. "I was an actress, Dray. Oh, I came from a famous theatrical family, we played all the best houses, and my way seemed set to follow in my family's footsteps. Then Marker came to the theater one night—and—" She looked at Pando, who was gazing at her, his mouth and eyes wide and the rich paline juice dribbling down his chin.

"Wipe your face, Pando! You look like an urchin!"

All the old adjustments had to be made by me. I was an urchin, a powder monkey who had climbed up through the hawsehole and trod the quarterdeck, bedecked with gold lace and a pair of shoes, cracked and with steel buckles, true. But urchins, to me, are comrades the two worlds over.

Tilda watched as Pando wiped. Then she said: "There is the Pallan Nicomeyn. He is old and wise. He was always fond of Marker—he tried to mitigate Marker's father's wrath; but uselessly."

A Pallan was the Pandahem equivalent of a minister of state, a name used, I discovered, also in Vallia.

"The Pallan Nicomeyn, then," I said. "Let us go and see him."

It was not as easy as all that to contrive a meeting, for we traveled under assumed names. But, eventually, we were shown into a small and windowless antechamber of the palace where guards—humans—stood at the folding doors. Presently the Pallan Nicomeyn entered. He was old, for his hair was gray and his face lined, destructions of time that do not overtake a Kregan until he is well past his hundred and fiftieth year. Whether or not he was wise remained to be seen.

As soon as he saw Tilda he turned and made a quick motion to the guards. Obediently they closed the folding doors and we were alone with him in private.

He wore a long gown of blue, girdled by a golden chain set with rubies, and he wore on his gray hair a flat velvet cap of a bright blue adorned with the blue tail feathers of the king korf. He carried a book which, I noticed, locked with a hasp and a golden padlock.

He advanced toward Tilda, his arms open to her.

"My dear! I never thought to see you again! You do not know the pleasure these old eyes of mine gain by once more gazing upon your beauty!"

They kissed and I thought this Pallan, this councillor or minister of state, showed some true feeling for Tilda.

"And is this—" He turned to Pando.

"This is my son, Pando."

"So," said Nicomeyn. "You are the young Kov—"

I said, loudly, so that they all jumped: "Pando is a fine boy. He doesn't know much, though."

"Dray!" said Pando, and he tried to kick me. I moved my

foot and he kicked the chair, and I smiled. "Sit quietly, you young imp, and listen while your elders talk."

He used the Kregish expression for grups, which I ignored.

"So he does not know, eh?" said Nicomeyn. He nodded. He wasn't too slow to catch on. "Perhaps that is wise."

Pando, defying me, said: "Will I see the king?"

"All in good time, dear, all in good time," said Tilda. She faced Nicomeyn. "You know the truth. Will you help us?"

He pursed his lips so that the lines indented deeply around his mouth. He put a long white finger to those lips, and shut his eyes, and thought. Just as I was about to become angry, annoyed that he should thus insult Tilda the Beautiful, he spoke his own salvation.

"There is no need to ask *if* I will help, Tilda. The question is—*what* to do best?"

"Oh, Nicomeyn!" said Tilda. "Dear Nicomeyn."

"Old Marsilus was a drinking comrade of my youth. It is dangerous to compare a king to his brother. I will not say more."

I stood up. "Well, that's settled, then, and pleased I am, too. Now Inch and I can get on. Kregen is a large place." I began to make a polite farewell to Tilda, with Pando staring at me as though I had grown another head, when Nicomeyn cut in.

"Please do not prattle, young man. I do not know who you are, but I assume the Kovneva Tilda employs you as a bodyguard. Your brute strength and your sword will be needed now, as it has never been needed before. So sit down and listen."

Then—with a great swoosh of air, I laughed. The situation tickled me. Inch looked most offended and Pando glowered at me, pursing his lips and fidgeting up and down on the seat; but I had my laugh out.

Tilda stared at me and her plucked dark eyebrows rose.

Most men, speaking like that to me, would have woken up in the far corner minus a few teeth. But the Pallan Nicomeyn was deep in conversation with Tilda, and patently anxious to help, so that I was completely disarmed. He did not know me, that is true, and so he escaped the deserts of his rash talk; besides, he was old and he wanted to help Tilda and Pando.

A plan was concocted but of it all the most important lay

in the few words Nicomeyn spoke to me. "I have labored long for this realm of Tomboram, and I know the family of Marsilus can play a great part in our future. My loyalties go a long way into the past. I would wish to see Pando where he belongs." I made no comment, frivolous or otherwise, on that pious hope. "If the usurper Murlock Marsilus can be deposed, and a fait accompli is presented to the king, then the law is clear. The rightful title lies—" He glanced at Pando, and finished: "The title lies where the law obliges it to lie, and cannot be challenged. But, the usurper must be deposed first. While he holds—possession counts for a great deal."

"And he's a bad lot?"

Nicomeyn made a face.

"I see. So we must first get rid of him and then it is plain sailing?"

"Yes." Nicomeyn looked at me. I was dressed in a sober blue tunic with leather shoulder straps rather like winged epaulettes, and my weaponry was belted about me as was my custom. Under the tunic I wore my scarlet breechclout, but that was invisible. I held the broad-brimmed gray hat with its curled blue feather on my knee. As though sizing me up in a different light from that with which he had first conned me, Nicomeyn said: "He is cunning, like a rast. He is strong, like a leem. He is stubborn, like a calsany. He will not be an easy person to dislodge."

Pando perked up, speaking his clear childish treble. "I don't know what it is you say, Uncle Nicomeyn. But if anyone can do anything, that one is Dray Prescot. I know."

I clumped my ex-assassin's boots on the floor and stood up. The part that Murlock would play was already clear; for he had sent the assassins after Tilda and Pando to make absolutely sure of his inheritance, that was patent. "We had better be about our work, then."

All the way out from the palace and into the suns-shine of Kregen I was hating myself. For I had once more engaged to do something that prevented me from rushing to my Delia, and claiming her before the world.

On the street with the busy pedestrians, and the zorca riders, and the calsany carts, and all the hurry and bustle of a great port that was also a capital city, Pando piped up "Why did Uncle Nicomeyn call you a Kovneva, mother?"

Immediately I took his arm and bent and whispered: "Did I not tell you, oh boy of little faith?"

He looked up at me and giggled and then tried to kick me whereat I spun him around and Inch yanked him back onto the pavement and a passing zorca bucked and its rider cursed. I looked up at him, and his curses stopped in midstream, and he swallowed and smiled—rather a sickly smile—and dug in his spurs and cantered off.

"You'll have to tell him soon, Tilda," I said as Inch and Pando went ahead. "If we are to rouse support for you, he is bound to hear—"

She nodded. "You are right, of course, Dray. We have much to thank you for—"

"You have," I said. "But say nothing of that until the job is finished. Then—" and I chanced it, and took a breath, and said stubbornly: "And then, Tilda the Beautiful, I must be on my way to Vallia."

She halted. "Vallia!"

"So you can see why we are like two nits in a ponsho fleece. We both have a zhantil to saddle." Which is the Kregan way of saying we both had our own secret and dangerous purposes.

"But, Dray! Vallia! What can possess you to go to that dung-heap of a disgusting rast-nest?"

When a woman as beautiful and respectable and intelligent as Tilda of the Many Veils spoke like that about the country that was the home of my beloved—what could I say?

"I have good reasons, Tilda. I believe I can expect of you some trust, to believe you do not think me an imbecile."

If she was about to make some unthinking remarks about me being a spy, she thought better of it. To take care, I hoped, of that eventuality, and already regretting that I had opened my big mouth, I said: "I have come to like and admire your Tomboramin, Tilda, I get along with your people. I shall be sorry, I think, to leave for Vallia, for there I shall do much mischief."

And, by Zair! That was true!

Inch, ahead of us, took Pando's arm, as I took Tilda's, to thread safely through the maze of traffic thronging the street as we crossed to make our way down to the discreet tavern in which we were lodging. *The Admiral Mauplius* was situated in the cooler end of a square, overlooking the sea and gathering most of the sea breeze. The temperature was somewhat higher here in North Pandahem than I had found it anywhere else I had so far traveled on Kregen. I have remarked that Zenicce and the cities of the inner sea are situated close to the same parallel of latitude, and Vallia, also, lies with much of her island bulk on those parallels. It is a strange fact that the temperate zones extend over far greater an extent north-south than they do on Earth. From the most southerly tip of the most southerly promontory of South Pandahem, the equator is not so many dwaburs farther south. From South Pandahem directly southwestward lies the coast of Chem. The equator runs through the enormous, dripping rain-forests of Chem in Central Loh. While I mention North and South Pandahem, it is worth saying that they are separated by a range of mountains running generally southeast to northwest in a dogleg. The mountains extend on into the sea to form the long chain of islands that terminate off Erthyrdrin in Northern Loh. But the mountains do not stop, for there, in Seg's homeland, they rear and convulse into that misty land of song and then, abruptly, collapse into a few islands across in the Cyphren Sea around which the Zim Stream swirls in its northward progress.

The problem we faced now has to hoist this usurper Murlock Marsilus out of his title and possessions, knowing that the king and the law would not help us until we had performed the deed, and knowing, also, that Murlock had all the aces on his side. He had the estates; ergo he had the money and the people tied up.

"We must do a little crafty detaching, Inch."

"With Ngrangi's help, that will be a pleasure."

Inch, as you know, came from Ng'groga, which is right down in the southeast of Loh, well south of the equator. I wondered if he'd want to go home after this. If he did, he'd try to talk me into going with him.

"Murlock," I said, firmly and with some bite. "We hit the top from the beginning."

So strikingly beautiful a woman as Tilda was surely going to raise men's eyebrows, inter alia, and she had taken to wearing a loose semitransparent blue veil, after the fashion of the women of Loh. When I asked Inch about Loh, and its mysterious walled gardens, and its veils, he chuckled and said: "I come from Ng'groga. There we are somewhat different folk."

"The truth is, Inch, everyone all over the world is somewhat different."

From the capital Pomdermam we took a coaster, a vile little ship smelling abominably of fish, to the westward. We touched at various charming little ports along the great in-curved sweep of the north coast which forms the extensive Bay of Panderk, voyaging steadily westward. On the third day we saw a swordship foaming toward us on a parallel course, the waves breaking clean over her long low hull as she wallowed and lunged in the sea, her oars bending with the strain, white spume skyrocketing high, all her blue banners and flags taut in the wind that bore us so comfortably on.

One of the crew spat overside. "A King's swordship," he said.

"The good Pandrite rot him," said another crewman, looking up from where he slapped dough to make the long Kregan loaves he would bake on the hot stove later during the morning. "My brother was sent to the swordships—for nothing. I'd like to—"

"Aye, Lart!" interrupted the first, scowling. "And your mouth is like to get you sent to join your brother in the galleys!"

I took note of this little interchange. Evidently, this King Nemo was not loved by all his subjects.

With the bread we ate cold vosk and taylyne soup. In the warmer weather here the cold soup was delicious, a thing I would normally never credit. Taylynes are pea-sized, scarlet and orange in their redness, and in conjunction with succulent vosk, superb.

"In Vallia," Tilda told me when we chanced on that awkward subject, "they drink their vosk and taylyne soup so hot it scalds their lips and mouths. Barbarous, they are, in Vallia."

She sighed. "Poor Meldi loved vosk and taylyne soup." Meldi was the bodyguard with whom she had fled from Tomboram, and from what I heard of him he had been a gentle giant, caring for Tilda and Pando, until sickness had carried him off just before my arrival in Pa Mejab.

On the fifth day we saw what at first I took to be a school of fish with tall almost-transparent dorsal fins. A cry went up and the crew rushed to the rail. Then, between the foam and the splashing I made out that this was all one huge and serpentine monster of the deep, with an oval body along the top of which grew that long fence-like fin. His head was impossibly out of proportion to his body, being immense, and equipped with a dredger of a fang-filled mouth.

"A sea-barynth," said Lart, whose brother rowed in a

"I made out that this was all one huge and serpentine monster of the deep."

King's swordship. "Now if we could catch it we'd feast right royally this night."

However, the coaster's skipper was no intrepid huntsman, and we left the sea-barynth far astern wriggling and curving in the water. It had two large paddle fins beneath its head. I was told that the barynth, of a similar size and ugly ferocity, one was likely to meet in the swamps of Pandahem as elsewhere, was equipped with four clasping claw-armed legs beneath its head.

I do not believe I have mentioned that the general word in use in Kregish for sea is "splash." The oddity of this perfectly sound onomatopoeic word in English ears, I think, is sufficient justification for the hint of a smile I summoned when I heard it, and why I use the word sea in its stead. There is another aspect of translation worth mention here. The word in Kregish for "water" in the sense of a drink of water is one that could never be uttered in any respectable company where English is spoken. To hear a wounded man calling for water, on Kregen, is to experience heights of the surreal.

In the shambles of the gun deck of a seventy-four which has just received a broadside from enemy thirty-twos, of course, one would hear through the smoke and confusion both words in just about equal proportion.

On the day before we picked up the pharos for what would be our penultimate port of call Tilda discovered nits in Pando's hair and nearly went mad, ordering up huge copper kettles of boiling water, and formidable bars of Kregen soap which is designed to scour little boys' eyes and the backs of their ears and necks. When Pando had been nearly scalped, she pronounced him fit to enter decent company once again. I thought of those running-alive ponsho skins of the Magdag swifters. Conditions of life are all relative.

From this last port of call before we reached Port Marsilus, the entrepôt for Bormark, we sailed in a little convoy of eight ships, accompanied by a vessel paid for and maintained by Bormark and her neighboring dukedom to the east for just this purpose of escort against raiders from The Bloody Menaham which lay far too close for comfort to the west beyond the promontory and islands that terminated the Bay of Panderk. The vessel was an argenter, if of a slightly leaner build than those that plowed the outer oceans, equipped with varters and catapults and with a sizable crew.

I studied her, and felt something could be made of her and her like.

From Port Marsilus, with Tilda still heavily veiled and under our assumed names, we hired two onkers for Tilda and Pando and two zorcas for Inch and myself. We rode to Tilda's home, a farm nestled among groves of samphron and muschafs, where her parents, having overcome their surprise, made us welcome. With a strict injunction to them to remain fast and not to stir abroad, and so be caught, Inch and I rode for the palace of Murlock Marsilus, the usurping Kov of Bormark.

CHAPTER TWELVE

Murlock Marsilus and King Nemo inspect my dagger

This Murlock seemed to me to be no atavistic sport of the family of Marsilus—despite all I had heard of Marker Murlock, and all I had observed of his son Pando—for the old Kov had been relentless in his rage and malignance against not only Tilda, the girl his son had married in defiance of his wishes, but against her family also so that they had given up the stage and gone farming with distant relatives in that pleasant valley. Now, we left the valley and our zorcas' hooves rat-tatted with a more purposeful sound on the paved road.

"Pando will turn out all right, Dray," said Inch. He reflected, and added, "If he lives."

"The story of the old Kov's recantation on his deathbed and the known desire of his to have Pando recognized as his heir," I said. "They are slender weapons, it seems to me; but they are all we have."

"If what the Pallan Nicomeyn says is true—I expect it is—those weapons will be enough."

"Once we have Murlock."

"Ah!"

The palace of the Marsilus family stood on the highest eminence of a block of red cliffs that fell into the sea with a stark sheer of cliff reminiscent of those cliffs of the Eye of the World where I had dived in order to go to the assistance of Seg and the others in our flight from the sorzarts. Verdant glowing vegetation clothed the heights. The castle and palace, as richly red as the cliffs, reared above. Many flags floated there, and armed guards strode everywhere. We heard, in the inn where we stayed for a dram of Tomboram wine, that the news was that the king was visiting Tomboram and was even now on his way, traveling with a great company, coming on the pleasant coast-road, journeying in state and great comfort, surveying the domains.

"There is no time to waste," I told Inch. "Once the king gets his lodging and board in the palace—"

"By N'grangi! We must strike quickly, Dray!"

So it was that that night we two, Inch, a gangling giant with his ax, and I, Dray Prescot, Lord of Strombor, with all my weapons about me, climbed that frowning red cliff in the light of the Maiden with the Many Smiles. We were gentle with the guards, for Pando, we hoped, would assume the overlordship of this pile and we did not wish to store up resentment against him. As it was, we left a trail of unconscious bodies until we penetrated clear through to Murlock's bed chamber, where Inch uprooted the nubile wench sharing his bed and I showed him the point of my dagger.

"You are coming with us, Murlock," I said, and at sight of my ugly face he flinched back. He was a fat man, but strong, and his jaws shook when I twiddled the dagger closer. "You may dress or not, as you please, but you had best make haste."

Shaking with the fear that must be torturing him with wonder how we two desperadoes had invaded his palace— for he could not know that Tilda had told us of the best secret ways in that she had learned from Marker—Murlock threw on his clothes and we three went out of his bedchamber leaving the wench neatly packaged in costly silks of Pandahem itself.

We carried him down the cliff on our backs, passing him from hand to hand like a carpet. He was near paralytic with fear; but he knew, for I had made it very plain, that a single cry would sink my dagger in his throat.

We loaded him aboard the spare mount, lashed wrist and ankles, and then we spurred in the streaming pink moonlight of Kregen along the metal-shining road. Tilda could hardly believe we had done what we had done. I shushed her up. Murlock had been blindfolded so he would not know where Tilda had hidden, and for this her people were grateful. We spurred hard toward the east, going through rich agricultural land, avoiding the farms, heading up toward the coast so that at last, with the coming of the twin suns, we were well on our way.

We rode for three days, keeping up a good pace, eating

provisions we had brought and not venturing near another
living soul. On the morning of that day we rode boldly into
the camp of the king. His people, servants, grooms, courtiers,
guards, were just rising and yawning and thinking about the
day ahead.

I selected the biggest tent of all, with its blue flags, and
jumped down before the guard. He was a man, in half-
armor, clad in a blue tunic, and for weapon he carried as
fancy a long-hafted spear as I had seen on Kregen. In
addition he had, of course, his rapier and main-gauche.

"Keep away, rast," he growled, and the spear blade
snapped down level with my stomach.

"Send a message to the king, insolent one, that the Lord
of Strombor wishes to speak with him on a matter of trea-
son."

The spear did not waver.

"Take yourself off, benighted of Armipand—" There
would have been more, doubtless of a foulmouthed kind,
but I stepped inside the spear, knocking it away, put a fist
into his jaw, didn't bother to catch him, and pushed through
the drapes into the tent.

In the anteroom with its bright silken walls other guards
started up, and their Hikdar strode forward, puffy as to jaw,
bloodshot as to eye.

"Hikdar!" I said, and my rasp sounded like a mill full of
buzz saws. "I am the Lord of Strombor. Rouse the king. I
have news for him."

The Hikdar hesitated and I did not miss the lifting of
weapons of his men. At that moment a short and exceedingly fat man wearing the robes and insignia of a Pallan
stepped out.

"What is going on?" he demanded, with some acerbity.
"The king is dressing and orders that whoever is creating
this disturbance shall be brought before him."

The Hikdar lost all his color.

"It was not me, Pallan Omallin, not me! This man—he
claims to be the Lord of somewhere or other—"

I pushed past them both, tripping the Hikdar, shoved into
the main body of the tent.

As I went I shouted back: "Bring 'em in, Inch! Come
straight through. Take no notice of this rabble."

The scene in the king's tent was much as I had expected.
Evidences of luxury lay everywhere. Rich carpets, brocaded
coverings, cushions, arras to double-wall the tent, weapons

glittering from the tent-poles, all I saw and ignored. On a sumptuously upholstered divan sat a corpulent man with a puffy face pulling on a pair of enormous black boots. Their spurs would cause agony to a zorca. His black bar moustache lifted as he stared at me. His eyes held a pale fanatical look. He licked his purple lips a great deal. I did not take to him, as you may wonder, for I am overly tolerant to other people until I read them through correctly.

This was the man, this King Nemo, in whose power I had placed myself and my friends. I knew of his bias toward Murlock; yet would he flout the law? There were witnesses, for the Pallan Omallin had scuttled in, gasping, after me, and the guards and their Hikdar also.

"You are the man creating the noise," the king said, speaking with a nasal rasp that irritated. "You will be taken to the cliff-top, flogged, and then thrown into the sea." He motioned to the guard Hikdar. "Take him away."

"You are mistaken, King," I said. I eyed him. "I am the Lord of Strombor. You know of the last wishes of your brother, the Kov of Bormark, concerning his grandson?"

The king reared up, puffing, scandalized, starting to shout. But Inch had walked in, and with his height ducking to get in through the tent-opening. He carried Murlock over his shoulder. Tilda followed, holding Pando's hand.

"You are mad!" shouted the king. "You will all die!"

"We are not mad, King, and I think you will listen—else it will be you who will die."

And with that I caught his fat greasy neck in my left hand and showed him my dagger in my right.

He gobbled.

I thought his eyes would fall out and roll like marbles on the carpets.

"I come in friendship, King. I would not harm you, but you must listen to me. You know what your brother, Marsilus, desired. The usurper Murlock is here, a dead man if he fails me. Also here is the Kov of Bormark."

Murlock emitted a shrieking groan at this and Inch threw him down on the carpet. He groveled there, and I had it in my heart to feel sorry for him.

"Mercy! Mercy!" Murlock yelled. "They are madmen!"

"Not so." With the king threatened by my dagger no one was foolish enough to make a move against me. I thought that these men here were most unlike that Lart aboard the coaster, who would probably have driven his dagger home had he been in my position, and damn the consequences.

"What do you want?" squeaked the king. "I can see the Kov of Bormark—Murlock—"

"Here is the Kov of Bormark," I said. Tilda pushed Pando forward. He stood there, clad in his zhantil-skin tunic, gripping the hilt of his dagger, and he looked wild enough; but, withal, there was about him in the cut of his jaw some strength that showed through. I know that the king recognized in Pando's young face the true lineaments of the Marsilus family.

"By the laws of Tomboram," I said, in a loud voice, "Pando, the grandson of Marsilus, is the Kov of Bormark. Banish the usurper, or he dies now, beneath my sword."

Inch had unslung his great ax and was swinging it up and down, whistling softly through closed teeth.

Murlock groaned and squealed and managed to croak out: "Do not kill me! Yes, I did it!" He knew what to say, for I had made sure of my facts first. "I did send men to slay Tilda and Pando!"

The king was in a cleft stick, in one sense, for he knew nothing of Pando, who was a young lad completely out of his reckoning. He had had Murlock under his thumb. I released the king's neck and stood back. The guards tensed, but they did not jump forward. By my actions I hoped to convince them it was all over. Tilda lifted her veil and smiled on the king.

Perhaps, when all is said and done, that smile did the business.

The king gave his judgment, there and then. It was for Pando. Murlock was given twenty burs to get out of Tomboram. He slunk out of the tent. I knew there would be trouble from him in the future; but there was little to do about that right at that moment, save kill him. And murder in cold blood is not one of my hobbies.

Now was the time for me to be properly apologetic for manhandling King Nemo. I managed this with a straight face, and when breakfast was brought and we sat down to a good meal, and Pando demonstrated that he knew exactly what being a Kov entailed—at which I winced a little— and Tilda got along with the king, as I thought then, I did really believe we had pulled it off. The king set himself to statesmanship at once.

"I was visiting Murlock because The Bloody Menaham,

may Pandrite rot 'em, are planning to invade my realm. They march alongside your borders, Kov Pando. I shall need many men and much money from you to defend the frontiers."

With the simplicity of youth and with all the fiery ardor of which he was capable, Pando cried out: "You shall have all the men I can raise, and all the money in the treasury, King Nemo! We will teach The Bloody Menaham a lesson. We will march against them! We shall fight them, and kill them, and burn their farms! It will be a great victory!" He swung to me, animated and excited and hardly a little lad of ten years old any longer. "Is this not so, Dray Prescot, Lord of Strombor?"

About to try to calm him down, for Tilda had somehow succumbed to emotion, and was sitting, drinking Kregan tea and sniffling from time to time, I was brusquely interrupted by the king. He was in a jovial mood. I saw through the reason for that. He had been looking forward to an interview with Murlock that would be painful to both of them, for however much Murlock may have been under the king's thumb, any Kov is cautious when asked for men and money. And now the new Kov, a mere boy, was giving away all he had by the handful.

I saw that King Nemo felt he had done a good morning's business. He spoke to me, later on, in much the same terms, except that he left out all advantage for himself that had occurred during my handling of him.

"You fight well, Kyr Dray nal Strombor. Right well. I have room for you in my guard. I need a man who is loyal to his employers."

Without hesitation—and in that I made a foolish mistake —I said: "That cannot be, King. I have a mission in life, and having discharged my obligations to Tilda, the Kovneva, and to Pando, the Kov of Bormark, I must be on my way."

King Nemo frowned.

For all my detestation of authority and sheer hatred of it when it is unfairly imposed and in tyranny and oppression destroys good simple people, much of my life on Kregen has been spent among representatives of those very people who wield the authority. I am as happy among a lower deck gang of sailors as among a palace full of Kyrs, finding good qualities in both. I was still very young and green then, as you will know from my previous narrative spoken into the tape recorder in the epidemic-stricken village of West Africa.

How I was to face Delia's father, the emperor, I had not yet decided. I simply could not stalk in and treat him as I had treated this flabby and shifty King Nemo. So I floundered on, then, in my ignorance, and only when the next morning, instead of awaking to the tent where I had been quartered, I awoke with chains galling my wrists and ankles, lying facedown in the bottom of a boat where bilge water sluiced over the floorboards, was the understanding forced in on me that I had sadly underestimated this King Nemo.

I was naked except for the gray slave breechclout.

I knew where I was destined.

The banquet the night before in Pando's honor had seen some agent of the king's slip a potion into my drink. He had not had me killed, despite the fact I had laid hands on him, and I guessed that, maybe, after my stint in the sword-ships, he would attempt to win me over again. If I give myself too much credit in thus thinking, there were good solid reasons for it.

In addition, he would be well aware that the punishment of a quick death would not satisfy him. The lingering agony of the slave benches would please him much more. Or so I tried to reason as we rowed out and were bundled aboard a swordship lying in the roads. I have told you of my life aboard a swifter as a galley slave. The differences now were there and noticeable, but the end result was much the same.

I raged and cursed and broke a few heads and swung my chains and was soundly beaten and came back for more, crippling a whip-deldar, and was flogged again and, at last, came to my senses. The previous experiences of being an oar-slave should have trained me far more rapidly into the required state of dumb and instinctively willing obedience. There would come an end to the torture of this life, hauling at the loom of the oar. There would have to be. I could look forward to a life of a thousand years, and here one of the drawbacks of that state made itself horribly clear—a thousand years of life as an oar-slave aboard a swordship of Kregen!

No!

That I would not tolerate.

The swordship on which I found myself was *Nemo Zhantil Faril Opaz*. This mouthful was itself an abbreviation, a kind of heraldic shorthand for a much longer name which meant, in effect: "King Nemo as courageous as a zhantil and be-loved of Opaz." For a laugh, and I sorely needed something to lighten my spirits in those dark days, I translated this out into English as: "King Nemo the lion-hearted, beloved of God." And so cursed and struck the loom of my oar, and almost despaired of ever seeing my Delia again.

We rowed eight to an oar, usually, five pulling and three pushing. The swordship, usually known as *Nemo,* and by we slaves with a spit and curse also, had commissioned for service up among the islands chasing pirate swordships. She was a moderately large vessel, although I did not then ascertain her measurements, not being in a position to do so; but she rowed in her single bank of oars arranged *alla scaloccio* thirty oars a side. There were marked differences between this swordship and the swifters of the inner sea, differences dictated by the altered circumstances of sea and weather and distances.

Whereas a swifter needed little freeboard, a swordship must be built with freeboard sufficient to cope with the deeper swell-waves and the greater violence of the outer oceans. Only one bank of oars was employed. The old-fashioned zenzile method of rowing was still found among the swordships, but it was rapidly disappearing. Because of this the oars were that much heavier and longer and were not angled so sharply into the water. Up front she possessed the curved bronze ram or rostrum that is still regarded by many sailors as the principal weapon of the oared galley, despite the problems of entrapping and swamping entailed in the rammed galley's apostis. The proembolion, the second projecting wedge designed to thrust the rammed ship off the rostrum, was as well-developed among the swordships as among the swifters. Above that the beak extended forward, and here, too, a difference was found. The swifter beaks were movable, being lifted or slung down into position for boarding, rather after the fashion of a sophisticated and modernized Roman corvus. The swordship beaks were permanent structures and built so that they extended forward short of the point of the waterline ram, and they were extended aft into the foot of the low forecastle.

All in all, as I sweated at my oar with seven oarsmen around me, I fancied the swordships were as good a bargain a navy might get from the always unsatisfactory attempt to oar a sailing vessel, or sail a galley.

Their underwater lines were nowhere as fine as a swifter's and they were deeper in draft, which made them sea cows to row. But they were still long, lean, low, and they were cranky and dangerous and wet and hideously uncomfortable.

Every time I hauled the oar I cursed King Nemo. To liken him to a zhantil was a ludicrous slander on a noble beast; if anything, Nemo was a leem—or a cramph.

This swordship *Nemo* boasted three masts, unlike most of the pirate galleys I had previously encountered, and the captain seemed to me to be as unhandy a sailor as any I had shipped with and always preferred to use his oars. This made life hard. We sailed north and west up along the island chain, calling in at various of the port fortresses Tomboram maintained there. We did not sight a single pirate swordship.

We saw three scraps of sail on a bright day of fine visibility; but we sheered away and later the buzz went around the slave deck that the swordships had been from The Bloody Menaham. They would have been a relief to me. Mind you, I was well aware of the horror and the shambles of the rowing benches during a fight, but my mood was black and vicious and by this time I was ready to tear the throat out of a leem with my bare hands.

Nemo Zhantil Faril Opaz got her comeuppance at last in a way that was so ridiculous that every time I thought about it afterward I cursed in delighted wonder.

We had touched in at an island that Valka, a captured Vallian and a man who appealed to me and to whom I had been closest drawn of all those oar comrades, said was deserted. A party was about to go ashore for water when, peering through the oar-port I saw a sight that created, at once, a great shout of surprise and admiration and lust all over the swordship.

Onto the beach dashed a horde of half-naked girls.

They danced down to the water's edge and they held out their hands to the swordship in supplication. Many and various were the oaths that floated fruitily into the hot air.

"By Likshu the Treacherous!" said a yellow Chulik farther along on our oar. "Were I not held by these chains!"

We mocked him. "Were any of us not held by these chains, oh mighty Chulik!"

"Mother Zinzu the Blessed!" rang a clear call from somewhere farther along the rowing deck, at which I felt all that old pang of remembrance. Many and varied, the oaths, fruity and blasphemous and calling on gods and demons and heroes from a score or more of different cultures. But we were slaves, naked and chained, filthy and mop-headed, bristling with hair and vermin. That rout of beautiful naked girls was not for us.

The captain and the crew brought not water from the island but rich wine in great round-bellied amphorae. The girls, clad in their strings of flowers and feathers, laughed and came out to the swordship as the twin suns sank in an opaz glory. We slaves crouched on our rowing benches and glowered and fed on crusts, an onion each, and a strip of old cheese like lenk. The Maiden with the Many Smiles rose before the suns had gone. A weird clashing of colors poured over the swordship. We slaves could imagine what was happening in the aftercastle and the forecastle now; we could hear the peals of silvery laughter and the great gusts of sailor mirth.

And then, gradually, the sounds quieted down. We heard a shrill scream, and then another, fainter. Silence dropped on the swordship. We did not even hear the watch calling the turning of the sandglass.

Valka said to me, "Something is amiss." He roused the Gon who was nearest the gangway, an unpopular position as he was nearest the lash of the whip-deldar. "Hey, dom. What's afoot?"

The Gon's great bristling, malodorous thatch of bone-white hair lifted. Gons habitually shave their heads skull bare. If that is because they feel shame over a mop of white hair, one must sympathize with their own foolish beliefs. As it was, this Gon experienced deep shame over his unshaven head.

"Let be, Valka. I want to sleep, and dream of those women."

"Look aft, you hairy nit! Is the watch by the lamp?"

The Gon stretched. "The lamp is not lit."

"By Vox!" Valka galvanized himself into instant action. "This is the one night . . ." He began to tear at his chains, desperately, until his nails tore and the blood poured forth.

So far I had found no implement with which to file through the iron chains, as we had done in *Grace of Grodno* when Zorg, Nath, Zolta, and I planned escape. Yet Valka was right. This one night *was* our chance! But, through the most simple and elementary precautions of the crew, nothing convenient for a slave to rub through his chains lay handily about the deck. We might all have lost our reason, then, tearing at our fetters and trying to keep silent besides. Already the unlit lamp proved the routine of the swordship had been altered, and when we were not hosed down for the night we knew beyond doubt that the crew was otherwise engaged—and in our lascivious dreams how wrong we were!

For—in the lambent pink floods of moonlight a girl stepped up onto the central gangway. Every head turned to look—but there were no cries of admiration or lust or, even, of wonder.

In absolute silence that slip of a girl walked all the way along the central gangway, from aft forward, half-naked, her limbs gleaming pink in the moonglow, swinging her burden lightly from one little fist. She held that burden by its hair. Sightless eyes glared out upon the rowing benches.

From the severed neck from which still strips of gristle and flesh dangled dropped the dark blood. Drop by drop as she walked the blood fell upon the gangway.

No chance guided her choice of head thus to parade.

Every oar-slave recognized that hated face.

The uncanny contrast between that lithe slip of a girl, all gleaming beautiful and pink in the streaming moonlight, and that hideous severed head, dropping its blood as she walked so gracefully along, with a swing of her hips, laughing, affected every single one of us profoundly.

Not a man so much as moved. No one spoke. Every eye fixed on her and her burden, glaring like the jungle denizens stare upon their prey.

Drop by drop the blood fell upon the planks of the gangway.

Every oar-slave recognized that hated face. In a deep and scarcely comprehending silence we watched the girl carry the head along, laughing, swinging her hideous burden.

We knew that dead face.

It was the face of the chief whip-deldar.

CHAPTER THIRTEEN

Viridia the Render

We were given the usual alternatives.

Given them, I do not believe a single oar-slave took the choice that would see his carcass hurled over the side and feathered with arrows in sport.

What others considered as an omen I took, also, I confess, as some kind of pointer to the future, for all the seven moons of Kregen floated in the night sky above as Viridia spoke to us.

"Never disdain the power of women," said Viridia. "For my fighting-girls have laid the whole crew of this King's Swordship low, and have taken her, and now she is ours."

I could not see Viridia very clearly, for the stump end of a varter interposed its ratchets and its winding windlasses and loosing mechanism between, so that I caught only fragmentary glimpses of her as she moved about, gesticulating. Seeing her like that, however, meant that I immediately recognized that gaudy, pendulous, barbaric figure as the one I had seen strutting the quarterdeck of the swordship when *Dram Constant* had been destroyed, and when I had indulged in that pleasurable contest with the blue-feathering bowman of Erthyrdrin.

Her girls had successfully seduced the swordship's crew, poured them drugged wine, and seen them off to the Ice Floes of Sicce. To me, the master stroke of psychology had been to parade the severed head of the man whom we slaves would recognize immediately as the instrument of our daily torture. Now we were members of the pirate band of Viridia. I hesitate, even now, and remembering her as I do, to call her a lady pirate. Viridia was no lady. She was a woman, wild, free, gross, sudden, a woman who always—or, nearly always, as you will hear—kept herself in complete

control. She knew what she wanted, she knew how to go
about getting it, and she did what was necessary; and if the
blood reeked along the blades of her people, both women
and men, halflings and beast-men, then that was the price
she was prepared to have them pay.

Her control was normally such that when she indulged
in her killing frenzies and heads rolled one who knew her
could almost judge to the mur when she would snap out of it.

The pirates who infested these islands where through the
geography of the region there would of necessity be heavy
maritime traffic did not employ slaves to tug their oars.
Through this area passed the commercial traffic from Pandahem and Loh, north and south, east and west. Many armadas tried to avoid the area as the admiral of the armada
in which Captain Alkers' *Dram Constant* had sailed had
attempted, and many ships simply avoided the islands altogether, as Tandy, the Hoboling, had so bitterly informed us;
but, despite all that, the needs and demands of cities and
peoples meant that ships must sail these seas. Viridia was
only one of a great host of pirate chiefs. And, she was not
the only woman pirate chief.

Everyone has heard of the famous women pirates of our
own Earth. Lady Killigrew, Anne Bonney, and Mary Read
all made the headlines of their day. Anne Bonney, who deserted her husband for John Rackam, the notorious pirate
Calico Jack, was powerful enough as a lady pirate to make
Calico Jack take second place in the fighting and boarding and
arguments that are inseparable from a pirate's life. Mary
Read, already a girl who had led an adventurous life in that
she had fought as a soldier in Flanders by the side of her
husband, was captured by Calico Jack. The joke was—at
least by Kregen standards—that when the pirates were taken
they were all drunk with the exception of the two women,
who alone attempted to fight off the British warship. A ray
of light does exist to alleviate the story in that both women,
although sentenced to death, were not hanged and did escape
Execution Dock.

"We carry no passengers," Viridia informed us. At her
back stood four immense fellows, all rolling muscle and
corded thews, bull-necked, their heads jutting forward so
that the two stumpy but formidable horns they carried on
their foreheads could jab in with ferocious power at an opponent's eyes. They had two arms and legs, massive and
bulky, it is true, and their bodies were recognizable human

torsos and stomachs, plated with muscle. They wore the gaudy clothes of the pirate trade. They also carried short swords of a heavier pattern than the merely cut-down rapiers often found among the pirates.

Rapiers and daggers also swung from their belts.

These were Womoxes. As I have mentioned previously, there are many and various peoples inhabiting Kregen beneath Antares, and I give some idea of any individual people, either halfling or human, when they come onto the stage of my narrative. By this time in my sojourn on Kregen I had seen many strange and marvelous peoples of whom I have given no idea here simply because I did not personally come into contact with a representative of them. When I did—then I describe them, as I believe to the benefit of your understanding. I had not previously encountered the Womoxes. They came from one of the islands off the coast of Vallia. They are a people at once fierce, independent, not overly original—their native art is markedly copyist of another people on an adjoining island—and much given among the males to head-butting contests to decide who shall do what or who shall mate with which maidens. In all this they never, at least to me, suggested very much of the bovine.

Perhaps I could mention here that I believe that the many differing races and peoples of Kregen are not distributed over that marvelous globe by any laws of nature that are easily discernible as they are on our own Earth. I believe, further, that the races of Kregen have been arbitrarily placed in the locations of their origin. If this be the work of the Star Lords, as I have more than half a mind it is, then more remains to be learned of their dark and secret purposes than I, even now, fully comprehend. I do not think the Savanti had a hand in the locations of the populations of Kregen; but their task, as I know, is the amelioration of the lot of all peoples.

There have been many ups and downs in my life and in this present situation, because for the moment there was nothing else to do, I flung myself into the business of being a pirate aboard a swordship plundering along the Hoboling islands. We took Pandahem ships and ships of Loh. Sorry as I was for the people who suffered, I had worked out a theory that of the Pandahemic nations none could be construed as friendly to me except Tomboram, and of that country only, really, could I look for real friendship from Pando and Bormark. I was worried over that imp's handling of his people. I hoped Tilda and Inch would be able to hold in check his very natural desires to go for a fight and cut a fine figure and make a name for himself. War, as I have learned, is not a game.

The nations of Pandahem, always at loggerheads, were driven in part by economic rivalries, partly by the ambitions of their kings to become emperors of all Pandahem. They had the bitter example of Vallia to spur them on. Vallia might make a treaty of friendship with one nation of Pandahem, and another would ignore that and raid Vallian shipping, with the consequence that Vallia quickly lost patience with all Pandahem.

I had to make a stand against casual killing of captives.

"You are throwing money away!" I said to Viridia. I stood with my hands on my hips on the deck of a fine argenter of Walfarg we had just finished sacking. The frightened people left of her huddled by the break of the quarterdeck. I wore a loincloth of that brave scarlet I favor, and a rapier and dagger taken from a prize swung at my sides. Viridia came to the quarterdeck rail and leaned on it and looked down on me.

"Stand aside, Dray Prescot!"

So she knew my name. I thought that odd, among so many new recruits to the render's trade. A render is a pirate, and yet the name carries overtones associated closely with the swordships. She was looking down on me as I glared up. An odd expression crossed her face. She was a large woman, bulky, with muscles that could swing an ax with the best, and I had always thought of her as coarse, bloated, careless as to her dress and manners, oafish, almost. She looked different, now, as we glared at each other, eye to eye.

"Listen, Viridia. You intend to kill these wretched people and burn the argenter. How foolish!"

A murmur of surprise and shock went up from the gathered pirates. I motioned to them, calculatingly.

"By killing and burning you deprive your fellow renders of their fair share of the prize!"

She roared down, her dark hair flapping about her face, her blue eyes fairly blazing with wrath. "Have a care how you speak, Prescot! I am Viridia!"

"Aye! And you cheat your comrades!"

Viridia put out a hand to stay the automatic charging response of her chief Womox. He was a veritable giant, a good seven feet tall, and a formidable antagonist.

"Explain yourself, rast, before you die."

"If I am a rast, then what are you, Viridia the Render? Send the ship into port, sell her for good silver dhems, claim a ransom for these people in our power. They are cash and they stand upon cash! Can you not see that, Viridia the Render?"

Some of the men at my back set up a yell supporting me, seeing the cash in their hands already, and chief among them was Valka, my oar comrade from Vallia.

"Silence!" shouted Viridia. Once she had fought her way up to captaincy she had not experienced resistance to her slightest whim or order. The experience came as a novel one to her. She frowned. I could sympathize with her. The problems she had overcome were capable of being overcome, as she, no less than Anne Bonney and Mary Read, had demonstrated. Birth control is well-understood on Kregen where beliefs are taught that teach it is better to have two or three fine healthy children for whom parents can give what of food and clothing and shelter is necessary, than it is to have a whole squalling brood of poor, undernourished, half-naked infants for whom there is not sustenance enough. Ignorant and wrong-headed religious feeling receives short shrift in these matters on Kregen, where what can clearly be seen to be so is taken as a guide. Because there are two suns in the sky images tend toward a dualism. Because unthought-out parenthood, selfish and cruel, can result in a family of misery, compassion and sympathy tend toward families of sizes where the children may receive all that is their due.

Now, no virgin but capable of love, unhampered, totally in command of her swordships, Viridia glared down on me and her knuckles whitened into skulls as she gripped the quarterdeck rail. In a second she could order me to be run through and tossed overboard. I would fight, of course, but there would be little of joy in that fight.

I had the impression that Valka, and one or two others, would fight with me.

"Why do you resist my wishes, Dray Prescot?"

"Because I know I am right and you are wrong."

Her broad face, tanned and strong, flinched with a muscle tremor beneath those blue eyes. "I do not take kindly to—"

"Do you want the value of this argenter and the ransoms of these prisoners, or do you want a heap of corpses and a pile of ashes, Viridia the Render?"

Valka shouted, "Dray Prescot speaks good sense."

The tenseness of the moment showed in the ridges muscling on the faces of the men gathered about, the way the Chuliks kept polishing their tusks, the Ochs twined their four upper limbs together, the Fristles kept stroking their fur. Viridia looked down on us and who of us could say how that mercurial brain of hers would decide to go—up or down in the scales of our judgment?

She was, as I have said, a large woman, and yet from the way she was standing and the drape of her gaudy and impossible clothes I caught the impression that she wore armor beneath that show, and the robes and clothes hung loosely outside, as though worn deliberately for effect. She half drew her rapier, and sheathed it—a motion that brought an instant reaction from her four Womoxes, a reaction as instantly stilled—and she put a hand to her mouth, which was large and generous, and pondered on the problems that I had brought into her ordered render life.

"And who would take the prisoners for their ransom? You, Prescot, you would? And would we ever see you again?"

"Aye!" shouted the men, swayed her way.

"Does honor, then, count for nothing, here along the Hoboling islands?"

A growl greeted this, and Viridia flushed darkly; but she knew as well as I that honor among renders was a matter of convenience. I went on, quickly, "Send someone you trust, if you do not trust me." Then, as though clinching the argument, I spread my arms wide. "I simply want all the cash that is due me and my comrades. That is all."

The upshot of it was that Viridia did not kill the prisoners but sent them in the argenter to Walfarg for ransom. We hung about off the coast, most uncomfortably, while her lieutenant transacted the business. But when he returned and the canvas bags were opened and rich fat gold coins spilled across the deck—Lohvian gold!—everyone roared their approval. Even Viridia the Render was pleased.

She called me into her ornate and stuffy aft cabin where zhantil pelts covered the settee, arms were stowed everywhere, bits and pieces of clothing lay scattered on the deck, and toiletries cluttered a side table beneath a port. She looked at me with an expression I tried to fathom, and could not.

I knew I trod a tightrope.

With her, her lieutenant glared up at me in open distaste.

He was a man called Strom Erclan, rough and yet with a remnant of faded culture and manners. For "Strom" is the Kregan title, I suppose, most nearly paralleled by "Count." He liked the men to give him his title when they addressed him. I had considered it a harmless fad; but now, as I looked at the pair of them, I realized that this hankering after a titled man as her second-in-command was all of a piece with Viridia. Powers of life and death she had over the crews of her swordships. She fancied herself as one of those fabled Queens of Pain of ancient Loh. I thought of Queen Lilah of Hiclantung, who had been a Queen of Pain, with no pretense, and I sighed for poor Viridia the Render.

"You're getting too big for your boots, Prescot," said Strom Erclan.

I glanced down. I was, of course, barefoot.

Erclan snarled at me. He managed his snarl as well as a leem. "Insolent cramph!"

I said, "I understood you wished to see me, Viridia. Do you allow a kleesh like this to mock your authority in your own cabin?"

Before Viridia could answer Erclan's rapier hissed from the scabbard and he was around Viridia's table at me. I drew, parried, twisted, and halted my blade at his throat.

I glared into his eyes. Almost, almost but not quite, I lost control and thrust him through.

"Kleesh, I said, Strom. Do you die now?"

Viridia shouted: "Hold, you fool, Prescot. If you slay him you'll never leave this cabin alive."

Then I saw, through the aft bulkhead partition, the sudden movement and the shadow of a Womox grasping a bent bow, the arrow nocked and drawn back to the pile.

I whipped my blade away and struck Strom Erclan across the face, open-handed with my left, toppled him squalling into a corner where he put his face into a great bowl of some nauseous ointment Viridia used to iron out the wrinkles on her skin.

Viridia—she shocked me, then—Viridia laughed.

"Oh, Strom Erclan, you onker! Leave this wild man and me to talk a mur or two."

Although the words bubbled through with laughter and Viridia clearly had abruptly snapped into a playful mood, Erclan was less than happy. Ointment smearing his face, he took himself off, glowering. Viridia lifted her left hand and the shadow of the bowman eased the bow and moved back out of sight.

"Don't try to toy with me, Viridia," I said. I remembered some of the vainglorious boasting the corsairs of the inner sea employed when promising King Zo what they would do to Magdag. "I've eaten bigger fish than that fool for breakfast, and spat out the bones. If he's the best you can do, forget him. And that horned Womox of yours—I can get to him and spit him long before his addled brains add up what's going on."

She bit her lip. Had she been what she pretended to be she'd have snapped her fingers to her Womox bodyguard and made me prove my words. So I finished: "Anyway, Viridia, I'd as lief stick you through as a Womox."

She rallied. She refused. She said, "I think I shall have you killed, at the end, Dray Prescot."

"But, until then, you wanted to ask me something."

"Not ask!" she flashed. "I ordered you to report to me so that I could tell you I want you to take command of the varters. Valka tells me you have some skill with them."

I nodded. But I did not answer.

"Well, Dray Prescot?" She was surprised and not a little mortified. "Have you no word of thanks?"

"For what? For being given the thankless task of drumming varter drill into the blockheads of your crew?"

Her bosom rose and fell, but with the constriction I had noticed before, as though armor cased her. "Take care, man! Viridia the Render is known through all the islands! My swordships take and burn and sink—we are feared wherever argenters sail—"

"Aye! And by ramming and boarding. I've seen your catapult and varter work. You're hopeless. If I am to train your calsanys, then I demand absolute obedience. Any man who argues back will be knocked down instantly. Is that clear?"

About to reply she was interrupted by a Fristle messenger who put his head in at the door and squeaked rather than shouted his news, his whiskers quivering.

"*Venus* is alongside and she's sinking!"

I give the name Venus to the swordship. I could not give her real name without causing offense. She was the ship in which, in company with a crew of oldsters and weird beings without interest in what they carried, the host of maidens of Viridia's renders was carried. They were female pirates, true; but I had already seen how their talents were best exercised in the delicate business of extracting largesse from the shipping of the islands.

We all raced on deck and there was *Venus* already shipping water and the lithe agile forms of her girls leaping aboard Viridia's flagship. I believe I have not given the name of Viridia's personal swordship, the flagship of her little fleet of eight craft. Seven, now that poor old *Venus* was sinking.

I know why I have not given it, for it displeased me. She had called her pirate craft *Viridia Jikai*. It made sense, of course; but I had been trained into a different school of thought where Jikai was concerned.

When all the pandemonium had subsided and *Venus* had sunk and Viridia started her court of inquiry, I was left to seek out Valka. He looked at me with a most ferocious grin, the while sharpening a nasty-looking boarding-pike.

I said, "You got me into giving drill to these calsanys. Hauling and winding and loosing varters, Valka. Well?"

He laughed and went on sharpening. "Certainly, Dray. I heard about you when they dumped you aboard the old *Nemo*." He looked up, suddenly. "Anyway, it gets us out of the rowing benches, does it not, dom?"

Well, there was that to be said for it—indubitably.

CHAPTER FOURTEEN

The fight on the beach

During this period of my sojourn on Kregen many incidents occurred, but I feel that my purpose will best be served by pressing on. I am, I fondly believe, a man tolerant of other people until they prove themselves unworthy of trust; perhaps I am tolerant to a fault. But when a task has been put into my hands I am intolerant—decidedly and sometimes cruelly so—of every phase of the task until it is completed. I made those renders of the islands aboard the swordships sweat blood over the varters and the catapults. I have previously told you of my attitude to gunnery; discipline and absolute efficiency alone count. Eagerness and willingness to work are excellent; indeed I welcome them as bonuses; but a gang of calsanys, given my methods, will stand to their weapons whether varters or thirty-two pounders, and fight a ship.

And, as I know from experience, by the time I have finished with a crew, no matter how recalcitrant and unusable they were at the start, by the end they are as keen and eager and willing in all genuine fervor to excel, as the best volunteer crew afloat.

As it happened I was afforded not enough time to turn Viridia's pack of sea-leems into gunners—if you will pardon the expression. We met one of the strange ships which sail up out of the southern oceans from whence no man knew, and fought her, and only a storm coming on saved us all from sinking. We ran with the gale and by the time we could shake a little more canvas out, the southerner had gone. I will talk more of these strange and terrible ships later.

The days floated by, and Valka and I hammered at the varter crews. We transferred from swordship to swordship, and when I rotated back to one I had given some instruction, and found the calsanys had forgotten it all, there were many bruised lips and black eyes. I was not popular. And yet, despite that, Valka told me that the men respected me, for they could understand my purpose.

"They know the risks involved in ramming and boarding. If you can force an argenter to surrender without their having to risk their hides, that will please them."

Valka, indeed, was a tower of strength to me in those days.

It was mainly through his instigation that I picked up, one from here, another from there, a tight little crew of men and halflings who in addition to their expertise with varters and catapults showed—again according to Valka—respect and loyalty to me personally. I was aware of the dangers. I handled these men carefully. The idea, simple, of course, of welding them into a crew, of obtaining a ship and of sailing away, occurred to me without any deep cogitation.

The deep cogitation lay in where I would direct the course of the ship.

Tomboram?

Vallia?

My duty to Tilda and Pando seemed to me to have been discharged.

I could, in all honor, sail for Vallia.

Valka, as a Vallian, would be invaluable.

I am a loner. I walk singly. And yet, I am constantly aware of this strange—power, attribute, thing?—call it what you will, this uncanny phenomenon I possess of attracting the utmost loyalty and devotion from men. It is passing strange. I do not seek it. Sometimes I am embarrassed by it. I notice that men look to me for leadership. Only can it be explained, in part, by the fact that I will never let a fellow down if it is humanly possible. Perhaps some of that personality trait is responsible. I do not know. But, there it is.

In tandem with this charisma there goes, I believe, its opposite. But you who listen to this narrative will already be aware of where that leads to . . . .

The dangers to which I alluded were simply that if Viridia or any of her lieutenants got wind of a knot of men devoted to me they would smell mutiny on the instant, and the steel would flicker red. So, in pursuance of plans, I must tread warily.

Despite all you may think of me as a hotheaded barbarian warrior who flings himself into action before thinking, this is not so. The first lieutenant of a seventy-four never stops thinking and planning, believe me.

This habit of thinking ahead and, in the night watches, of planning how to react to every foreseeable disaster must have been the root cause of my decision not to attempt to seize the ship. She was surrounded by six of her consorts. Even if I captured Viridia and threatened to kill her unless we were given free passage, I had the hunch that the captains of the other swordships, Viridia's lieutenants all, would still attack and let Viridia take her chances.

One fine morning we espied a sail on the eastern horizon and bore up in chase. The swordships did not sail well on any point; but, as Viridia observed, they sailed well enough for the renders' purposes, and they could row at top speed when it mattered, which an argenter could not do.

We gained on this chase with a rapidity which led me to believe her bottom must be fouler than most. The cut of her sails was strange to me. She bore away but ever and anon kept trying to edge to the west and so reach the islands. Valka came up beside me at the fore starboard varter platform and stared across the tumbling sea. The weather was fine and the smartish breeze cooled the air gratifyingly.

"What do you make of her, Valka?"

He looked surprised. I had given him very little of my history, as he had given me none of his; our friendship, fragile as it was, was based in its entirety on our mutual slavery at the oars and now our positions as varterists. That varterist I had shot from *Dram Constant* in his passing had, weirdly, left the way open for me now.

"You don't recognize her, Dray?"

Incautiously, I said: "Should I? She has two masts, rigged square, and a bowsprit, and she looks a trifle unhandy. Her stern looks high but narrow. I fancy I'd redistribute the stepping of her masts had I the need to sail her any distance."

"She is from Zenicce."

"Oh," I said, and could say no more.

Zenicce! That great enclave city of a million souls, threaded by canals and boulevards, where Delia and I had been slave, where Princess Natema lived, happily married now to Prince Varden! Where I had met Gloag, my comrade who, although not a man, was all the more human for that. Where I had slaved in the black marble quarries. And where now my own powerful enclave of Strombor no doubt wondered what had happened to their Lord. I hoped that Great-Aunt Shusha—who was not my great-aunt—ran Strombor in my stead, as was her right.

Then I saw the colors of the banners.

They flaunted there, purple and ocher, blazing in the streaming light of the twin Suns of Scorpio.

"Pontheu," I said. "She is of the House of Pontheu."

Well, Prince Pracek had led my Delia to the altar to wed her, although his plans had tumbled at that point. Pontheu was an enclave aligned with the foes of Strombor. So . . .

Valka said, "Now how can you tell that, Dray? You must have visited Zenicce, to know the colors of the houses—"

"Not so, Valka. Any sea-leem knows the colors of his victims."

"True. Still, it is passing strange. All the Zeniccean colors are alike to me."

So Valka had not heard of me all he might that night I had been dumped down into the slave benches of the old *Nemo*.

We took her without trouble. I must give her name, for it was, having regard to her speed, ludicrous on two counts.

Her name was *Splash Zorca*.

She was clinker-built. Swifters and swordships and argenters were all carvel-built. This made me ponder.

That same day we made the island of Careless Repose where lay our renders' nest. We had made a good cruise and the men were in the mood for relaxation. Viridia wanted to negotiate with another pirate captain for a new swordship to replace the ill-fated *Venus*. From this island with its entrance hidden by a small and unsuspected vegetation-clothed islet and with its beach of white sand and its village of comfortable houses we would sally forth on our roving raids against the sea commerce of the area. So far, no King's Swordship had discovered the anchorage.

The pirates, like any good Kregan given half a chance, started in carousing.

I went for a stroll along the white sand of the beach by the light of She of the Veils, brooding to myself. As was my custom I wore my scarlet breechclout and my weapons slung about me. In the warm weather of these latitudes that was ample clothing, even at night. By the pinkish light of the moons—for a lesser moon hurtled past above—I walked on with bent head, pondering.

Strom Erclan almost caught me.

He leaped on me from a boulder beside the vegetation's edge and I saw the wicked flash of his dagger. I got his wrist in my fist and jerked him back; but he kicked me low down and sprang away, ripping out his rapier as he saw he would have to fight me for real.

I drew.

"You stinking cramph!" This Strom was reputed good with a rapier and main-gauche. I had seen him in action when we boarded and he showed no fear. I put myself in a position for fighting and waited, for I had no wish to kill him——then. "You mildewed rast! You lump of offal!" He went on shouting for a space, hoping, no doubt, to enrage me.

After a bit, I said, "Kleesh. Walk away quietly, or you are a dead man."

Whether his breeding goaded him into madness, then, whether he was simply mad clear through with jealousy, matters little. He threw himself on me, his blades whirling and thrusting in a positive flurry of action and a fury of venom. I parried, caught him, twisted; but he eluded that one, having been caught once before. A swordsman need only see a fighting trick once to know it again. If he doesn't, he is dead, of course.

Our blades crossed and slithered with that teeth-vibrating screech of metal. He leaped, I forced him back, I thrust, he took my blade on his dagger and held and thrust for me to take his blade on my dagger in turn. For a space the four slivers of steel slanted up in the pink moonglow, evil and slick and lethal, smooth and unbloodied.

Then, quick as a striking leem, he withdrew his dagger and thrust low. I swayed sideways, recovered and once more we fell into our fighting stances.

He was good. There was no doubt of that. I thought of Galna, whom I had fought in that corridor in what was now my own palace of Strombor; yes, it is all a long time ago, now; but I can still feel the jar of steel on steel and I can hear yet again the ring of blades as they met and crossed. Then he essayed a complicated passage, and I took him, and in the pink wash of moonlight from She of the Veils Strom Erclan slumped with my rapier through his heart.

CHAPTER FIFTEEN

I give an opinion
at Careless Repose

Raucous shouts and good-humored arguments broke the stillness of the night as the renders of the islands caroused in the wooden houses of the pirates' lair.

In the fringe of the vegetation back along the beach lay the skewered body of Strom Erclan. Very soon the creeping crawling denizens of those woods would convert his body to bones and then these, too, would rot away until all that remained to show a man had existed would be the memory other men might carry in their minds.

I knew no one would mourn Strom Erclan for very long.

In the wooden barn-like house where most of the higher ranks in Viridia's confidence were carousing, the atmosphere billowed thick with the fumes of wines culled from the freight holds of a hundred ships. Heaping platters of food loaded the heavily-timbered tables. Disheveled wenches darted in and out avoiding clutching hands in giggles or shrieks or abuse, each according to her nature. Food appeared on the tables in bounteous abundance, and disappeared down gullets with fascinating speed. The wine that was drunk! Men would suddenly screech and leap up and dance a wild jig, or leap head-over-heels across the floor, or two would fall into a deadly dagger fight that ended with one coughing his guts out bloodily across the floor, the other ready to face the render court of inquiry. Other half-men half-beasts drank and caroused in their own ways, and all were equal here, under the captains.

To this select company Viridia had bidden me, Dray Prescot.

As I approached where she sat at the head of a long

143

"This Chulik captain was trying to sell a swordship to Viridia.

table, quaffing her wine and roaring like any jack-booted man of the sea, I noticed Valka sitting at the lower end of the table, his nose in a blackjack. He looked up as I passed, and winked. Shades of Inch, I said to myself, and planted my feet down on a clear space among the litter of bones and discarded meats on the floor.

One blessing there was in all that pandemonium and guzzling and drinking and wenching, one evil we were spared; the only smoke in the room came wafting in from the glowing cook fires or rose from the succulent dishes covering the tables.

"Dray Prescot!" shouted Viridia, lolling back. Her blue eyes were not clouded with wine and I saw in their depths a deep and shrewd intelligence; yet her body lolled and her head jerked and she laughed shrilly, as though she were drunk. Near her a Chulik captain sat, a mass of gold lace and crimson silk, his tusks gleaming and—a fashion I had noticed before—tipped with gold. He was plying Viridia with wine. She laughed and drained the cup, and thrust it forward for replenishment.

In general Chuliks can be trained into seamen; of the halflings the Hobolings are unquestionably the finest topmen in the business, and I wouldn't give berth space to a Fristle, be wary of an Och, and detesting Rapas as I then did, would haul up the gangplank before letting one aboard my command. I knew that the Relts, those more gentle cousins of the Rapas, went to sea as supercargos and clerks, but I doubted even them.

This Chulik captain, one Chekumte, was trying to sell a swordship to Viridia. His ploy was transparent to me, and, I saw, to Viridia also. I fancied she could drink him under the table.

"She is a fleet craft, and nimble, Viridia," Chekumte was saying. He spilled wine as he slanted his cup in eagerness to lean forward in friendly converse. "She rows a hundred and twenty oars and sails like a king korf!"

"A hundred and twenty oars," said Viridia, properly contemptuous. "Zenzile fashion!"

"And what of that? She has served me well; but I have captured a new swordship from Walfarg, and my force is balanced so that I no longer need her."

"And you seek to dispose of your old scows to me, Chekumte."

I stood there, listening, for listening brings information.

Viridia lifted her cup to me. The fingers she wrapped around the glass stem glittered with gemmed rings. Her tanned face was, minute by minute, growing more flushed. "Dray Prescot! You are not drinking."

"When I find out what you wanted, Viridia, I will find some wine."

She scowled as though I had insulted her, but heaved up and glared sullenly at me.

"Have you seen Strom Erclan? I want him to discuss this business. Chekumte is a wily rogue, for a Chulik."

Chekumte guffawed, polished his tusks, and quaffed wine. I would not lie. "I saw him up the beach half a bur ago."

"Wenching again, I'll be bound." Viridia slumped back, that sullen expression on her face turning all her features lumpy. "I keep my render maidens locked away from the likes of him."

I did not say: "You will have no need of that anymore."

It would have been a nice line, but I wanted no more trouble. If I had to tear the hearts out of all those here, I would do so if that was the only way to return to my Delia. But only a fool buys trouble.

Instead, I said, casually, "A zenzile swordship would not fit in with your squadron, Viridia. And if she rows only a hundred and twenty oars she must be short, and if short then narrow to retain her speed, and if narrow then useless in a sea. I can't get your calsanys to shoot straight from the deck of your flagship as it is."

Chekumte surged up. His eyes were bloodshot. His thin lips ricked back from those gold-tipped tusks. Little of humanity is known to a Chulik. About the only thing I have heard in their favor is that they are loyal to whoever pays them.

Mind you—that is a valuable attribute in any mercenary.

Now this Chulik glowered down on me and spouted obscenities at me. He rounded on Viridia. "Do you allow Likshu-spawned offal like this to teach you your trade, Viridia the Render?"

Viridia was annoyed. She twiddled with the hilt of her rapier. As though transmitting her anger to her Womoxes who stood in partial shadow at her back, she herself stood up. For a moment we three stood, confronting one another, and gradually the uproar died as the roisterers realized the tension gripping us.

Chuliks make a habit of adopting the weapons and customs of the race employing them. Now Chekumte was a render captain in his own right and he had adopted the weaponry of his peers. He drew his rapier and, slowly, pushed it forward until the point touched my breast. He did not prick the skin.

"This thing must be taught a lesson, Viridia."

I looked at her. This was a test for her. I knew that. I wondered if she had realized that yet.

"For the sake of the cursed Armipand, Chekumte! Leave him alone!"

"Not until he grovels on his knees and begs my pardon."

So far I had not moved. Still I looked beneath lowering brows at Viridia. Her bosom beneath that armor heaved. She was clearly in distress—and I marveled.

"Leave it, Chekumte! I will buy the swordship. There! Will you shake hands on it?"

But the Chulik kept his rapier point pressed against my breast.

"Not until this cramph apologizes!"

I said, "This island is called the island of Careless Repose. I did not expect to find a quarrel here."

"There is not a quarrel, cramph! You, Prescot! Down on your knees! Lick my boots! Beg my pardon else I run you through."

"Now, Chekumte!" protested Viridia. She began to lose her temper and a spark of that wildness flared. "I have men here! Would you drench our safe haven in blood?"

"This is a point of honor, Chulik honor! By Likshu the Treacherous! I'll have his tripes!"

Still I glowered down on Viridia the Render—and still she would not meet my gaze.

A ruffianly towheaded pirate down the board laughed and yelled. He was of The Bloody Menaham or Menahem—either spelling conveys the meaning—and he had no love for anyone of Tomboram, from which country he believed me to originate. "Stick him now, Chekumte! What are you waiting for?" He waved his goblet and spilled wine over the brilliant blue and green cummerbund he wore, the blue and green of his national colors.

"Hold!" shouted Viridia. Her blue eyes blazed on me now with a violence of passion I knew would break out any moment and that would be followed by a battle royal and bloody corpses strewing the pleasant island of Careless Repose.

"There seems no holding the Chulik, Viridia," I said. With a quick and startlingly sudden movement I stepped back so that Chekumte was left with his rapier pressed against thin air. I lifted my voice and shouted. "Listen, renders of the islands! I will fight this rast of a Chulik in fair fight! It lies between him and me! In all honor is this not so?"

After a great deal of yelling and cursing and argument, the general opinion was that, indeed, the quarrel lay between Chekumte and myself. He leaped the table and advanced on me.

"You have held me up to ridicule, human! Now you will die!"

I drew and faced him.

As Strom Erclan had been, as long-dead Galna had been, he was a master swordsman. The moment our blades crossed I felt the power in his thick wrists, and knew that I must put out every ounce of effort. And yet—and yet I sometimes wonder if I exaggerate the qualities of swordsman opponents in order to aggrandize my own prowess. I do not know. I know that I have faced many master swordsmen and fencers of high renown, famous in their own lands, and have bested them, every one. Is this the beginning of paranoia? Yet each time I cross blades with an opponent I know that this time, at last, I may have met my match. I think it is this tingling zest of the unknown, this awareness that every combat may be my last, that gives me the nervous energy to go on. I have met swordsmen who through years of absolute victory have thought themselves invincible and so they fought in order to kill and gloat in their killing. This, to me, is the mark of the beast. I detest killing, as I have said many times. If I thought that I could never lose a fight—where would be the fun of fighting? If, Zair forgive me, fighting is ever fun.

Chekumte the Chulik was extraordinarily good, as I remember, as I believe. He would have disposed of Strom Erclan in a mere passage or two. Chekumte came from one of the many Chulik islands that stretch northeastward up the coast of southeastern Segesthes, with the island of Xuntal in the south of the chain. There they train their children in all the varied weapons they are likely to encounter when they reach adulthood and sally forth as mercenaries, for this is the chief occupation of Chuliks. Chekumte had been well-trained, and by a master I would like to meet. In addition, he had turned pirate, which was unusual for a Chulik, and had fought his way up to the captaincy of his own band of renders.

We fought in a great glittering of blades, thrusting and parrying, rapier against main-gauche, whirling about and sliding and slipping on the discarded bones and meats of the floor.

But, in the end, I had with as pretty a passage as I recall forced him against a table so that he bent backward to escape being transfixed. He catapulted out, his dagger low, his rapier high. He feinted a thrust with the dagger and then, as swiftly as a striking leem, slashed diagonally down with his rapier. Here was the Jiktar and the Hikdar working in sweet unison. I heard a shrill chopped-off scream. Then I had taken that swooping lethal blade on my main-gauche and in a screech of steel deflected it and the next instant my own rapier stood out a foot past Chekumte's backbone.

In almost the same motion I withdrew and Chekumte dropped his weapons. He looked down in wonderment and then placed both his hands over the blood-seeping hole in his chest. My blade had gone through cleanly, without fouling bone; but he was done for.

"You fight well," he said, before the bright blood frothed from his lungs and out of his mouth in a gory stream. "For a human."

Then he fell.

Without a pause I strode across the floor and stood before the towheaded man of The Bloody Menaham. I showed him the stained blade of my rapier.

"You were saying?"

He eyed me. His face was corpse-white. "I said nothing, Dray Prescot."

"That is good. Make it so."

Chekumte's render band would choose their own new captain and I wanted none of that. They were an unsavory bunch. After the room had been tidied up the carousing began again. Some had not stopped drinking throughout the whole argument and fight. Later on Viridia sent for me, one of her Womoxes padding gigantic in the misty pink moonlight from She of the Veils. I went and I went alertly, for presumably Chekumte had friends. Had he comrades willing to fight for him, I did not meet a single one.

Her room in the pirate village was furnished in much the

same barbaric splendor, the same untidy womanly bric-a-brac as her cabin aboard her flagship. She looked different as the Womox ushered me in and then retired. Then I saw she had taken off that armor—and it was as I had suspected. She did indeed wear armor, a pliant mesh-steel shirt that came, I guessed, not from an armory of the inner sea but from the mysterious and progressive land of Havilfar.

Now she stood by the samphron oil lamp, her tanned face highlighted and wearing makeup that suited oddly. She wore a long white shift that reached her feet. Her dark hair had been combed—and that was a job for Kyr Nath, the Kregan Hercules, if ever there was one—and her blue eyes looked on me with a melting expression that at once alerted and alarmed me. I had seen that look in the eyes of women before, and I knew the trouble it brought. I braced myself.

She advanced and held out her hands.

"You fought right well, Dray. Chekumte was feared throughout the islands as a swordsman." Her voice was not steady.

"You might have told me, Viridia, before," I said. I spoke lightly. I tried to be casual; but Viridia the Render had her own dark and secret purposes which were transparent and unwelcome to me.

"Do you then so much dislike me, Dray?"

"Of course not! You are what you are—"

She bit her lip. Her mouth was very generous, soft and sensuous in a way quite different from the voluptuous mouth of Tilda. Now, with Tilda, I had had no trouble at all. . . .

"That is not—gallant."

"Why not? You choose to walk around as a render, a pirate captain, and you dress for the part. I understand you must be tougher and stronger and more violent than your men. So—"

"So now I am changed, Dray!" Her blue eyes caught the mellow gleam from the samphron oil lamp. She was trembling. "I have combed my hair, and I have taken the baths of nine, and I am clean and fragrant—and—"

"You are very beautiful, Viridia," I said, for this was true, as incongruous as it sounds. Her body thrust with firm bold curves against the sheer white robe. The material of the shift, some fabricated silk from Pandahem, was very sheer, very smooth, almost transparent. Her bosom rose and fell and the silk ruffled with her movements.

"Then why do you scorn me? You must have seen with what favor I have treated you——"

I did not laugh, but I felt my harsh lips curving into a gruesome smile. "Training a bunch of calsanys with heads of lenk! Fighting the most noted swordsman of the islands! Oh, yes, Viridia the Render, you have treated me with favor!"

She blew up then.

She jumped for me and began beating me on the chest with her fists, shouting and sobbing, the dark hair swirling all into my eyes, pins and priceless gemmed hair ornaments flying in all directions. She even, like Pando, tried to kick me. I grabbed her wrists and brought her arms down and so inclining toward me, we stared face to face.

On her cheeks thick tears coursed. Her rich lips shook and quivered. "Dray Prescot! I hate you! I hate you!"

"I do not hate you, Viridia. But, I do not love you. That cannot be so."

All the passion and fire left her. She sagged against me so that our gripping hands were trapped between our bodies and I could feel all the firm softness of her. She moaned.

"Say that is not so, Dray! Please! I am Viridia the Render! My word is law! I can have you taken out and tied up and my men will loose at you for sport! Do not say you do not love me!"

"Nothing your men can do could make me change my mind by a single degree, Viridia. And you know it, by Zair! You know it as well as you know my affection for you! But love—that I cannot give you."

She drew back and I let her go. Her sheer robe tautened against her as she pulled her shoulders erect. That maddening dark hair swirled now about her face and with an impatient gesture and the flash of a gem-encrusted white wrist she pushed it back.

"You do not know what you are saying——"

"I know. I will faithfully support you, Viridia, in our render raids. I will be a loyal member of your pirate band. Beyond that, it is forbidden for me to go."

I saw the glitter in the lamplit blue eyes. I saw the way her body tensed, the deep breath she drew, the way her hands hooked into claws. I poised.

"Get out! Get out, Dray Prescot! Oh, you fool! You fool! Get out! *Get out!*"

And so, for the love of my Delia of Delphond, I left Viridia the Render shaking with passion among her pirate trophies.

Truth to tell, I felt remarkably sorry for the girl.

CHAPTER SIXTEEN

Of a wooden long sword
and a cargo of Jholaix

The next morning a macabre scene was enacted on the beach fronting the village of wooden houses with the sword-ships riding over their reflections in the harbor. The weather was fine and hot, with the twin suns pouring down molten rays of ruby and jade. Everyone flocked down to the beach to witness the punishment of a dozen men who had been caught stealing a boat with the intention—as they freely confessed—of sailing to the nearest fortress port of the islands. This fortress port happened to be one belonging to the country of Lome, situated in a triangle at the extreme northwest of Pandahem. Lome was not overlarge as nations go, but her colors of blue and green horizontal stripes were to be found fluttering from swordships. Even in this matter of policing the Hoboling islands and their renders' nests, no unity of action was displayed by the fractious countries of Pandahem.

I will not go into details of the fate of these poor unfortunates. Whether they were paid spies, whether they had merely become sickened of the pirate trade, or if they had had an argument with their render chief, I never discovered. I turned away as soon as the executions began and took myself off to think. Clearly, any plan to escape to Vallia must be thought out with exquisite care, else I would end up like those poor devils on the beach.

In the event, when we put to sea again I took care to take myself aboard a swordship that was not Viridia's flagship. We dug in the oars, for everyone took a turn on the rowers' benches, and for all that I was now varterist in chief—the varter Hikdar—I pulled and tugged with the rest.

My idea that I could for a space escape Viridia's observation through my duties as varter Hikdar were soon dispelled. Her flagship cut water perilously close to our oars, and a stentor bellowed across, in much the same way as the stentors bellow a passage for the swifters passing Sanurkazz from the Sea of Marshes into the inner sea.

"Dray Prescot to co-ome abo-oard!"

So, rather like a ponsho-trag with his tail between his legs, I was rowed across. Valka and the men whom I had trained, ostensibly as my varter cadre, were rowed across, also.

Viridia was not on deck when I stepped aboard. A fine tall man with the red hair of Loh greeted me. He had been a lieutenant and now wore a smothering extra layer of gold lace and so I gathered this man, Arkhebi, had been promoted into Strom Erclan's place.

Overside the swordship I had left gathered her boats in and then, all as one, her oars struck into the sea and with a heaving surge she took up station again. I did not feel in the mood to sweat at an oar any further this morning, and so I said: "If you'll muster a broadside crew, Arkhebi, I'll start in giving them a little training. I'll make 'em jump!"

Arkhebi smiled. He was, as I remember, a ruffianly fellow; but he loved a good fight.

"The captain ordered for you to come across, special, Dray. But she's said no more and she's closeted in her cabin." He clapped me on the shoulder. "You steer small, Dray Prescot!"

"Aye, Arkhebi, I'll do that. And congratulations on your rank." I nodded to where our six consorts plowed the sea. "You'll be in command yourself, soon."

"Aye, I will be!" he said with a brightness I found charming. Reavers and rovers all, those renders, but genial, with it—some of them.

With the starboard broadside crew I was soon hard at work on the varters. I concentrated more on them, for with the ballista-type weapon one could obtain a flatter trajectory than with the catapults—they were of a formidably varying nature and kind with a plethora of technical names—and I sought to obtain the kind of accuracy and rate of fire I would tolerate on any ship I commanded. It may seem a strange and crankish thing to say, but I sometimes missed the deep-throated thunder of the broadsides of our Earthly guns.

Presently the breeze increased enough for the oars to be

shipped and all the canvas to be set. Courses on fore and main, crossjack on the mizzen, topsails on the fore and main, and the spritsail ahead on its mast and yard on the bowsprit, we surged wet and uncomfortable through the sea. Swordships are a pestiferous kind of sea-animal. I would as much have them rowed as sailed providing I am not lugging an oar. As it was, she lay over and the spray lashed our faces and solid sheets of water were shipped green. But we flew along. This was what being a render of the islands was all about: discomfort and danger and, at the end, prizes and jewels, silks and wines. . . .

Our first victim bore fluttering at her masthead the diagonal stripes of blue and green that denoted an argenter from The Bloody Menaham. We bore down on her. A few accurate shots from our bow varters knocked away some spars, we saw the flash and gleam of weapons along her decks, and we were about to bear down, our keen bronze rostrum foaming through the sea, when Viridia, who had not appeared when called, stepped on deck.

"Avast, you dogs!" she roared, all her old callous roughness fully in evidence. "Prescot, you great calsany! Get your pestiferous varters going! Earn your plunder! Knock over that fat ponsho for me and save the blood of my men!"

To all that I simply shouted, "Aye aye!" and bent to the nearest varter. It was fully wound, a chunk of rock in the slide as big as a vosk-skull.

I touched the trigger as the swordship rose to the swell.

The rock flew true. A great shout went up as the mainmast of the argenter toppled, leaned, and in a weltering smother of canvas and cordage plunged overside into the wake.

After that it was simply a matter of boarding, of brandishing our weapons, and of cleaning up.

We took spices, and silks, great jars of Pandahem ware, chests of jewels, weapons and trinkets, and amphorae by the score. Rich wine of a dozen different vintages was carried aboard by the happily sweating crew and the frightened passengers who were now our prisoners.

"We can soon jury-rig her," I said to Viridia, without really taking too much notice of her, as we watched the busy scene of activity. "She will bring much Lohvian gold."

"Aye, Dray Prescot. And does gold please you? Is that all you seek?"

I faced her. "Whatever you think, Viridia, I will be loyal to you and your renders. Never fear."

"You had best be, Dray!"

We sighted no other sail for the next two days, and Viridia was contemplating a return to our island of Careless Repose. We were running under all our canvas and the sea was such that oars would have been impracticable. Despite my disdain for mere wealth I knew I had, personally, amassed a fair-sized sum in these piratical pursuits. I just had to find a ship to take me to Vallia. This life was seducing me.

"Sail ho!"

An excited rush to the rail and up the ratlines confirmed the sail, a triangle of white on the horizon. We took the wind with us as we bore down on her and soon the tall superstructures of a great argenter came into view. She was a fine tall vessel, her three masts clad with billowing canvas, her flags all standing stiff and taut in the breeze. We had the heels of her, if none of our rigging carried away. The hands began to discuss just what prospects of fortune she carried, and if she would strike under varter bombardment or if we would have to board in steel and blood.

Then I saw the flags standing so proudly from her mastheads.

All blue, they were, a bright proud blue. And, in the center of that blue field glared the yellow-orange head of a zhantil, ferocious, roaring, untamed.

I knew that flag.

"She's from Tomboram!" shouted Arkhebi. As a Lohvian from Walfarg he would know the Pandahemic colors as well as he knew his colors of Walfarg, the flaunting horizontal stripes of red and gold.

"Aye, Arkhebi," I said. "And not only from Tomboram."

For I knew, for Pando had told me, with many a boyish twitch of muscular excitement, that he was going to charge a brave zhantil on the blue field of his flag, a zhantil in memory, so he said, of the zhantil-hide tunic I had had made for him, the courageous zhantil, he had said, that reminded him of me.

"Booty, there, mates!" roared a squat-bodied Brokelsh, laughing, pointing, the black bristle hairs on his muscular body all slick with sweat.

I remembered *Dram Constant* and her blue flags, and how we had waited for the onslaught of the sea-leems, and of how Captain Alkers had fought this very swordship on which I now found myself. I could imagine the horror aboard that argenter from Bormark in Tomboram now.

My conscience is a slippery beast. Going a-roving had seemed perfectly respectable to me when I plundered, as I believed, the enemies of Vallia and of Bormark. But, now, I was faced with the task of capturing and perhaps destroying a ship of a friend. There was no alternative, no choice, about my dilemma; the problem was how to carry the thing off without having my head parted from my shoulders by a Womox.

"Haul that sheet tight!" roared Arkhebi in high excitement. Hands rushed to the sheet and hauled. We were catching all the breeze there was and we were overhauling the argenter as a zorca strides past a vove.

Our four consorts—for one had been sent away with the captured argenter of Menaham—were left far in our wake. They had been dragging their heels all the way. Now it was between us and this proud argenter of Pando's. I saw his face in my mind's eye, I saw Tilda's—but I truly believe it was memory of Captain Alkers that spurred into action what little of conscience I possess.

I picked up a long and stout length of timber that fitted snugly into my two spaced fists. I held it in my left hand and walked across to the bulwark. A boarding ax glittered in the hand of a man who stared with a leem-grin over the shining sea toward his prey. I took the ax from him without a word, swung around, and brought the keen glittering edge down across the main course braces and, in a motion so fast the ax blurred into a silvery circle in the hot air, sliced down across the main yard halyards.

In a wild flurry and tangle of parting braces and lines the main course billowed up with a gigantic snap, and the main yard smashed down across the deck.

At once everything was confusion.

Viridia screamed orders, Arkhebi ran shouting and gesticulating. I walked quickly forward and repeated my actions on the foremast.

"Dray! You madman! Stop that!"

Viridia came leaping across the deck toward me and her four Womoxes followed, shaking out their swords, their ugly faces blank with anticipation of bloodletting. I knew they did not like me, and they were ferocious and powerful in the extreme.

"We cannot take that argenter, Viridia, that is all. The damage aboard here can be cleared up in no time."

Men surged in confusion, and the ship rolled, falling off as her crossjack swung her around so that any moment she would be in irons. I didn't care. Just so that I gave Pando's ship time to make good her escape. Immediately she had seen our plight she had at once worn and gone haring off across our bows, heading for the shelter of the islands which were smudges low on the western horizon.

If I had hoped that Viridia harbored any sentiment for me that would halt her vengeful orders I was mistaken.

Valka and the other men of my little group I could see clustered a little to one side and, quite clearly, they were at a loss. They couldn't understand my actions.

"That ship was from a country friendly to me!" I roared. "No man ravages my friends. Remember that!"

"And no man stands between me and plunder!" shrieked Viridia. She was absolutely furious, her face as red as my breechclout. She jerked her hand at her bodyguard.

"Seize him—do not kill. I will talk to him when you have bound him in iron chains!"

I saw two redheaded men lower their longbows, and so I knew I had a chance.

I threw down the ax.

"I will not kill, then, also!" I shouted.

Then the Womoxes charged.

They sought to beat me down, to wound, not to kill. They rushed in with so furious an onslaught that I was beaten back and half to my knees. I used the length of timber to push myself back onto my feet. Then, gripping it as I would my own Krozair long sword I jammed the splintery end into the guts of the nearest Womox. Before he was down, vomiting, I had swung my wooden long sword full at the head of the next. He ducked with the instinctive grace of the fighting-man, but the timber cracked against one of his horns and splintered it redly from his head. He screamed. I was already dodging and weaving away from the blades of his fellows, and with that scream ringing in their ears they were out to kill. Blood-lust dominated them completely.

They thrust now with every intention of spitting me.

I heard Viridia yelling. I ignored her. By rapid and eye-deceiving movements, by a constant flow of action and blows I held the two Womoxes off until I could lay that wooden long sword across the ribs of one and then, as he doubled, short-arm the splinters into his face.

He reeled back, spraying blood.

The second had recovered from the loss of a horn and bored in. The last lowered his head as he fought and sought to rip my eyes out with his horns. I skipped back, swung the timber, cracked his skull wide open. The first one, who had been winded, joined his comrade and they rushed me together. Here was the danger. I circled them, weaving the wooden long sword. I do not believe they had experienced a long sword in the grip of a man who knew how to use one before. I dazzled them with a series of passes, ignored their daggers, which took skin from my ribs and slashed my wooden brand down across the face of one of them. He reeled back and I back-struck at the last, smashed in his rib cage and then leaped forward and finished off the sole survivor.

The fight had been hot and brisk, but nothing was settled yet—or so I thought.

Viridia was standing with her hand to her lips, her body gross in the swathing robes and armor.

"Dray . . ." she whispered.

"I bear you no malice, Viridia. But your bodyguard no longer exist."

At that moment I heard Valka's voice, high, screeching.

"Dray! Behind you!"

I whirled. The Brokelsh, an ax high, was swinging at my defenseless back. I sprang aside and as he lunged on with all the vicious power of his swing, I smashed the timber down upon his own back. He went on into the deck. But my wooden long sword, sorely abused, snapped clean across.

"You men!" I roared, brandishing the splintered stump. "We are comrades. There are plenty of fat ponshos sailing the seas. Another will be borne by the wind any time!"

Viridia stood as though turned to stone. Even then I did not fully comprehend the disaster to her personally. I stepped close to her side. I tried to speak gently, although, Zair knows, that was difficult enough with the reeking blood splashed upon me.

"Please, Viridia. Try to think. Only do as I ask in this, that you respect the flag of an ally, and all will be well."

"You do not understand, do you, Dray Prescot?"

Before I could answer, a hail reached us.

"Sail ho!"

The reaction was immediate and unthinking. Everyone rushed to the rail, so great is the greed for plunder in a render's breast.

She was a broad-beamed argenter from Jholaix, as we could tell from her blue flag with the bright red amphora in its center. At sight of her I was inspired. Jholaix was fair prey.

I sprang up into the ratlines. I threw away the splintered stump of that long sword that had served me so well, albeit the brand was wood, a mere length of lumber. I drew my rapier.

"See!" I roared. "See what the gods have brought! Did I not say so?" I pointed with the rapier. "And you all know, you sea-leems, what a ship of Jholaix carries!"

"Aye!" they yelled back. "Aye, Dray Prescot! Wine of Jholaix, the best in all the islands!"

With that we set to like maniacs to repair our rigging. The task was accomplished with much cursing and bellowing and by the time our main yard was up and the canvas sheeted home our consorts had drawn level. Together we bore down on the wine ship from Jholaix. She offered not the slightest resistance, and we took her without loss of life.

By the time the twin suns had set across the sea with the distant humps of the Hoboling islands rising against that sheeting crimson and emerald glory most of the hands were rolling merry with bellies full of Jholaix wine. The ship carried a fortune in fine wines.

I drank a little of the best, and was well pleased.

Viridia approached me as I stood by the taffrail. She carried no sword. Her armor hung over her arm, limp, a sheen of mesh-steel in the growing light of She of the Veils.

"So, Dray Prescot, you have taken command."

I was astonished. "Not so, Viridia the Render—"

"Do not mock me, Dray Prescot! You are captain now."

"Why should you suppose that? Because you chose to set your beasties on me and I was forced to dispose of them? I want nothing of command of a crew of cutthroats like this! They are yours, still."

"They follow you, now. You have proved yourself. You are a lucky captain, for you conjure the best wine of Jholaix from the sea, when we have not seen an argenter from there for many a long cruise."

"I am a man of peace, Viridia."

"So I notice." In that flood of moonlight the slight curl

to her upper lip was pronounced, and distressing. I did not, then, and I admit this with some strangeness, relish Viridia the Render's contempt.

"Put your armor back on. I do not wish to take your crew or your ship from you. You will find other bodyguards."

She stared at me. "I told them not to kill you, and so they did not use their Womox swords. But then—"

"They tried to kill right enough, Viridia. You saw that."

"Yes."

So we stood for a space, and I do not know what she thought.

Looking back, it occurs to me that perhaps you are wondering, as I was so obsessed with the desire to sail to Vallia and claim my Delia, why I did not assume command of the pirates. Then I would have a ship and could command my men to sail to Vallia. It would not have been as simple as that, of course, for a swordship would have made heavy weather of the passage. I can only say that such a course did not occur to me as being a course with a grain of sense in it. Why this should be I do not know. During the night I heard a harsh and ominous croaking from the moonshot sky above; but when I looked up I could not see the Gdoinye with the scarlet and gold feathers I knew was circling up there in wide planing hunting circles.

So, in uneasy alliance, Viridia and I sailed back to the island of Careless Repose.

CHAPTER SEVENTEEN

A zenzile swordship
displeases Valka

My changed status aboard aroused considerable contro-
versy and speculation among the hands until I told Valka to
lay it on the line for them. Viridia the Render was still the
captain, still in command. We had had a little disagreement
over plundering the ship of a friend of mine. That had been
amicably settled. Now I was going to knock varter-work
into their thick skulls—and they had seen the way I had
dealt with the four Womoxes with my only weapon a wooden
long sword—and they heeded my words. Valka wanted me
to take over. I regarded him with a curiosity I did not conceal as we ran into the harbor and the anchorage and the
hook plummeted into the calm water.

"You say you are from Vallia, Valka. You have told me
nothing of your history." Among the render crew we dropped
into the longboat and brawny arms dipped the oars and we
fairly flew over the still waters to the white beach. "I do not
expect you to tell me anything of yourself, but I am curious,
I admit. Of what use would it be to you if I took command?" He began to speak in his quick and volatile way, but
I held up a hand. "Remember, Valka, it would mean the
death of Viridia. That is certain."

"So, Dray Prescot! That is why you did not take the captaincy! For concern of Viridia the Render!"

If he chose to think that, let him. Maybe I should have
disabused him, then and there; but I am not a one for giving
confidences to any but those I know and trust.

We walked up to the village and were soon well into a
bottle taken from the argenter of Jholaix. The stuff was
smooth and mellow and, perhaps, it loosened Valka's tongue.

"You know Vallia, Dray? You have been to that beautiful and wicked land?"

I considered for a moment. Then I said, "No, never."

He sighed and drank deep. "It is a land where anything the heart desires may be found—but only for those in the privileged positions of power and wealth and authority."

"That is everywhere the same."

"True, true, Dray, my old dom." He looked up and his eyes misted. "In the north of Vallia are the mountains— the wonderful mountains of Vallia! From them flow mighty rivers, pouring in a refreshing flood down to the coasts on east and west and south. Ah! The south coast. Nowhere in all of Kregen is there a place like it."

He was waxing semipoetical on me now; but I listened with care.

Delia had told me something of her homeland and I had heard of these mountains before. They were not the Blue Mountains. Valka drank and wiped his lips. "The whole island is connected with a network of canals. Canals flow everywhere. As a consequence, the roads are usually abominable. The canal folk are my folk. We form a community—" Then he stopped, and hiccuped, and roared some obscene jest at a render who grabbed a serving wench, and missed, and fell into a waste bucket. Full-flavored accidents like that often amuse the Kregans.

Then he said with as much bitterness as I ever heard him speak: "I offended against a law. The Racter party are all powerful. They do as they please, them and their mercenaries. So I ran away to sea. And was captured. And ended up here."

"And would you return to Vallia, if you had the chance?"

He grimaced. It was not a pretty sight. "By Vox! I miss the canals. But if I return home, they will hang me, for sure."

"The Racter party will, or the government?"

"Government?" He spat. "The emperor wields awful powers. He is a devil. But he must walk small when the Racters frown."

The noise of carousing bellowed on about us as we talked. Soon Valka had drunk enough for him to join in with the songs the renders yodeled out. They sang songs I had never heard of until then: "The Worm-eaten Swordship Gull-i-mo." The part song, "The Wines of Jholaix," which they were sober enough to sing more or less correctly through, swordship crew and swordship crew taking parts. "The Maid with the Single Veil," which brought on a rash of giggles from the serving wenches. And they sang the old ones, too: "The Bowmen of Loh." They even had a shot at various musicked stanzas of "The Canticles of the Rose City," but by that time most were too far gone for exact rendering of the cadences of those old myths, three thousand years old if they were a day.

When I wandered off to the room I had been assigned Valka and the knot of men I knew now were faithful to me, for I had seen their reactions during the aftermath of the fight aboard the flagship, accompanied me. They would sleep next door. I went in and the samphron oil lamp was lit and there was Viridia, smokily lovely in a short orange shift which showed her legs and her knees—which were dimpled, I swear it!—reclining on the bed.

In her combed hair a blaze of jewels reflected the light and glittered magnificently. I heard Valka and the others laughing. Viridia pushed up on her arms.

"You were asking Valka of Vallia, Dray." She smiled and that sensuous mouth parted enticingly. "Come and sit by me and I will tell you of Vallia, also."

"You are a Vallian?" In truth, I had heard a story that she was, but had doubted it.

"I will tell you, Dray; but come, sit by me."

I did not relish a repetition of that scene I had endured with Queen Lilah. I discounted women like Natema and Susheeng in this equation; because Viridia fancied herself as a Queen of Pain, which Queen Lilah had in truth been. If I give the impression of Viridia as being less of a person than she was, then I do her a disfavor. She was a real person in her own right, vibrant, alluring now she had tidied herself up, and a genuine force to be reckoned with. I fancied she wanted to place herself under my protection, now that her Womoxes were gone. As I thought of them I gave an involuntary shiver, for they had been gruesome and powerful antagonists indeed.

Viridia started up.

"Dray! You have a fever?"

"It is nothing, Viridia the Render. Now, listen to me, and listen to me carefully. I shall not tell you again."

At this she sat up on the bed and meekly put her hands together, down between her knees. Her tanned face, warm under the mellow light, assumed an expression of subservience, the eyes downcast. If she was playacting, she did it well. There were no slaves among the renders, but I guessed from this display that Viridia had been slave in her time.

"I listen, master."

About to bite her head off, I stopped. Very well, if this was the way she wanted to play it, so be it.

"You are now defenseless, except for the strength and skill of your own arms, Viridia. I know you can fight and swing an ax, for I have seen you. But men lust after you."

"That is true, master. I desire to be your slave. You must chastise me if I am bad, punish me with the knotted cord. I have killed many men who attempted me. But for you I will do as Chekumte desired you to do for him, and kiss your feet."

I began to think she meant it.

I was naked to the breechclout; but I began to get hot under the collar.

"Listen, Viridia. I do not want your Makki-Grodno pirates! Keep them, and the swordships. If you want me to be your master and carry on in this foolish fashion I shall lift that short nightie of yours and spank you soundly—"

She looked up and her eyelids flew up.

"Oh, yes, please, master!"

With a furious roar I scooped her up, opened the door with my free hand and then found that I could not, as I fully intended, throw her out, for she had wound both her naked arms around my neck. The next instant she had kissed me, a full, wet, soft kiss that—I confess—was pleasurable, most. Then, automatically, images of my Delia floated into my mind in a torrent and I laughed. Yes, I laughed.

"It is no use, Viridia. I like you exceedingly well. But I do not love you. Now go to your room and Arkhebi and Valka and I will stand turn and turn about at your door. You will be safe."

"But, Dray, my master." She said this with a charming pout. "I do not want to be safe from you."

I marveled. From the fierce tough she-leem of the seas, she had metamorphosed into this teasing, sensual, alluring woman. Just how much of an act was it all? Would she, when I was suitably disarmed, slip a dagger between my ribs?

The last thing she said was: "If I am to remain in command, Dray Prescot, then I will set you in command of the swordship I have just bought."

This sounded more promising.

Once I had a crew under my orders and was free of the other swordships, without their seeking a lead from me, I might plan escape.

"So be it, Viridia the Render," I said, and carried her to her room and threw her inside. I slammed the door. Then I roused out Valka and Arkhebi and we stood guard turn and turn about all that night.

The next day I went down to the anchorage to inspect thes newest addition to Viridia's squadron and my future command.

The moment I saw her I exclaimed: "A sea scow! Viridia, you cunning she-leem! She's a zenzile! Old, ancient, leaky—a veritable tub!"

The smile Viridia cast at me upward and the way her blue eyes caught mine through her eyelashes made me want to spank her in very truth. I put my hands on my hips and jutted my beard out to the swordship.

"Yes, Dray Prescot—you may think she is all of those things. But, if you wish to command a render ship in my squadron—that is the swordship for you."

Valka, at my side, guffawed, so I said without looking at him: "Laugh all you like, Valka. Just remember, you'll be commanding her varters." At which Valka stopped laughing.

It had been my custom in the Eye of the World to name any swifter I commanded *Zorg*. This in memory of my oar comrade. Other swifter captains had known this, and respected my wishes. But I would never dream of calling this swaybacked old zenzile swordship *Zorg*.

Without another word to Viridia I strode off toward the nearest of our beached boats and my men, after one look at my face, clambered in silently and bent to the oars. I did not look back at Viridia. I knew she was laughing at me. But, in truth, this old zenzile swordship was not all that bad and she was a weapon of the sea, long, lean, low, lethal.

The old-fashioned zenzile way of rowing incorporates what was a wonderful invention when it was first used—and just how long ago that was let the academic pundits argue—of slanting the benches diagonally so that their inboard seat is farther aft than their outboard. With three oarsmen on each bench and using oars of different lengths so that the blades formed those impeccable parallel lines in the water, the swordship presented from the beam an impression of a single bank of oars arranged in clumps of threes.

One man rowed one oar, three oarsmen to each slanted bench, and the centers could be anything from three feet six inches to four feet apart, depending on the whims of the naval architect who designed the ship. There were twenty benches a side and thus a hundred and twenty oarsmen in all. I began to think, as I mounted the side and put my foot on the fantamyrrh and so stepped aboard my new command, that Viridia had indeed bought the scow Chekumte had been trying to sell her.

If she had, she had done it to spite me.

Well, that was a game two could play.

Valka was making unpleasant comments on the swordship and with the group of men loyal to me strode about the central gangway and hurdled over the benches and prowled the apostis, looking over the side, for she was of the anafract variety.

"Don't be too hard on her, Valka. Galleys like this have fought in many great engagements—aye, and they will continue to do so, just so long as men believe in them."

"Give me a good long oar and half a dozen men on it, any time," said Valka, with a curse.

"This is a zorca of the seas," I said. "At least in theory. This zenzile arrangement is fine for smaller galleys; when you come to a swifter—a swordship—of large size is when you need the packed power that *scaloccio* rowing gives you."

I suppose the last time galleys had been constructed after this pattern on the Earth of my birth had been back in the sixteenth century, for the *alla scaloccio* system had been dated, I gathered, to 1530. The Venetians were great galley men of the Mediterranean. Zenzile rowing died out on this Earth; but I suppose these seafaring folk of Kregen clung to their own ideas with a stubbornness I could recognize.

The name of this wonder craft was *Strigicaw*. A strigicaw is a powerful fast-running carnivore with a hide striped as to the shoulders and foreparts and double-spotted as to belly and haunches, in a variety of brown and red camouflage colors, and although looking not unlike a leem has only six legs instead of that voracious beast's eight.

She was a hundred feet in length—any more would have been too much for her power-propulsion—and had just the two masts, a main and a fore, both rigged with courses

and topsails. At least, she did boast a rudder and whipstaf
This is a clumsy system long superseded on the ships o
Earth; no doubt soon the naval architects of Kregen wi
develop the wheel and cylinder steering gear. I strode abou
her, and, despite all, despite that she would need constan
pumping, I began to get the feel of her, and to know sh
was my command.

After the sinking of *Venus* Viridia's render maidens ha
been shipped aboard another of her squadron, whose crev
had been distributed among the remaining ships, so tha
we had been crowded. Now I would have to look to bar
gaining and cajoling and arguing in order to obtain the crev
I wanted.

As we so stood surveying our new swordship a boomin
horn note rolled weirdly over the anchorage. All the bus
noise of hammering and shouting, of singing and whistling
all human sounds ceased.

Again that booming note mourned across the water.

"The alarm!" shouted Spitz, a redheaded archer from
Loh. I had marked him from the first, and sought to wo
him for my little company, for in his quiver he carrie
arrows fletched with the brilliant blue of the king korf—an
also arrows fletched with jetty black feathers—feathers
knew had been set by Sosie na Arkasson—and given to me
and loosed by me against Spitz, and so retrieved by him fo
further use. "King's swordships!"

We tumbled down into the boat and rowed ashore in
welter of foam. The swordship—or swordships—prowlin
around the island of Careless Repose might come from an
nation; but we usually dubbed any swordship attempting t
police the islands the King's swordship. Viridia met us on the
beach. She looked excited, her tanned face flushed, he
strong body in the mesh steel armor firm in the sunlight.

"Be ready to repel them if they venture past the conceal
ing islet!" she rapped out to her lieutenants, captains of thei
own vessels, of whom I was now one. "I and my warrio
maidens will seek to do their business for them." She laughed
throwing her head back in the light so that the dark hai
swirled. "As we have done before!"

"Aye, Viridia!" the man yelled. "Hai, Jikai, Viridia the
Render!"

There was no malice in me, no regret, for the use of tha
great word here. Viridia, in that moment, was a lady pirate
indeed.

She took her girls off to the other side of the island and the swordship crews repaired aboard their craft and made ready to pull around the point if Viridia's plan did not work. As I had no crew, apart from my own small company of loyals, I took them, with weapons in our hands, across the island after Viridia.

She might welcome a little help, when it came to the time.

As it happened, she needed no help, least of all from mere men.

A repetition of what had happened to the old *Nemo* took place. This swordship, commissioned to hunt down the renders and sailing out of the chief port of The Bloody Menaham, was taken in exactly the same way and by exactly the same means.

I daresay it was the same half-naked sprite who ran along the central gangway carrying the dripping head of the chief whip-deldar.

The King's swordship was rowed around the point and past the concealing islet and so into the anchorage where the slaves were freed from their oars. They set up a wonderful hullabaloo. All, I knew, would take the alternative of joining the pirates.

I studied the new ship. She was a smart and efficient-looking vessel, with three sails and a spritsail on her bowsprit. Her bronze ram was fashioned into the likeness of a mythical bird of prey, something like a falcon, although, of course, the hooked beak had been smoothed into a single shaft of cutting bronze. Anything like a hook, as of an accipiter's beak, for a ram is idiocy. One has to be able to backwater and shove off from a rammed vessel, with the aid of the proembolion, before the water rushes into the cleft in her hull and the apostis, the rowing frame, settles down over your ram and drags you under.

As for her spritsail, that was a sailor-like rigged job, nicely forward and yet well clear of her beak. I watched the ex-slaves being ferried ashore. Among those on the beach I saw a group forming around some object on the sand, and I heard loud guffaws, and hearty laughter, and many merry curses. I strolled down.

A man, a very tall man, was upside down on the sand, his legs rhythmically bicycling in the air. Some of the men were attempting to push him over. He did, at that, look a sight. I heard him yelling. "Clear off, onkers! I must abjure my taboos!"

A guffawing render—a towheaded man from one of the islands past Erthyrdrin—pushed the tall upside-down man and he rolled spraying sand.

Instantly, he was upside down again, his long fair hair sand-clogged, his legs rotating.

The renders and ex-slaves roared.

"Taboos!" They yodeled, getting set for their next prank.

I sighed.

I strode over and unlimbered my sword.

I stood before Inch.

"If any man wishes to push this man over while he abjures his taboos, he must pass this rapier first."

After that, Inch could get on with it, and I could only wait until he had worked all the accumulated taboo-breaks out of his system before I could ask him all the news.

CHAPTER EIGHTEEN

The yellow cross on the scarlet field

Strigicaw prowled the seas in search of plunder.

"I never believed, Dray Prescot, that any man could claw back from the Ice Floes of Sicce."

"Since I don't believe in investigating that shivery region for many years to come, Inch, your surprise is unwarranted."

"But, man! You just disappeared!"

"Evidently, what happened to me happened to you." I told him, briefly, how King Nemo had disposed of me and he sighed and said: "Much the same. I suppose I was getting too big for my boots. When you vanished, no man knew whither, Tilda insisted I stay on. I had to—you see that, don't you, Dray?"

"Of course. It was the honorable thing to do."

My swordship, making a most unpleasant business of beating into a devilish strong wind from the wrong quarter and with a sea that made the use of oars out of the question, pitched and rolled. Spray drenched us. My flags flew stiff as boards.

Being anafract, that is, without armor protection for the rowers, my artillery—for I may use that word of varters—must be concentrated forward. We were far more a galley than a galleass, like the other swordships. The others of Viridia's squadron were sailing far more weatherly than we and were pulling away across the tumbled sea. Again I looked up at my flags. Up there the yellow cross of my clansmen had been charged on the scarlet of Strombor. A brilliant yellow upright cross on a scarlet field. Yes, those were my colors. A momentary stab of an emotion I did not want to recognize shafted through me as, from the truck of the main, floated the render flag, a shaft of conscience, almost, that the pirate flag should wave in company with my own.

Inch had given me the news. He had tried to assist Tilda, and keep Pando under some sort of control; but the wild zhantil had taken his newly-won status as a Kov to heart, and had lavished money and armament on the king and, with a great levy, had gone to war. I ached that I had not been there to help him—and by helping him to draw him back from the folly of war.

"I spoke out, Dray, and the next thing I knew was chained on the rowing beaches of a swordship—and, mark me—a swordship of The Bloody Menaham."

"I had noticed. They sold you, it seems."

"The war was not going well when I—ah—left."

"If that idiot Pando gets himself killed—although," I spoke hopefully—"I expect he would be held for ransom."

"We didn't handle him the best way. The Kovnate went to his head a little."

"Agreed. And, Inch, that was my fault. I was a fool."

Inch had not broken any taboos as yet since boarding *Strigicaw*, and I had swiftly adjusted to remembering. Now he shook his head. "Not so, Dray. You could always control him, and in the best way, without a strap. I tried. But after you went he turned wild. There was no holding him."

"Tilda?"

He smiled. "She is a good mother, and a wonderful woman and a superb actress. But I think being a Kovneva was a trifle out of her experience. She tries to cope, but she has been drinking—"

"No!"

"I am afraid so."

"We'll have to go back, Inch, and sort them out."

"Yes. It seems to me that is a task laid on us, for our sins."

"For our sins, Zair be thanked."

And so—what of Vallia? What of Delia of Delphond? The strongest doubts existed that this wallowing swordship *Strigicaw* would ever live through a passage across the open sea. She was a swift galley built for coastal waters, up among the islands. Now, through the sheets of spray, our consorts were a full dwabur upwind of us, and going hull down. Vallia would have to wait. Delia—I know I prayed she would understand and forgive me. But I was tortured by the thought that her resistance had been broken down, and she had given

nto that imperial majesty, her father, and married the oaf
of his choice.

"By Ngrangi!" exclaimed Inch as the ship rolled and the
wind tore at our canvas and water slopped green. "This tub
will founder beneath us!"

"Spitz!" I yelled to the archer from Loh. "Before the flagship disappears! Hoist the white flag from the main yard!"

With a yell Spitz ran to obey.

That white flag from our yardarm, plus the simultaneous
hauling down of the pirate flag from the main truck, would
indicate to Viridia, if her officers could pick the signal out,
that we had been forced to return to Careful Repose.

In the midst of giving the orders that would turn our head
toward the easiest point of the compass for the ship, Valka
sprang up through the canvas coverings we had spread over
the rowing benches to keep the sea out and raced along the
central gangway toward me. He glared up to the quarterdeck.

"Only just about in time, Captain, if you ask me! The
seams are working something horrible. We're shipping water
faster than the pumps can clear."

"Muster a baling party," I told Valka. "See they jump to
it. I'm taking this ship home—never fear—unless something
better comes along."

They all laughed at that, as though it were a jest.

The new course, off the wind and sea, eased the ship and I
made a tour of inspection in the wildly leaping vessel, feeling
her working in the sea, and realized just how close we had
been. The inspection I had given her before we sailed had
not been as thorough as I would have liked, and now I
could see that Viridia had been cheated—although, no doubt,
that troubled her not a whit. The new swordship she had just
taken would be fitted and ready by the time she returned
from this cruise. Much of the underwater planking was rot-
ten, and I could push the point of my dagger into the wood
with ease. I began to entertain a conviction that the bottom
would drop out before we made port. And all through the
rush of departure!

Thinking baleful thoughts I climbed up on deck again and
ordered a tot of good red wine for every man.

When Spitz, having hauled down the white flag, began to
rehoist the pirate flag I growled at him. "Belay that!"

Certain ideas were meeting and melding in my head. I
knew I was sick of the pirate trade—and yet, its fascination

and its rewards, given that we would plunder only enemies, could not be denied.

"Sail ho!"

I stood on my ridiculous quarterdeck as we pitched and rolled and struggled in that sea, with a scrap of canvas showing to keep us from being merely a waterlogged lump of drifting wreckage, and watched as, on almost a reciprocal bearing, so close to the wind was she, a magnificent ship foamed toward us. She passed like a queen of the seas. She took absolutely no notice of us at all. In reality, working as we were, boarding would have been an operation too costly, as I judged. As it was that beautiful ship beat past us, leaning over, all her canvas as taut and trim as a guardsman's tunic, her colors snapping out insolently.

I gazed on that ship and on those colors.

A galleon, jutting of beak, sheer of line and curve, bold in the sea, built low with forecastle and quarterdeck and a small poop, four-masted, raked, aglitter with bright gilding and flamboyant colors. She moved surely against that sea in which we floundered. A galleon. A race-built galleon.

And the flags! A yellow cross, a saltire, on a red field.

I glanced up at my own flag.

That yellow Saint Andrew's cross on a red ground—I knew it. I knew from whence that proud ship hailed. From Vallia!

The galleon from Vallia roared past and was gone and was soon hull down and then the last scrap of her canvas winked over the sea horizon to the east.

"Damn the Vallians!" said Spitz. He held his Lohvian longbow in his hand, a kind of nervous reflex. "They think they own the sea and all who sail on it! By Hlo-Hli! They think they've been anointed and given the scepter of all Kregen!"

We struggled on and, to our vast relief, the sea went down, the wind backed, and we were able to make better weather of it. The twin suns of Kregen were slipping down toward the western horizon, first Genodras and then Zim, and soon the nightly procession of moons would arch through the swarming stars.

Again came the hail that warms a render's heart.

"Sail ho!"

She was a swordship from Yumapan, the country south of Lome, on the other side of the massive mountains that divide the island into North and South Pandahem, Her colors of vertical bars of green and blue in keeping with Pandahemic tradition fluttered in the dying breeze. She had seen us and was closing fast, and even as I watched she sprouted her oars and the long looms held, as though ruled parallel, like wings on either beam, before the drum-deldar gave his first stroke and the oars dipped as one.

Valka yelled at me, pointing.

"No oars!" I shouted back.

Now Spitz and others of my officers were shouting. I leaped into the main shrouds and roared them to silence.

"They are big and powerful and can take us—and who among you wants to row for the Yumapanim? Eh? Any volunteers?"

There rose a few scattered, uncertain laughs.

Yumapan, being situated across the sea to the east from Walfarg, had been one of that robust nation's first conquests on her road to empire in the long ago. Now that Walfarg's empire had crumbled, the Yumapan remembered, and aped those old ways; and they had long memories. Men even said they preferred a queen on the throne in Yumapan, in remembrance of the old Queens of Pain of Loh.

"But, Dray!" shouted Valka. "No oars! How can we fight?"

"We let her ram us, of course, you hairy calsany! Let her stick her rostrum up our guts—poor old *Strigicaw* is done for, anyway! Then, my sea-leem—*then!*"

"Aye!" they roared it back at me. "Then, Dray Prescot—*then!*"

And so, rolling like a washtub in the sea, we awaited the bronze-rammed shock from the Yumapan swordship.

When it came, with a roaring rending of wood and the screeching of bronze against iron nails, the smash of white water and the solid reeling shock as we nearly overset, my men knew what was required of them and knew the plan. Before the swordship captain could back his oars and draw free we were up over our side. Grapnels flew. Men leaped down from our rigging.

With Spitz in masterly control of our bowmen we shot out their quarterdeck. I went in at the head of my sea-leems, handing up over the bronze ram, up past the proembolion which was fashioned in bronze in the likeness of a zhantil-mask, up to the side of the beak and so, with a heave and a squirm, over onto the beak gangwalk. I snatched out my sword and, roaring and shouting, led my men down onto the central gangway. We fought. Oh, yes, we fought. We knew that if we failed we would either die and be tossed overside or be chained naked at the rowing beaches.

This was a fight that had some meaning to it.

This was a fight we had to win.

I saw Inch with a great ax, almost the equal of his own mighty weapon he had lost back in Bormark, smiting and smiting. In expert hands the great Saxon ax of Danish pattern is a frightful weapon of destruction. It cleaved a red path through the Yumapanim. Many men leaped overboard, shrieking, rather than face the tall form of Inch with those incredibly long arms smashing that gory ax in swaths of destruction.

And, obeying my orders, selected hands of my crew were jumping down between the rowing beaches, kicking away the ponsho skins, smashing the padlocks and breaking the chains. How those oar-slaves rose to us! With snatched-up weapons parceled out by my men, the ex-slaves vomited into the battle. We began at the prow and we finished at the taffrail, and all between was mine!

Of course, looking back, how can I take a pride in all that destruction of life? How can I feel a glow of satisfaction that good sailormen had been slain and thrown overboard? But then, at the head of my sea-leem, my bloodstained rapier in my hand, I felt the full tide of gratification and lust of conquest. I had scarcely heeded that this was a part of the render's trade. Yumapan was a foe of Vallia, was a foe of Tomboram—and, as I knew, was a foe also to Zenicce and Strombor. It was all part of the struggle that, all unbeknown, I was waging on Kregen under the Suns of Scorpio.

Poor *Strigicaw* was almost gone.

Before the waves closed over her we took what was necessary and transferred our goods and chattels to my new command.

That brave flag of mine, the brilliant yellow cross on the scarlet field I personally bent and hoisted, high, high at the truck of the mainmast. And there it blew, proclaiming to all that this swordship was mine!

Pride, and possession, and power—disastrous, disastrous!

The released slaves would join us.

The name of the swordship had been a long and complicated farrago of high-flown pomp and circumstance, which boiled down to her and her captain being the best on the sea, and the queen of Yumapan being the greatest Queen of Pain who had ever lived. I gave orders for the whole name to be expunged, and this was done by a certain amount of high-spirited chisel work and a triple splash in the sea.

I gathered everyone aft and addressed them from the quarterdeck, which was wide and spacious for a galleass, and ornate with fittings that already I had my eye on as further consignments to the deep.

"This swordship is now named *Freedom*."

They cheered at that.

"We return to Careless Repose. There is work set to my hand, work that will bring rich loot, plunder beyond your wildest dreams, prizes—gold, silver, wine and women! Do you follow me, lads?"

"Aye!" They roared it out. "Aye, Captain Prescot. We will follow you to the Ice Floes of Sicce!"

I saw Inch looking sideways at me, and I did not wink; but I know he took the gist of what I meant.

Freedom was indeed a fine ship. She rowed forty oars a side, and there were nine men on each bench—according to the Kregen and not the Earthly way of reckoning. So that meant seven hundred and twenty men hauled and pushed the oars. Also, there were the sailors, and the marines—so that she had to be a large vessel. Quite unlike the swifters, with their dangerously low freeboards and their serpentine lines, she had some run to her underwater lines, and with her three masts and spritsail could hold a wind. Compared with a galleon, of course, she sailed like a barge. Even then, even then, that proud and haughty Vallian galleon could not match the qualities of a first-class frigate of my own day, let us not forget that!

Her freeboard seemed immense, and her varters and catapults mounted on the broadside had a superb arc of training and commanding height. I felt I could sail her to Vallia, if the need arose—*if the need arose!*

How far I had come! Tilda and Pando must be sorted out and when that task had been accomplished to my satisfaction, then, then I would turn the proud beak of this beauty north-eastwards to Vallia!

Inch was let into all the plans I had formulated, with the exception that he knew only that I intended to sail to Vallia, and, being a footloose mercenary warrior, that suited him fine. Valka and Spitz and the other of my officers were told enough to keep them happy. They were well-primed to do their work. I knew that by the time we arrived at the island of Careless Repose I would have a whole swordship crew devoted to carrying out what I wanted done, demanding, pleading, desperate to sail on my business.

If I have a good ship's crew ready to my hand I sometimes fancy I might move mountains.

At the pirates' lair we talked and held out dazzling promises and suborned good men. The big breakthrough came when a swordship brought in an argenter from The Bloody Menaham. The renders had taken to copying Viridia and instead of butchering their prisoners and burning the ships, ransomed them instead. Now I heard that The Bloody Menaham were on the attack against Tomboram, had marched in to invade Bormark, had crossed that Kovnate and were advancing on the capital, Pomdermam.

"Let us hit these Bloody Menaham, where it hurts, at home!" I urged the sea-leems. By the time Viridia returned, with but a poor coaster to show for her efforts, and thoroughly out of sorts, she was, willy-nilly, swept up in the feral enthusiasm.

By careful sea passages we could reach south of the islands, coast along the north shore of Pandahem, come storming in on the rear of The Bloody Menaham, from a quarter where they least expected assault. There was a great deal of flashing blades and shouts of "Hai! Jikai!" but I kept busily preparing plans for every swordship captain, and as the news of a great venture whose final destination was a secret from all but the captains buzzed around the islands, swordship after swordship nosed in until the anchorage filled and they had to lie up in secondary harbors.

For some time, everyone said, the renders had been aching to go on a great Jikai. Now, all agreed, was the time.

If you think me blind to what I was doing, then, in all humility, I suppose I was. But I wanted to get to Vallia, and I could not leave until I had honored my promise to Tilda and Pando.

The great day came at last. We had filled every quiver. All the ammunition lockers were filled to overflowing. Wine, water, food, arms, everything was crammed into the swordships. In a great fluttering of flags and booming of stentor horns, we lifted our hooks and pulled for the sea and Pandahem.

CHAPTER NINETEEN

The Scorpion returns

As we shipped our oars and from the yards the topmen let fall our canvas and we began to heel to the breeze, I saw above me and flying in those familiar wide planing circles the gorgeous scarlet and gold form of the Gdoinye, the raptor sent as observer and sentinel by the Star Lords. Although I did not see the Savanti dove, I was heartened by the sight of the Gdoinye, taking it as a good omen for my venture. In this, as you will hear, I was foolishly naïve.

We made a fine passage south and east, swinging wide of the northwest tip of Pandahem where the land of Lome meets the sea, and cruising eastward to make the island of Panderk which lies off the western end of the enormous Bay of Panderk, immediately north of the border between The Bloody Menaham and Tomboram. Here we sent spies ashore.

The news they brought back infuriated me—and drove me to commit a folly that nearly destroyed the fleet of render swordships and would have totally undone me; but then I believed I was acting out some small part of the scheme the Star Lords planned for Kregen, and so I believed that I would not fail.

The spies reported that the Menaham army was slogging on toward the capital of Tomboram, Pomdermam, and thereby keeping in play King Nemo and all his forces. But, secretly, across the wide waters of the Bay of Panderk, a mighty armada of ships of all descriptions was sailing on, packed with men, to come upon Pomdermam from the sea and in a sudden and savagely unexpected onslaught rout the Tomboramin utterly.

This was bad enough. But, at least for Inch and me, there was far worse information. One of the spies, an agile pirate who hailed from Menaham and had been consigned to the galleys and subsequently followed the usual path to the island of Careless Repose, reported a choice tidbit of gossip. The Kov of Bormark—"a mere stripling!"—and his mother had been forced to flee and were hiding somewhere, Pandrite knew where.

I said one word: "Murlock!"

Inch nodded. "It would be like him, the obvious thing for him to do."

"But he must be mad! Blind! Cannot he see that Menaham will use him and then toss him aside? He'll never recover his estates and his title, by the Black Chunkrah!"

"Murlock Marsilus," said the spy, his blackened teeth exposed as he smiled knowingly. "That's the name. But he is not with the fleet for Pomdermam. He was seen—a girl I know told me, with many giggles—heading for Pomdermam itself, astride a zorca that he roweled as though Armipand himself, may Opaz rot him, was after him."

Then, bringing the problem squarely before me, the Menaham pirate nodded over the bulwark to the northeastern horizon. Black thunderheads piled there. All about our island anchorage the water lay listless and still, glassy, unbreathing.

"By Diproo the Nimble-fingered!" said the pirate, and spat —by which I knew him to have been a member of the thieves' fraternity. "That fleet may just scrape through to Pomdermam, but no ship will follow for days!"

Everyone, it seemed all of a sudden, was looking at me. I could feel their eyes, like scarlet leeches, sucking at me.

An instant decision would be easy, perhaps fatally wrong. Just how far these pirates would follow my lead remained also a factor to be considered. I grunted something to Inch and Valka and went into my cabin. I automatically looked around for the scarlet-coated marine sentry at attention with his musket and bayonet—so far gone aboard ship was I in problems.

This was Kregen, four hundred light-years from the nearest Royal Marine and his musket and bayonet. I already knew the answer, in truth, this atypical and cowardly hesitation was merely my self-excuse for once again failing Delia. I loved Delia, and Delia loved me. We both knew each loved the other. Therefore there could be between us none of these adolescent lovers' tiffs of immature passion, those fits of jealousy and rage—no lovers's quarrels. So much of the literature of Earth no less than Kregen is consumed by these juvenile lovers' quarrels, and disbeliefs, and worries over faithfulness. I knew Delia would not despair of me and I knew she would not marry of her own free will; it was chicanery that I feared for her, the deep plots of her autocratic father. She would know my duty lay with Tilda and Pando for the moment and then—then to face her father. I would have to be ruthless with him. Have to be . . .

Love gently forces one to adjust mental horizons. If love is selfish, crying: "She is *mine!*" and one destroys lives and hopes for the sake of this spurious love, one cannot truly love. Love demands sacrifices, it makes giving easy. And, in turn, it means that receiving, also, is a part of love.

I went out onto the quarterdeck and everyone fell silent. All those eyes leeched on me as I stood, holding myself up, my left hand gripping my rapier hilt, and I know my beard jutted out in its swifter-ram arrogance, and my face wore its old ugly look of devilish power. But, that is me, alas.

"There is much loot aboard the armada of The Bloody Menaham. That loot will be ours. Afterward, we will smash The Bloody Menaham and take from them wealth enough to make us all rich for the rest of our lives."

I turned to Valka, who stood now in the position of my first lieutenant, Spitz taking the responsibility of varter Hikdar. "Make the signal to weigh. We sail at once."

For a long moment there was complete silence.

Had I failed? Would they disobey? Then Inch tossed his hat in the air. "The Bloody Menaham!" he roared. "We rend them utterly! Hai, Jikai! Hai, Dray Prescot!"

After that it was a matter of getting the hook up and of setting all our oarsmen at pulling and heaving. One by one the other swordships followed our lead, for they recognized a strong hand at the helm and had no other plan. As we gathered into our stride a longboat rowed alongside, her oars splashing frantically. A tossed rope hauled up a chest and on its second cast fished up Viridia. She bounded onto the deck, shook the dark hair out of her eyes, and declared roundly: "By Opaz, Dray Prescot! You won't get rid of me so easily!"

Nodding to that ominous blackness all across the horizon, I said so that only she could hear: "You may have joined me for your last voyage, Viridia the Render."

She laughed recklessly, tossing the hair out of her eyes. "And if I have I would sail on that last voyage to the Ice Floes of Sicce with no other man than you, Dray Prescot."

The black storm clouds whirled up into the zenith and the opaz light of the twin suns was blotted out in a hell of roaring wind and smashing seas and of a blackness like an impiter's wings enfolding us. We battened everything down and held on under storm canvas. Now the swordships must prove if they were sea boats or not. Some render captains turned back, out of cowardice, out of prudence, out of dire necessity of a sinking vessel beneath their feet. But *Freedom* held on across the wide Bay of Panderk, and with her sailed through those bitter seas a goodly proportion of the render armada.

If we failed to get through, then Pomdermam was completely lost, and with the capital the country, and with the country Bormark, and Tilda, and Pando. We fought the sea, for we must not lose.

Relieving tackles were rigged so that more men could throw their weight on the rudder. Lines were rigged across the decks. I stood lashed on my quarterdeck, spray-drenched, soaked, the wind whipping through my hair and beard and stinging into my eyes, conning the ship. We fought all the elements that the ocean could throw at us, and on the second day we emerged, sorely bruised and battered but intact, and sailed on into a subsiding sea and a dying wind.

And then—"Sail ho!"

Ahead of us and spreading across the horizon in a great cloud of canvas toiled the armada from Menaham. They straggled. They had caught the outskirts of the gales's violence. The twin suns were sliding down into the sea, staining the vast expanse of ocean in bruised rubies and jades. Signals flashed from swordship to swordship, so that my fleet held back, riding out the last of the swell-waves, repairing damage, giving the tired crews time to rest and recuperate. Signals among shipping on Kregen had not reached to the sophistication of the signal book as invented by Kempenfelt and Popham; but by flag and lamp I was able to get my message across.

The fallacy that ships may be drilled like soldiers still holds among landsmen, and although the Navy had achieved remarkable evolutionary prowess, navies still could not under the conditions of sail and oar take up long neat lines of upward of a thousand ships, in four ranks, with outraiders and scouts, as though they drilled on Salisbury Plain. For one thing, the length of lines of galleys, marshaled abeam, makes for vast acres of sea coverage, and the distances are such that signals take a good long time to reach from the commander in chief to the outer horns of his lines. So I had simply adapted a Nelsonian piece of advice: "Sail or row toward your enemy whenever you see him. Any render captain who places his swordship into the guts of his opponent will not do wrong."

Perhaps, at another time, I will speak more fully of that battle in the Bay of Panderk off Pomdermam.

With the coming of the twin Suns of Scorpio the sea woke to long swaths of crimson and emerald. Birds flew low over the water, screaming. The sea lay heaving in glassy swells after the storm, and the wind died to a zephyr, so that it was all oar-work, and rowing, with the men standing and flinging themselves against the oars. Benches are provided aboard swifters and swordships where anything from four to ten men may labor at a single loom, and these benches are thickly covered with ponsho skins. There is nothing of the genteel sitting in your seat and resting your feet in slides and rowing as though you pulled an eight in some university boat race. The one-man-to-one-oar zenzile craft share something of that finesse. Not so the swordships. Here men stand and grip the loom and thrust it down and then, lifting it high, hurl themselves bodily backward, crashing down with numbed buttocks onto those benches and those thoughtfully provided ponsho skins. The benches exist to prevent them from smashing back to the deck, to support them for the next convulsive effort of jumping up and thrusting down. All the body is used in rowing a swordship or a swifter. Every ounce concentrated on dragging those massive blades through the water. So we thrashed on through the water. So we thrashed on through the glassy swells, the white water creaming from our bronze rams, bearing on in lethal pursuit of the armada of The Bloody Menaham.

The greatest problem would be that of individual renders taking an argenter and stopping for plunder.

The drum-deldar thumped out his booming and commanding beat, bongg, bongg, bongg. A single beat, as is used aboard a swordship as opposed to the double, bass and treble, employed in swifters. Quicker and quicker the beat rose as I urged the oarsmen on. We foamed through the sea. Ahead of us spread the blue and green diagonally striped flags of the Menaham, fluttering from a hundred staffs. I selected our target. The helm-deldars swung the whipstaff. Our ram curled back the white running water. I measured the distance. . . .

"Prepare to ram!"

Spitz's varter men hauled back and braced themselves. A single shining instant of poising hush, a fragile bubble when everything coalesced and rushed together—and then we smashed into the stern of the argenter and the world revolved in a rending smashing and a bright chaos. On the instant I released my handholds and leaped. From our beak I crashed forward and in through the stern windows of the argenter, to be met by a flickering wall of rapiers and boarding-pikes. With my sea-leems at my back we went through the defense and roared out onto the quarterdeck. In a few murs we had taken the ship. We battened the crew below and left a small prize crew and then it was back to the benches and more of that straining, lung-bursting heaving at the oars with the whole body flung backward to drag the blades through the resisting water. We took another argenter, and then avoided the deadly thrust of a Menaham swordship, and raked her all along her side so that our cat head pulped her oars even as our own rowers shipped theirs.

For the rest of the day we were engaged in chasing Menaham shipping and taking or sinking everything that flew the diagonal blue and green flag.

By the time the Maiden with the Many Smiles floated into the night sky and Inch wound a great turban around his fair hair, we were masters of the sea.

"And this is the great victory you promised, Dray!" cried Viridia, flushed, dripping blood, her gaudy clothes ripped and slashed away to reveal the mesh link armor clothing her firm body.

"Only a part, Viridia, only a part. Now we must land in Pomdermam!"

When we had invested the treasures of *Freedom* after we had taken the swordship I had found, safely wrapped in tissue in great lenken chests in the aft stateroom, a great quantity of armor. Remember that *Freedom* had been a Yumapanim vessel and the Yumapanim aped the ways of old Loh, so the armor was of that refined and decorated kind I had worn when fighting for Queen Lilah of Hiclantung. Now I stripped it off, chipped and dented and blood-smeared as it was, and let it drop to the deck. I hung my rapier on a hook on the bulkhead. I was tired, but no more tired than I have been a thousand times in my life. Viridia stared at me, her eyes unreadable.

"Tomorrow, Viridia the Render, or the day after, we land

at Pomdermam. After that we drive The Bloody Menaham
back to their own frontiers—or beyond—or kill them all. I
do not care which."

She said, "Why do I do this for you, Dray? Why do the
renders of the islands follow you in such desperate ventures?"

"Plunder."

"Aye. That—and more."

I knew the fragility of the links that bound the renders
to my schemes. They were pirates. They would seek always
easy victims. They must be cajoled into following me against
the army of Menaham. But they would follow me. I was
determined on that.

"Once the renders are let loose in The Bloody Menaham,
Viridia, I believe they will find ample reward."

She cocked her head on one side. "And why shouldn't we
rend the Tomberamin?"

"Because, if you do, yours would be the first head to adorn
a spike over the walls of Pomdermam!"

Because the bountiful and marvelous paline grows everywhere it possibly can on Kregen it follows there must be
different varieties, generally distinguishable by slight varia-
tions in the yellow of the fruit. A Kregan could tell you
where a paline had grown by the color, and I was already
picking up the knack. There are two main sorts, divided into
those that grow their fruit on the old growth and those that
grow it on the new, and it is of the latter variety that one
may pluck a paline branch and sling it over one's shoulder for
the journey. It is a nice custom of seafarers to take a pot-
plant paline with them, hoping their water will hold out, and
there was a wondrous specimen aboard *Freedom*. Now Viridia plucked a paline and set it between her teeth, and
crunched, and sucked juice.

"You wouldn't, would you, Dray?"

"Don't try me, girl."

With that she gave her reckless laugh and began to strip
off her oiled steel mesh which was as befouled as my own
armor. I sent her out into an adjoining cabin, for the swordship was marvelously well-off for accommodation in her
after-parts, if the men slept wrapped in furs and silks between the rowing benches and on the central gangway.
Watches were set with a naval efficiency I saw was strictly
kept.

From the Island of Panderk in a straight line to Pomdermam is about a hundred dwaburs, and what with the gale and

the battle I figured on our making landfall the day after next. Some of the render captains had taken their prizes and gone roaring it back to the islands; but I was gratified to note that many still followed me, and their sails made a brave show against the brilliant sea and sky.

The first sight of Pomdermam, as is so often the case with any port of Kregen, is always the pharos. At Pomdermam there are two, one maintained by the government, the other by the Todalpheme of Pomdermam. These Todalpheme, the mystic mathematicians and philosophers of the oceans of Kregen, calculate the tidal effects and issue almanacs to give warning of impending high tides. The Todalpheme of Pomdermam wore purple tassels. Since the Hostile Territories through which I had traveled had no seaboards, there had been no Todalpheme there for me to ask: "Do you know of the scarlet-roped Todalpheme? Do you know of Aphrasöe?" That had been one of my first questions when Tilda, Pando, Inch, and I had stayed here. A shake of head was sufficient answer—sufficient! Sufficient disappointment.

I directed the course of our armada into a little cove someway to the west of the city. Although Kregen possesses a larger landmass than does Earth, there are fewer people, which is pleasant from the point of view of breathing space. No one as far as we could ascertain observed our swordships as they plummeted their anchors into the smooth water of the cove and the captains and the crews rowed ashore. I held a meeting; it was more an order group. I specifically ruled out any form of council of war. I do not, in general, believe in those.

"You render captains of the islands! You have fought well. You have sailed through a storm that would sink a sea-barynth. You have some wealth. Now we go up against The Bloody Menaham, and the booty will be enormous." I glared around on them, speaking from my perch atop a boulder. "If any one of you from Menaham wishes to pull out, that I understand. He is free to go, he and all his crew."

No one moved.

"Very well. We take the Menaham in the flank. They will not expect us—they think an army is coming to aid them across the sea instead of you shaggy sea-leems!"

There rose a gust of laughter at this. By Kregan standards that was a jest of high carat value.

So we set off, marching for we had no mounts, heading for Pomdermam. We were a motley bunch. Men and half-men

of many races marched in that straggly army. But one thing
we shared in common. We were all warriors of the first rank.

In the event we did not take the army of The Bloody
Menaham in the flank.

We struck them from the rear.

They were engaged in storming the city and tearing down
the walls and setting fire to the houses. The Tomboramin had
fought well and stubbornly, but they were overwhelmed and
beaten back. We saw the smoke and flames as we charged in.
Everywhere the diagonal blue and green waved the renders
charged like sea devils. Rapiers thrust and slashed. Boarding-pikes skewered past upraised arms. Our bowmen sleeted
their feathered death into the ranks of our foemen. For the
Tomboramin this last-minute rescue was unbelievable.

Through all those wild scenes of carnage I fought at the
head of my men, my loyals about me, driving on wedgelike
into the enemy ranks. Above our heads floated my flag, the
brave yellow cross on the field of scarlet. Viridia fought at
my side. Inch and his incredible ax were there, striking and
smiting. Valka, with a rapier like a blur of steel, thrust with
me, thrust for thrust. Spitz and his bowmen cleared the
path. Onward we drove and soon—very soon, to the destruction of the Menaham—we had them on the run and
they were fleeing and we were looking about for booty.

"Touch nothing of the Tomboramin," I had told my render
captains. "Any man found looting will be hanged." I remembered Wellington and his ways. "When we strike Menaham
they will yield all the plunder you can imagine, for their
armies will have been destroyed. The whole country will be
yours." In that, I remembered Napoleon.

A stubborn knot of fiercely-resisting Menaham cavalry
still clustered about the palace of King Nemo. Their zorcas
were down and they fought afoot, and they fought savagely
and well. With perilously few men left to me I led the final
charge upon them, driving into them, with the yellow cross
on scarlet biting into the ranks of diagonal blue and green.

"That flag of yours leads men on!" panted Viridia as we
hacked and hewed together. The cavalry wore armor, and
we were making heavy weather of it. But, as though, indeed,
that flay did lure men on to victory, we poured over a shattered breach and ravened in among the Menaham. Now, we
could thrust with care, aiming to drive our blades between
the armor joints.

"Follow the flag!" screamed Viridia. She had flung down

her rapier and now gripped the flagpole, the shaft all bloody in her fingers. The yellow and scarlet flamed above us. "It is superb! Superb! On! On! Jikai! Jikai!"

Following that magnificent girl with her flaring dark hair and her steel-mesh clad figure waving the flag aloft the men bellowed over the last of the Menaham cavalry. Now were left only those who had run into the palace, ready, like cornered cramphs, to fight and die.

"She is superb!" grunted Inch, flicking blood drops from his ax.

"Aye!" said Valka, waving his rapier. "And so is the flag!"

We raced up the marble stairs, hurdling the dead bodies, and so came into King Nemo's palace.

As I had known I would, I found Murlock Marsilus.

Viridia, gripping the flag in her bloodied left hand, her right now wielding a fresh snatched-up rapier, used her booted foot on a double folding door, kicking it open with a crash. Spitz feathered three shafts into the room and then Inch and I leaped in. Half a dozen Menaham gathered there, three with Spitz's blue-feathered shafts in them. The other three went down before Inch, Valka and me. Then I saw the tableau in the adjoining room, clearly visible through flung open drapes.

Murlock was there, gripping a rapier, about to drive it down into Pando's back as he clutched his mother about the waist.

Tilda faced Murlock bravely. She swung a wine bottle at his head, reeling, and with a savage laugh Murlock smashed it away. But the diversion had been enough. He heard our entrance and swung about—and I reversed my rapier, hefted it, balanced, and hurled it as I had hurled javelins with my clansmen on the great plains of Segesthes.

The rapier flew true.

Murlock screamed, and the scream was choked off as my rapier transfixed his neck. He stood for an instant, staring, his face as horrible a mask of hatred and disbelief as any I have seen. Then he fell.

Tilda and Pando, with wild and abandoned shrieks, flew across the room, through the drapes, and flung themselves into my arms, all bloody as they were.

"Dray! Dray!" they babbled, grasping me. "Dray Prescot! You have come back to us!"

Viridia, all blood-smeared, grasping that old flag of mine,

tared at me. Her tanned face with the dark hair flowing contrasted with the classical ivory beauty of Tilda and her etty mane of gorgeous hair. Pando was gripping me and obbing convulsively.

"So," said Viridia. "This is what you tricked me and my renders into! A woman and her brat! It was all for this that you schemed and fought!"

"Not so, Viridia the Render. This is Pando, Kov of Bormark. And this is Tilda, his mother, the Kovneva. They are my friends, and if you are my friend and comrade, then they are your friends, also. Do not forget that. As for me, my destiny lies elsewhere."

"Do not say it, Dray!" sobbed Tilda, grasping me, as Viridia stared at me with her wide blue eyes all aglitter from the samphron oil lamps' gleam. "Say you will not go to Vallia."

"Vallia!" said Viridia. "What is this of Vallia, Dray Prescot, render?"

I felt the cold anger in me, the desire to turn and smash everything in sight. Not for this petty wrangling had I risked all and turned my back on Vallia and my Delia, my Delia of the Blue Mountains!

"Vallia is where I am going, Viridia. And neither you nor Tilda can stop me." I lifted Pando up. He wore his old zhantil-hide tunic and belt, and I marveled. Tilda's long blue gown was torn over one shoulder, and an ivory globe and collarbone showed, gleaming, alluring, even there, in those circumstances. "Pando. You will stop all this nonsense of going to war, and fighting for pleasure. You are a Kov. You must rule your people wisely and well, and you must listen to your mother and to Inch. Otherwise I shall strap your backside. As for you, Tilda. You must smash the bottles of Jholaix. Pando needs guidance. You must listen to Inch. He knows my views."

If that sounds pompous, tyrannical, banal, blame yourself, not me. I spoke truths. Truths were needed then; for I could hardly hold myself under control. Vallia! Delia! The need for her flamed in my blood, drugged me with desire. Too long had I betrayed her, and dillydallied with renders and Kovs and all the petty glory of sailing a swordship sea under my old flag.

"You—will not desert us, Dray?" Tilda tried to wipe away the tears staining her cheeks. Her eyes rested on me in a new glory, and I knew that if I stayed I would now have the same trouble with her as I had with Viridia.

As for that pirate wench, she stood with my old flag draping her shoulders, her rapier all bloody, glaring at me.

"And if you go to Vallia, Dray Prescot the Render, what is to prevent me from going, also?"

I sighed. I tried to speak calmly.

"There is nothing but heartbreak for you in Vallia, Viridia."

"And is she so much more beautiful, more desirable than me, Dray?"

"Or me?" demanded Tilda passionately.

There was no answer that a gentleman might make, and although I am no gentleman, although a Krozair of Zy, I could make no answer, either. But my silence told them both. The moment held, awkwardly.

Then Pando broke it. He struggled free, wiping blood from my armor caught tackily on his hands down that zhantil tunic.

"And would you beat me, Dray?"

Then I laughed.

"I would flog you, Pando, you imp of Sicce, if you did not behave like a true Kov and have a care for your people of Bormark! Aye, flog you until you sobbed for mercy!"

Before Pando could answer the chamber filled with the pirates who had followed me here. They crowded in, forming a great excited mass of milling men and glittering steel about me. Arkhebi, his red hair all tousled, shouted the words, words taken up by the others in a flashing of lifted rapiers.

"Hai, Jikai! Dray Prescot! Hai! Jikai! Jikai!"

Well, they were happy in the knowledge that immense plunder awaited them in Menaham. I listened to the uproar, and that slit between my lips widened a trifle, hurtfully.

That glorious mingled sunshine of Antares flooded in from the tall windows to lie across the rich trappings, the colors, the steel of blade and armor, the flushed excited faces, the blood. The samphron oil lamps blinked dim. Someone had thrown back the shutters from the windows and all the opaz glory of the Suns of Scorpio poured in.

I looked through the windows into that bright dazzlement and saw a giant raptor, its scarlet and golden feathers brilliant in the streaming mingled light of the twin suns.

And coldness touched my heart.

Jerkily, moving with the stiffness of rheumatic old-age,

I pushed through the shouting exultant renders, entered a small side room. I was vaguely conscious of Viridia and Tilda following me, suddenly anxious, but if they spoke I did not hear what they said. Behind them, I guessed, Inch and Valka and Spitz would be treading on fast, and Pando would be working his way through to catch me.

I felt dizzy.

Then—how I recall that moment of horror, of despair!—across that empty room before me I saw the scuttling running form of a scorpion.

A scorpion!

I knew, then. . . .

I was to be returned to Earth, banished from Kregen beneath Antares, hurled back contemptuously to the planet of my birth.

As that cursed blue radiance limned all my vision and the sensations of falling clawed at my limbs, my body, my brain, I cried out, high, desperately, frantically.

"Remember me, remember Dray Prescot!"

And when I tried to shout my defiance of the Star Lords, and of the Savanti, who were so callously flinging me back to Earth, and to scream that I would not return to Earth, that I would stay on Kregen, no sound issued from my rigid lips.

The blueness grew.

It took on the semblance of a gigantic blue-glowing scorpion.

I was falling.

In my mind, unuttered, tearing and bursting with passion, I screamed: "Delia! My Delia of Delphond! My Delia of the Blue Mountains! I will come back! I will come back! Delia, I will return!"

I would return.